Z's Legacy

October, 2135

Cascadian Intelligence Mission Agent, Zakaya Kalu—better known as "Z"—travels to the United States to visit her mother. But when her young friend, Zeena, sees the men who took her two years earlier and soon disappears, Z vows to find her and bring a ring of human traffickers to justice.

In this sequel to Legacy 627, Z finds herself teamed with, and attracted to, a man she does not entirely trust in order to assist the local police in solving strange murders by a suspect known only as the Kind Killer. By agreeing to assist in this case, Z demands access to evidence in cases she believes will lead to the rescue of Zeena.

Still wanted by the Americans for her part in destroying a dangerous chemical they hoped to weaponize, Z must guard her connection to CIMA and tread carefully as she poses as an ordinary police detective and closes in on the traffickers.

Through it all, Z learns one valuable lesson: No matter who they are or what they have…

Everyone leaves a legacy.
Everyone.

Also by RLM Cooper
Legacy 627

Z's Legacy

RLM Cooper

A Black Opal Books Publication

DEDICATION

Human trafficking is a heinous crime
that exploits the most innocent
and vulnerable in every society.

This book is dedicated to the brave men and women
of every nation who hunt these criminals
around the globe and bring them to justice.

And to the very special men
who bring sunshine into my life:
My husband, Lawrence
and
My wonderful son, Garth

1

May, 2135
A Mall in Crimson City, Alabama, USA

He sat back in the armless chair he had installed in the darkened cubby, idly picking beneath his fingernails with a pocketknife. Waiting.

He watched closely from behind the two-way mirror as the girls rushed into the fitting room, arms cascading a chaos of color in the tulle, lace, and satin of prom dresses. Both girls giggled excitedly over their upcoming dates. Both were fifteen years old. One brunette, one blonde. Both pretty. The blonde was a bit on the chubby side while her brunette friend was beautifully proportioned with that blushed and glowing complexion that made her skin radiant. And valuable.

He rose slowly, carefully, and stood quietly appraising the girls through black-dark eyes, coldly calculating their value on the market. He had hit the jackpot on this particular day. The weeks leading up to prom had always been lucrative. So lucrative, in fact, that he could afford to be selective taking only the very best. He pocketed the knife and tapped out a short note on the tele-communicator strapped to his wrist, then became so distracted by the brunette that his finger lingered above the t-com, the message temporarily unsent.

The girls were holding the dresses up, admiring themselves in the mirror—unaware they were, themselves, being admired from the other side—just inches away.

"Oh Kit!" the blonde said. "You look so beautiful in blue! I wish I was thin like you."

The brunette—Kit—answered her friend generously. "Don't be silly, Connie. You're beautiful! What do you think of the pink?"

"I like it."

"Do you think Andy will like it?"

The blonde Connie laughed. "Andy likes you. I don't think he cares what you wear."

They both laughed and placed their dresses on the wall hooks in the order they wanted to try them on.

This mall, like so many in the United States over the years, had fallen into disrepair as many of the stores had either canceled their leases or just gone bankrupt and were forced to vacate. It had subsequently been sold several times until a recent purchaser had gotten the bright idea to sell off the individual spaces, pocket the money, and be done with it without worrying whether or not it would succeed or fail yet again.

The purchaser of this particular shop had had very special renovations in mind that would make it doubly lucrative.

This particular fitting booth—a former storage room—had been outfitted from floor to ceiling with mirrors on three of its sides and was large enough to contain both girls comfortably as they began to undress.

T-shirts were excitedly pulled over their heads and jeans were pushed down and leg-tossed into the corner. Next came the bras, releasing tender, young breasts with pink, upturned nipples. It was all he could do to contain himself at the sight of the brunette. His tongue licked out at the thought of those nipples between his lips and he could feel himself growing hard.

But she was not for him. She was worth far too much. This was business. Dangerous but extremely lucrative. He pushed his hardness down in an effort to concentrate on the job at hand and, at last, remembered to press the "send" button on his t-com. Then he waited. And watched.

The dispatched t-com note was short and to the point. It read: *Lose the blonde.*

The blonde would bring much less and he rejected her out of hand. Not that he cared one way or the other about her. Or about any of them, for that matter. After all, they were just fickle little pieces of fluff who would one day marry some yokel, have a bunch of squalling babies, and complain incessantly for a new sofa. Girls were all alike. Little flirts. Teases. Then they dump you for some lawyer's spawn or a misfit in a motorcycle jacket. Well, he had made more than a few of them pay over the past several years.

Self-centered, money-grubbing little airheads.

He retrieved the knife from his pocket and again began scraping beneath his nails, intently watching the brunette as he waited. She leaned into the mirror and pursed her lips into a pout, then giggled at herself and unzipped the gown, once again exposing her breasts. He groaned silently and tensed, nicking himself with the knife he had forgotten was in his hand. He sucked the blood from the cut on his thumb and continued to watch as a second man silently slipped into the cubby through a small door behind him. He turned and frowned at the new arrival, temporarily placing the bloody thumb on the back of the chair.

"You're late! You risk everything coming in like that." He whispered in the angriest tone he could muster and still remain virtually silent.

The other man, shorter and rounder than himself, said nothing. He handed over a small bottle and a folded square of soft cloth, then waited, motionless and silent just inside the cubby door.

Before the girls had time to try on the next of their dresses, the saleswoman appeared and informed the blonde she had found the perfect dress for her. Store rules, however, insisted she bring out one of the dresses she had already tried before she could bring in another. The girl happily re-donned her t-shirt and jeans and preceded the woman out of the dressing room in excited anticipation. The saleswoman, perhaps once pretty but now careworn and furrowed, looked back at the brunette, then into the mirror. She sighed, turned, and closed the dressing room door behind her.

The brunette, Kit, was now alone.

He moved fast. He soaked the cloth with the contents of the bottle, and with the flick of a switch engaged a lock on the dressing room door, trapping her inside.

Hearing the click of the door, the girl turned toward it but saw nothing. Still happy and excited, she was reaching for the dress hanging just to the right of the door when he pushed open the left-side mirror-wall and grabbed her from her blind left side. Stunned, she had no time to scream before his hand covered her mouth with the Octo-flurane-soaked cloth. She was rendered unconscious almost immediately. His partner, still waiting patiently by the cubby door, took her over his shoulder and out the back room of the dress shop. He watched for a moment and then casually gathered up her handbag and clothes to take with them.

The prom dresses were left in a frothy ocean of pinks, greens, and blues about the room. There would be no inventory shortage for store audits to ponder later and no sign the girl had ever been there. Finally, he released the lock on the dressing room door. In fewer than twenty seconds the girl was loaded into an unmarked and windowless van parked just inches from the shop's rear door. The sliding door was slammed shut and the van slowly pulled away from the building, turned right at the mall entrance, and disappeared into the ordinary flow of traffic on the main thoroughfare that ran through the shopping district and out of town to the southwest.

Not two minutes later the girl's blonde friend, Connie, came bursting through the dressing room door, arms loaded with lavender tulle and taffeta.

"Kit! Look what I foun—." She stopped and turned to the saleswoman. "Where did she go?"

"I don't know. Maybe she got tired and left. Her clothes are gone. See?" The woman gestured toward the corner of the booth where the brunette's clothes and bag had been. "Were you supposed to meet somewhere after shopping?"

"No. That's really odd. That's not like her." The girl frowned, obviously worried.

"Well, I wouldn't worry. She's either out looking for more dresses or just got tired and went home. I'm sure you'll find her soon." The woman began gathering up the discarded prom dresses to return to the racks in the store. "Let me know if you need anything else."

It had taken all of eleven minutes and twenty-three seconds from the moment the girls first walked into the fitting room, and it was over.

2

Late October, 2135
Cascadian Air, Flight 0042
San Francisco, California, Cascadia - to - Montgomery,
Alabama, USA

Zakaya was jittery on this flight and the newspaper headline wasn't helping. It shouted in bold lettering: **Another Young Girl Missing!**

She managed to catch only the first few lines of the article before the man in the four-seater section across the aisle folded the newspaper and shoved it into his carry-on. She hadn't been able to determine the location but, apparently, it was believed the girl was a runaway, fed up with parental control and most everything else as well. Teenagers. The same everywhere. Maybe the writer of the article was correct. Maybe the girl was just a runaway. Still, a creeping unease began nagging at her.

Of course, she told herself, a runaway wasn't hard for her to believe. After all, she had done that very thing when, at the age of 18, she had headed west from Alabama, working odd jobs along the way, until she ended up at the U.S.-Cascadian border along central California, and soon after became a Cascadian citizen. She hadn't run from parental control, however. She'd had other reasons. Back then she was a small, wounded animal but had covered it well under a layer of false bravado and stubbornness.

She looked across to the pair of seats facing her where Zeena was fast asleep. Zeena was another small, wounded animal who had come into Zakaya's life two years earlier—living proof there were other reasons a young girl might disappear.

Zeena had been more nervous about this trip than Zakaya herself, and hadn't wanted to come at all. But "Miss Z" was going with or without her and she didn't want to be separated from her even for a day.

Zakaya couldn't help smiling as she watched the girl sleeping. All arms, elbows, and gangly legs, Zeena was beginning to gently round into a lovely young woman. Her fondness for the girl had only grown since the day she had discovered her chained to a filthy bed in an out-building at a seedy Florida beach motel and freed her. It had all played out during the final moments of an incredibly dangerous mission—a mission that had taken her and her team of Cascadian Intelligence Mission Agents from Cascadia to Atlanta and down to the beaches of the Florida panhandle where the pursuing, and determined, Americans had finally caught up with them and engaged them in a fierce firefight before the team was picked up and whisked back to Cascadia.

She hadn't regretted a single one of those final moments even though she had been wounded in the skirmish. She had not only freed Zeena from the clutches of human traffickers but had, along with her team, helped to save the world from a potentially diabolical chemical weapon at the same time. Such was her job as a Mission Agent for the CIMA-2 team in the CIB—the Cascadian Intelligence Bureau. And, for the past two years, she'd had the responsibility and the honor of being a surrogate parent to Zeena. No, she had not a single regret. It was one of her best day's work ever.

Still, she couldn't deny her nervousness at returning to

the United States. It had been five years since she had entered the country legally under her own name. She had come then, as now, to visit her mother in Selma, where she was born. But it had been only two years since the mission when she had entered the country under a false identity, traveling, so she had told the suspicious airline clerk, to Atlanta to meet her sister, a person who did not actually exist. The false identification had been impeccable and not challenged, yet she knew the Americans were not stupid for all their decision-making that had caused the country to decline over the past hundred years. She would be a wanted person by both the CIA and FBI. Americans, she knew all too well, had long memories and could hold a grudge.

She made an attempt at shaking off her nerves and looked around the aircraft. This Cascadian Air flight was not full so she and Zeena had a 4-seat section all to themselves. The seats on all Cascadian aircraft were in groups of four—two facing two. One class. Everyone treated equally. Like Cascadia itself, where no one had ever seemed to take any notice of her skin color. Or, more recently, Zeena's. This had been the way of things since Cascadia had become an independent nation in 2038 when the Western states of Washington, Oregon, California, and Hawaii broke away from the near third-world country the United States was fast becoming and dragging them down with it. Oddly, the breaking-away had been done without a single shot being fired. The American military leaders had refused to order their soldiers to fire upon those who were still U.S. Citizens—many of them friends and relatives.

And so Cascadia, once established, began the process of recovery, slowly digging itself out of the ruin in which the United States had left it. It became a place of opportunity, peace, and equality. At least as nearly as possible when dealing with human beings.

Even though the U.S. had managed not to be blown up, nor to blow anyone else up, except minor wars here and there, the country had still managed over the years to alienate nearly every ally except the United Kingdom, who held on to them as to a wayward black sheep child. Domestically, however, the country was a shambles, slowly deteriorating in a sort of one-step-forward, two-steps-back kind of political *danse macabre*. Abortion, birth control, and divorce were all made illegal in a devastating blow to women's rights. Many people fled to Canada and Mexico and parts beyond. But the poor had few resources and fewer options. Their lives had become a black-and-white photograph of hope-tinged misery.

There was no getting around it. The USA of 2135 was a very gray and dangerous place. Especially for women. Zakaya was not only a woman; she was a Black woman. This very obvious fact presented its own limitations and challenges. Since the United States had never been able to rid itself of its racist past, she knew she would have to be especially cognizant of everything and everyone on this visit.

Once this plane landed, she would be at risk.

3

Though born in Selma, Alabama, Zakaya's home had been Cascadia for over twelve years and, for that, she was grateful beyond measure. Even so, there were times she felt nostalgically sad for an earlier, grander United States she had read about but never actually experienced. One thing for which she was especially grateful was the fact that the United States and Cascadia both loved, and resented, each other like a couple of siblings. This made travel between the two fairly easy.

She sighed and reached into her bag on the adjacent seat next to the window. She pushed aside the sizable bundle of American dollars she had gotten for the trip in exchange for Cascadian credits and withdrew a small, antique velvet box. Her legacy.

She turned it over and around, examining it slowly, feeling it, and admiring the old dusty rose color and how the pressure of unknown fingers had long ago permanently depressed portions of the velvet into flat little ovals on its surface.

She smiled as she remembered meeting the Sage of Legacy Hall for the first time. She had spoken with her via t-com, of course, and she knew of her through her sister Alex's descriptions, but it wasn't until her own thirtieth birthday when she had become eligible to claim her own legacy, that, urged on by Alex, she had reluctantly made the trip to Legacy Hall and met the woman herself.

Her reluctance stemmed from Alex's unusual legacy that became the catalyst for the mission two years earlier. It was true, of course, that Alex could not have known what the contents of the legacy box she chose would be. Nor could she have known those contents were going to lead her, and the entire CIMA-2 team, on a dangerous mission—a mission that ended with them both wounded along with Alex's team partner, Parker West. He had gotten the worst of it, too—hit in both the shoulder and the leg—while she and Alex had suffered only a single bullet wound each. Only. As if that hadn't been enough.

But that was two years ago. The really good thing that had come out of that mission—aside from the recovery and destruction of a deadly chemical and potential weapon the U.S. Military had badly wanted—was sitting directly across from her, fast asleep.

Zeena had been the victim of human trafficking and bound for a life nothing short of horror until Zakaya had, in the final moments of that mission, heard her cries, broken down the door of the rickety out-building behind the beach motel, and hustled her away to the safety of Cascadia. It was the run, hand-in-hand with Zeena, down the beach to the waiting rescue boat piloted by her CIMA-2 team partner, Gray Hawk, that resulted in her being wounded as the Americans closed in, firing upon them. But the team had all made it, and once back in Cascadia, Zeena had been welcomed by all and dubbed "Little Z" by the director of the CIB—much to the amusement of everyone. She smiled at that memory and turned her attention back to her legacy.

As she examined the velvety box, her thoughts returned to the Sage at Legacy Hall.

The woman had been amused at the differences between her dark-eyed self with her section-twisted 'fro, and her adopted, hazel-eyed sister with the short, spiky blonde hair and had been genuinely surprised when Z told her it didn't matter which legacy box she chose.

There had been eleven boxes whose timers had recently ticked off the final seconds of their seventy-year countdown, automatically unlocking their inner doors with a click. The unknown "Legacies" behind those eleven doors were all available for Zakaya to choose. But, unlike Alex, she hadn't agonized over the ten that would be forever lost when she chose the eleventh. She was nothing if not pragmatic. Since she couldn't know what was in any of them, she had chosen the first one she saw at eye level. The Sage had unlocked the outer glass door with her master key and stepped aside to let Zakaya open the already-unlocked inner door so she might discover the legacy for herself.

Z glanced at the still-sleeping Zeena, then opened the small box. Inside, cushioned in age-yellowed white satin, was a lovely old brooch with blue stones. Maybe aquamarine. Maybe something else. They could have been anything from blue topaz or zircons to sapphires. Even diamonds. She didn't really know gemstones very well and in her line of work they weren't something she often wore. The brooch was set in either white gold or platinum. She didn't know which of those, either. She only knew it wasn't silver.

There had been a note inside the box, but it hadn't identified the stones. It was handwritten by a man who explained the brooch had belonged to his wife, Linda. She had been the love of his life and when she passed away, far too young, there had been no daughters to inherit it. He hoped the person who claimed it as their own, many years in the future, would also love it and know that it had been cherished by someone once. He had signed his name, simply…Benjamin.

Zakaya decided her mother was going to love it.

She ran her index finger over the stones. They were smooth to the touch between the sharp-edged facets. She liked knowing the brooch was something that had been loved. Something treasured. The Cascadian tradition of leaving something for future citizens in those tiny time-capsules called "legacy boxes" was a good one, she thought. What legacy she would leave, in turn, was still a puzzle. She had thought a bit about it, but still had no answer. She had few possessions and none of real value. Her work as a CIMA-2 agent was her whole life. She closed the velvet box and returned it to her bag.

Settling back into the seat, she watched Zeena as she slept.

She looks so young and vulnerable. She's so tiny for her age. So fragile looking.

She wondered if she was doing the right thing, bringing the girl back to Alabama considering what she had only recently been through. Human trafficking flowed like a dark undercurrent in the United States, and she had no way of knowing what they would encounter once they arrived.

Even though Zeena was still traumatized by her experience in those short weeks before her rescue, Z felt she should go back and see her mother. The girl, however, had begged not to be taken there. Zeena had argued her mother was not a good person and did not want her, but Z felt maybe she was exaggerating. What if it had been just a mother-daughter tiff? In any event, the truth, whatever it turned out to be, would be uncovered on this trip. With any luck, everything would work out for the best.

During the two years since the girl's rescue, Z had tried to get Zeena to tell of her abduction, but she could get no genuinely useful information from her. Zeena had said only that she had been walking home from school and a really good-looking man and his friend had stopped her and told her how cute she was and maybe they would put her in their next movie. They had encouraged her to hop into their car and they would all go to the *Cream and Cone* to talk it over. They had tricked her, she said, because she had been taken to a large house but she didn't know where it was because they had given her something to make her sleep before they got there. When she woke up, the men who took her were not there, but there were other young girls in the house and different men who acted as jailers and guards. She told Z she could hear the others crying but she didn't know how many there were. She had been kept in a separate room and, after a few days, she had been taken away by a man who wore a ski mask, so she never saw his face but, unlike the men who took her, this man was Black like herself and Z.

Speaking of it had only served to upset her so Z had not pressed for more. But she had something. A few small tidbits. The traffickers were Caucasian. A middleman, it seemed, was Black. There was a large house with at least several other girls, and guards who watched them closely. It was possible that was all she would ever learn. And maybe that was for the best. Zeena was safe now and in her care. Besides, she was coming back to Alabama to visit her own mother, whom she had not seen in five years. She was not coming back to investigate criminals.

She checked the time. It wouldn't be much longer before they landed. She closed her eyes and attempted to push her uneasiness aside. After all, she kept telling herself, this was only a visit. She would not stay. She would never stay again. She had found her place in this world. She was a Cascadian citizen and a member of the top CIMA team in the entire CIB. She was Zakaya Kalu,

Cascadian Intelligence Mission Agent. And one of the best.

She turned and watched out the window as the plane descended through thinner and thinner clouds, finally hitting the runway a bit roughly before it settled down to a smooth crawl. It taxied off the runway to the Montgomery airport gate reserved for Cascadian Air and both the British and French airlines, as well. This airport wasn't as large—or as busy—as the one in Birmingham, but it was closer to Selma.

Zeena, awake now, gathered her scattered belongings, which consisted of two books and a sweater. She shoved them into her backpack and sat quietly on the edge of her seat, waiting for Z's signal to exit the plane.

Z took a deep breath, reached for her own bag and stood up to exit. She made a silent attempt at reassuring herself. She told herself once again she was only coming back for a visit. Just a visit. Small tidbits of information about Zeena's abduction weren't enough to act upon, and in the United States she would have no authority to pursue them, anyway. Besides, her involvement in the mission two years earlier now put her at great risk should her connection to CIMA become known to the Americans. So, no. She was not coming back to investigate criminals.

Or so she thought.

4

They disembarked the aircraft through the boarding tunnel directly into the arrival area. At the same time, a plane arriving from Texas at the adjacent gate was unloading a couple dozen young people headed for the football game on Saturday. This noisy crew pushed and called to each other happily as Z and Zeena picked their way through them. Z was burdened by only her shoulder bag and a small carry-on, so they headed to baggage claim down a long corridor carpeted in a nasty brown that had apparently never been introduced to either a vacuum or cleaning solution. The whole area reeked like the inside of a stinky athletic shoe.

Lining the right-hand wall, just outside baggage claim, stood a row of five old-fashioned telephone booths. Landlines, it seemed, were still in operation here. Z dismissed them after an initial and partial glance between the passing football fans.

A small mistake.

In the middle booth a rather handsome-looking man watched the two of them closely as they passed, then faced away and spoke into the receiver.

"I have eyes," he said.

He nodded in agreement with whatever was being said in response and repeated an address, apparently committing it to memory since he wrote nothing down, then hung up the receiver and exited the booth.

He followed Zakaya and Zeena into baggage claim, passed them by without looking their way, and exited through a side door.

ⱷⱾⱷⱾ

Zakaya knew there would be no car-bots here as in Cascadia, so the only option was to head for a rental desk where an ordinary gasoline-powered car could be hired. The United States had no infrastructure in place for advances in technology such as the car-bots in common use in Cascadia. In fact, the only bots known in the U.S. were those in the Washington D.C. area servicing government buildings. That area had been completely cordoned off with a wall after the People's Uprising of 2083 during which more than a dozen senators had been killed and the White House fences demolished. The president had managed to escape via Marine One before the swarm but had resigned shortly thereafter. The Vice President had then taken office and promised things would be better, but change was hard to come by in the short term.

Now, fifty-two years later, some progress was being made but the country was still a violent and unsafe mix of haves and have-nots, each at war with the other.

At the car rental desk, Z presented her identification to the counter clerk and waited. The clerk, a pock-faced young man wearing a rumpled blue uniform shirt, gave her a stony stare and then looked with obvious distaste at the thin girl standing close by her side. Z put a protective hand around Zeena's shoulder, pulled her close, and braced herself. She knew what was coming. She had experienced it in many ways and in many other situations.

The clerk examined her ID. "Your name is Zakaka?" he

said, with no attempt to hide a smirk.

For one split-second she was taken aback. She was used to people mispronouncing her name, but never in a manner so rude and so hatefully deliberate.

"No. It's Zakaya. Za-KY-ya. Ky. Rhymes with sky." Her words were direct. Clipped.

Smirk erased, the clerk narrowed his eyes. "What is it you want?"

Z leaned slightly to her right, looked around him and up at the sign on the wall just behind his head. The sign read: E-Z-CAR RENTAL. Then she looked back at the clerk—a look that said, "one of us is an idiot, and it's not me."

He held his gaze on her and shifted from one impatient foot to the other. Z met his gaze dead-on without flinching and waited.

"What size car?" he asked. Finally.

"What do you have?" Her tone was deliberately pleasant now.

"We are short on stock right now. Just a van, a pickup, and two sedans."

"We'll take one of the sedans."

He looked her up and down. "How long will you be renting it?"

"A couple of weeks. Maybe longer. But let's just say two weeks."

The clerk was silent for long enough that most people would have been uncomfortable. But, smiling pleasantly, Z kept steady eye contact and waited. He was, in all probability, wondering where she had gotten the money to rent a car at all—much less for two weeks.

He told her the price, then added, "And another hundred and fifty for taxes and fees." He gave her a condescending smile. "Cash."

Z reached into her bag, pulled out a fistful of American

dollars, and peeled off the correct amount. "I'd like a receipt for that, thanks."

The clerk, eyebrows raised in surprise, turned away, stowed the cash, made out the paperwork, and, at last, slid the keys and receipt across the vinyl countertop. She took them without comment.

Later, as she was fiddling around with the buttons and gadgets, familiarizing herself with the elderly vehicle, Zeena said, "He wasn't very friendly, was he? It seemed like he didn't want to rent the car to us at all."

"Yes. That's true, Button. But he has to. The company wants the money, and they don't really care who they get it from. Greed always seems to win over everything else. Always follow the money. That's one lucky break for us in an ocean of idiotic discrimination." She winked at Zeena.

At last comfortable enough in the driver's seat to proceed, she took the car out of the rental lot at a nice, slow roll. At the exit, she took a side road and entered highway 80 west to Selma, coming up from the south.

As she drove, her mind wandered back to Cascadia. Work was never far from Zakaya. She sometimes felt she was born to do her job. Justice and fair play were like breath and heartbeat to her so it was difficult to let it all go. For a fleeting moment she wondered what her partner, Gray Hawk, was doing without her at CIMA, but she pushed the thoughts aside. Right now she hoped to forget about work and enjoy this long overdue visit with her mother. To relax and be her mother's daughter again would be really nice. A well-deserved vacation. Yes. It would be really nice.

But it wasn't going to be.

5

A short distance just south of Selma, Z drove the rental sedan past fields and widely-spaced houses, never noticing a car pulling onto the shoulder of a weedy side road that cut through a couple of fallow fields.

Two men were driving an old repurposed black-and-white. Old police vehicles were often sold at auction and the man on the passenger side had purchased this one, painted it by hand, and named it "Orca" since it now more closely resembled the whale than a police car.

The driver of the Orca watched intently until Z's rental was well out of sight then pulled forward a few yards and stopped.

The man on the passenger side opened the door, eased himself out, and casually walked to the rear of the car. Tall and good-looking, he walked with assurance. Unhurried. He bent slightly and opened the trunk. Looking around, he slipped on a pair of rubber gloves, then lifted and shouldered the body of a young girl. Several steps beyond the road's deteriorating and ragged-edged asphalt he tossed her into the weedy growth of the ditch. The driver remained in the car and watched as he kicked and pushed the body until it was mostly hidden beneath an overturned and rotting wooden wheelbarrow apparently tossed there some time ago. No one had bothered to remove it so the weeds had grown high around it and served to mostly obscure the body from casual view of anyone driving past on the main road. Satisfied, he stood upright and dusted his hands in that universal sign of finality.

The driver leaned over and called out through the passenger side door left open when his partner had gotten out. "Come on!" He was impatient. "We have to get out of here!"

He looked back at the driver, annoyed, and pulled something small and blue from his pocket. He wiped it clean with his shirtsleeve then bent down and flung it into the weeds several yards beyond the upturned wheelbarrow that now mostly covered the girl's body.

"Relax," he said as he slid back into the car, calmly shutting the door. "Nobody much uses this old side road. You worry too much." He removed the rubber gloves and stashed them in the side pocket of the door.

The driver frowned at him. "I didn't sign up for this kind of thing. I don't like it."

His partner began digging beneath his fingernails with a pocketknife. "You like the money well enough. So stop whining."

"I still don't like this. This just ain't right. And it's too dangerous."

Partner laughed out loud. "*This* isn't right, but the other stuff we do is okay? You are really are messed up, you know that?"

The driver mumbled to himself as he shoved the already idling car into gear. Finally he said, "We need to get back to work before we're missed."

They eased away from the site, turning north on a side road. Skirting Selma, they drove into Crimson City where they headed up Alaska Avenue.

Neither had looked back at the girl's body lying in the ditch.

✑✑✑

Z could sense Zeena's anxiety as they rolled past houses and fields that were most likely very familiar to her in spite of her two years in Cascadia. The girl seemed jittery. Nervous. She was very quiet.

"Don't bite your nails." Z reached over and gave her a friendly push of the shoulder. Zeena tilted her head until it rested on Z's hand.

The fields along the highway were a mix. Some were great blankets of defoliated cotton, acres of scattered popcorn on a lake of brown debris. Others were long-neglected, fallow fields of bitterweed. The houses were a mix as well. Some were no more than shacks that had never seen a paint brush. Others gleamed as white as the cotton in the fields surrounding them.

Z's eyes grew wide and wider the closer they got to Selma. The intermittent shacks were slowly disappearing until there were none. Now the houses, though small and mostly quite humble, were tidy and well-kept. Some had little knee-high fences corralling wildflowers and late-blooming roses. Emerald lawns, recently mown, were neatly edged.

They passed a group of little girls jumping double ropes and chanting as they darted in and then out again between the thick, rotating strands of hemp. Boys were tossing a football in an empty lot. Neighbors were talking to each other over property-dividing fences, and some stopped and waved as Z and Zeena drove past. A few blocks more and they had reached the city limits of Selma just at the entrance to the old Edmund Pettus Bridge.

Zakaya eased on the brakes and stared. Blocking the bridge was a band of armed Black men who appeared not at all friendly. She looked over at Zeena and told her to stay put while she got out to meet, head-on, the largest of the group who was already approaching the car. She had no weapon with her on this trip so she would have to play along to see what they wanted. There were four of them, all armed. Armed Black men in the United States were so unusual and unexpected these days that she was taken off-guard. She was definitely out-gunned here, and out-numbered. This rarely happened to Z and that prickly feeling in her armpits warned of danger. Still, she met this apparent leader eye-to-eye, showing no signs of fear.

As she approached him, he slipped the rifle from his shoulder and held it with both hands in what could have been judged a more than intimidating move had he pointed it directly at her.

Z looked him over. The distance between them was close enough that she could easily disarm him with a kick but his index finger was not on the trigger and he appeared relaxed. He was much taller than her so she had to look up to meet his eyes with her own. She stood silent and waited for him to make the first move.

"Who are you?" he finally asked.

"Who wants to know?" She answered as boldly as he had asked.

He laughed and looked back at his comrades. Then he turned back to her, serious once again.

"You're obviously not from around here. So what are you doing here?"

Z studied him for a moment. There was something there. In his eyes. He had large, soft, deep-brown eyes. He was clean-shaven and wore his hair in shoulder-length dreads.

She said, "I didn't know I needed a passport to come to Selma, Alabama."

Amused, he suppressed a smile yet couldn't hide his dimples.

"Let me ask again," he said. "What are you doing here?"

She put her head to one side considering her next move, then decided to take a chance with him.

"I was born here and I've come to visit my mother."

"Is that your girl in the car?" He lifted his chin in Zeena's direction.

Z looked back at Zeena then turned back to him with narrowed eyes. "Yes."

"Where you live now?" he asked.

"Cascadia."

His eyes widened and he looked her up and down. Z wasn't sure he believed her but she continued to hold her ground, her five feet, three inches dwarfed by his height. He seemed impressed.

"Cascadia. You just have one branch of military there, don't you?"

"Yes. It's like your Army, Navy, and Marines rolled up into one. It's the Cascadian Corps. It's made up of seriously trained good guys. A lot like you, maybe." Z noticed his face soften almost imperceptibly. She stopped talking and waited.

He reached up and stroked his chin. He was deciding something. She continued to wait.

"Who's your mother?"

"What?"

"You said you were here to visit your mother. Who is she?"

"Annie Kalu."

He jerked back as though dodging a punch. "Shit, girl! Why didn't you say so? Hey guys!" He shouldered his rifle once again and turned to his buddies. "This is Mrs. Kalu's daughter!"

The group behind him shouldered their rifles as well and all came up to her, extending their hands.

Z wasn't sure what was going on, but she was pretty sure she was in no danger now. She shook each hand in turn and asked why they were blocking the road.

"We keeping Selma safe," one of them told her.

"This country gone nuts, but you probably know that," the leader added.

"Yes. Unfortunately," she told them. She wondered how they knew her mother, but decided it was a small town so it wouldn't be unusual. Besides, she didn't want to engage any more than absolutely necessary.

"Here." The leader reached into his pocket and withdrew a blue card with a silver circle surrounding the words "Selma Blues." At the bottom of the card, printed in black italic was his name—*Eli McClain*. "Take this," he said. "If you leave Selma while you are here just show it to the guards at any city limit when you come back and you won't have any trouble." He looked at her for a moment, then said, "Welcome back, Annie Kalu's daughter." He smiled then for the first time, displaying dazzling white teeth.

"Thanks." She never broke her eye-to-eye gaze as she accepted the card.

As she returned to her rental car the four men parted, two to each side of the road, allowing her to pass.

Zeena asked if everything was okay and Z assured her there was nothing to worry about as they headed over the bridge and deeper into the heart of Selma past ever-neater homes and yards.

This was new. This was an oasis in the desert of gray the United States had become over the last hundred years and Zakaya could not stop gawking—first at one side of the street and then the other. Street after street until she finally arrived at her mother's little house on Levoy Avenue. She hardly recognized it. The house number didn't lie though, so she was positive she was at the correct address. The house appeared freshly painted a very light green. The open porch was supported by four small columns painted a crisp white and the steps of washed red brick were placed dead center in line with the front door. Between the porch foundation and the lush green of the lawn, stood a pretty little boxwood hedge.

As they pulled their rented sedan into the driveway, Zakaya's mother flew out the door with arms spread wide. "Zakaya! Z!"

Z got out to meet her. They hugged. They backed off and looked at each other. They laughed and hugged again. And backed off. And hugged some more. At last, Mrs. Kalu looked over and spied Zeena still sitting in the passenger seat hugging her backpack with both arms. She motioned for the girl to come on out.

Zeena opened the door and came around to meet them, her backpack slung onto her right shoulder.

"This is Zeena, Mama." Z put her arm around the girl protectively and pulled her close.

"Hello, Zeena. Welcome!"

Zeena smiled but clung to Z like a baby possum.

"Well, come on in the house. You must be starved. I've cooked up a mess of black-eyed peas and collard greens. Cornbread's in the oven now. I need to check on it. Come!" Mrs. Kalu motioned to them both and the three of them filed inside.

6

News traveled fast and it wasn't thirty minutes before Z's Aunt Juanita came flying through the front door screaming, "Z! Z! Where are you, girl!" Z felt every muscle tightening in order to brace herself for the onslaught she knew was coming. Aunt Juanita had always been the black cloud of doom. Z shuddered.

"We're in the kitchen!" Mrs. Kalu yelled as she opened the oven door and bent down to check the cornbread. She straightened back up and announced, "About five more minutes. Zeena, go set the table. There's a good girl. The plates and silverware are in the sideboard in the dining room."

Everything went fairly well through the meal. They talked of little things like how warm it had been in September when it used to be such a temperate month, but how it was cooling now that it was almost November. They talked also of the barbecue her mother had planned for next week to welcome her home, and how wonderful the house looked. Z swore she'd hardly recognized the place as she drove up. In fact, the whole town looked marvelous.

"That's your mama's work," Juanita said in her usual clipped manner that brooked no opposition. She added, "These peas are too salty. Sister, why you put so much salt in everything?"

Mrs. Kalu ignored her and passed the collards to Zeena and Z.

"Mama, I haven't had cornbread this good since I—" She stopped.

"Since you left." Her mother reached over and patted her hand. "It's okay, Baby. It's okay. Tell us about your life in Cascadia."

Z smiled. She had told this story more than once. But her mother either forgot or never tired of hearing it.

"Well, I have a cute little house in a little town called Cotati in California. It's just a cottage, really, but plenty big enough for me."

"And how is your sister?"

"She's good, Mama. She's the best. I've got a recent picture of her here somewhere." Z began digging in her bag for the photo.

"You mean that white girl?" Juanita asked. It wasn't really a question. It just sounded like one.

"Yes, Aunt Nita. That white girl. That white girl whose father rescued me and adopted me when I needed somebody—when I needed help. And they both gave me a wonderful life that I would never have had without them." She glared at Juanita and then her face softened as she turned and handed the photo to her mother.

"Here it is. It was taken only last year."

"She's pretty." Her mother looked over the photo. "And her scar you told me about is hardly even noticeable. Needs to comb her hair, though.".

Z laughed. "Yes. Her hair always looks like that." There was no denying the love in Z's voice as she spoke of the blonde, spiky-haired Alex with hazel eyes, so different in appearance from herself.

Juanita had to get in her two cent's worth. "Yours could use a bit of a combing, too, Z. It looks like one of Uncle Bo's aloe plants stuck on top of your head."

This remark stung. But it wasn't because Juanita dissed her hair. It was the mention of her Uncle Bo. Memories flooded over her, yet she forced herself to a quick recovery.

"Why, thank you, Aunt Nita. You are just too kind."

Juanita snorted but sat back and hushed for the moment.

"Who is that in the picture with her?" her mother asked.

"That's Gray Hawk. He's my partner at work."

"My word. He's a handsome thing, isn't he?"

Z laughed. "Yes, ma'am, he is that. And he thinks the planets revolve around the sun only because Alex is on one of them."

"Well, they look good together. Just completely different. But still, good."

"Let me see!" Juanita commanded. She took the photo and gave it a good once-over. "She ain't really your sister, you know. And he ain't all that good-lookin' either. Looks like a girl with all that long hair hanging down. He's some kind of Indian, right?"

Zakaya reached out and snatched the photo from Juanita's hand. "She *is* my sister." She turned to her mother. "Take care of Zeena for a couple of hours, will you? I need some air." Z's anger stirred in her a truth she knew with certainty: you don't have to be born of the same parents to be sisters and brothers.

Mrs. Kalu followed Z out to the car and leaned in the window as she was starting the engine. "You shouldn't let Juanita bother you," she told her. "She's just jealous is all. You have a life now. A purpose. Juanita's time has come and mostly gone. She's bitter. She doesn't mean half of what she says. She doesn't mean to hurt you."

"I know, Mama. I won't be long. Get Zeena settled in will you? Put the two of us in the same room, please. She's vulnerable right now and I want her to feel safe."

She kissed her mother on the cheek and backed out of the drive. She had no idea where she was going and, right now, she didn't care. She just wanted to get away from Juanita and get some air. Coming "home" always had its drawbacks even though she always missed her mother. She wondered if it was like that for everyone. Probably. When you are grown and away from home, you're an adult. You're capable. In charge. But the moment you step within your parent's home again you become a child once more. It's inevitable. Parents never seem able to see their children in any other light. At least that's the way it felt to Z. Maybe it wasn't true for everyone, but somehow she didn't believe it.

She drove to the center of town and then right on through to the northernmost outskirts where Crimson City had collided with it some dozen years back when all the small towns between Selma and Tuscaloosa had agreed to incorporate and form one large city to keep Tuscaloosa from gobbling them all up as it continued to grow.

About three miles inside the Crimson City limits, she spotted a place called Brassy's Bar and Grille and pulled into the parking lot. She cut the engine and laid her head on the steering wheel for a couple of minutes. No telling what she would encounter inside. She was Black. And there was no forgetting that. Not in a United States that had marched steadfastly backwards for over a hundred plus years.

She raised her head and looked around. It must have rained here earlier, she decided, because the parking lot was shiny with wet. Even the potholes had disappeared beneath the puddles and the air smelled that fresh-washed clean smell that comes with a good dousing. She stepped out of the car and looked up and down the parking area at the people who were about. Habit.

Always be aware of your surroundings.

She noticed nothing unusual. A woman with a little boy tugging at her and whining about something he wanted.

An elderly lady struggling with groceries she was hefting into the trunk of her small car. A lone man entering the bar. A laughing couple heading past the doors of Brassy's, probably on their way to the drugstore at the end of the sprawling strip-mall. The usual assortment of cars scattered among the spaces. A rare few were new. Most old. A couple with dented fenders. Nothing out of the ordinary.

She turned her attention to the double doors of the Bar and Grille. They were frosted glass, each with "Brassy's" emblazoned in black-shadowed, gold script and set at an angle. They appeared to swing in either direction. She took a deep breath, pushed open the right-hand door, and stepped inside.

7

It was refreshingly snug and dim inside Brassy's. Just what she needed.

Looking around as she entered, she saw not one face that wasn't white unless you counted the guy at the back of the room mopping the floor and rearranging the tables and chairs. He looked up and nodded at her. She nodded back.

The place was certainly appropriately named. There were what appeared to be brass railings around the bar at both counter level and along the bottom, serving as a footrest. The lights were softened by brass shades, perforated here and there in an abstract floral design. The seating was green leather, a good choice that went well with the brass. In all, the place looked quite prosperous and was a pleasant contrast to the dilapidated look of most small businesses in the States. Even though it was still early, there were a few patrons already settled in and enjoying the food and drink.

Several people were sitting at tables by themselves. A couple of big scruffy guys sat toward the front of the room drinking beer. Along the right side of the room, a lone drinker was perched on the last stool around the far end corner of the bar. She remembered seeing him enter just a minute or two earlier. His choice of seats would have been hers had he not been there since, from that position, a person could look all the way down the business side of the bar and also take in the entire room at a glance. Finally, there was a couple, huddled at a table in the corner so close to each other that she concluded they either weren't married—at least not to each other—or were getting ready to be. All eyes except theirs were watching her as she made her way inside, but no one said anything.

She headed over to the bar and slid onto one of the stools near the center of the long, shiny counter. The bartender looked friendly enough and raised his eyebrows in a what'll-you-have gesture.

"Whiskey sour," she said. "Jack Black." Alex's drink. She smiled at the thought.

The bartender nodded and set about making her drink then set it down in front of her. She sipped it. "Good one," she told him. He nodded and busied himself wiping up a spot several feet down the counter.

She closed her eyes. The drink really was good. And she was glad to be away from her aunt and her depressing negativity even for a short while. It was nice here in the dim lighting of the bar. It was quiet. She sipped the whiskey sour and realized she had forgotten to give her mother the legacy brooch. She would do it this evening. After Juanita had gone home. She didn't need her Aunt Juanita's comments on her gift. But right now she just wanted to relax and enjoy the drink in the peace and quiet.

As often happened in the States these days, when race, religion, or politics were in play, the peace and quiet didn't last long.

The two beer-drinking bruisers she had passed when she entered got up from their table and approached her.

"Hey you! Gal!" The biggest and homeliest of the two called to her as he came close, making sure his voice was loud enough that everyone could hear. He was swaggering and looking around, smiling. Showing off for the other customers.

Z looked up at him. Unimpressed. If there was anything Zakaya Kalu could not stand it was affected macho and swagger. She turned and looked back at the whiskey bottles lined up in front of the giant mirror mounted to the wall behind the bar and, for just a second or two, sized him up in the mirror. Big. Probably more than two hundred and fifty pounds. But all of it fat and flab. She returned to her drink and ignored him.

"Hey! I'm talkin' to you!" He poked her in the ribs on her right side.

She turned toward him. Slow. Deliberate. "Don't touch me."

This appeared to amuse Big Ugly to no end. He grinned, displaying a mouth full of tobacco-stained and rotting teeth, and turned to his companion. "Be careful! Don't touch her!"

The second guy, a little flabbier, but just as big, laughed. He said, "What's she gonna do? Bite you?"

Big Ugly turned back to Z. "I know exactly what to do with you." He put his left arm around her shoulders, his hand reaching down to fondle her left breast.

His touch was repulsive. Still, she forced herself into a professional calm. She looked down at his hand and released the drink she had been cradling with her right. In the mirror behind the bar she could see him watching her. He was smiling. She smiled back. Slowly reaching up, she stroked her hand down his forearm gently. Calmly. When her fingers reached his own, she took his hand and, with considerable force, drove her thumbnail into the flesh about halfway between the joint and the nail bed of his own thumb. He screamed and tried to pull away, but she slid off the barstool and went with him like an angry ferret refusing to let go. She kept up the pressure for what must have seemed an eternity to the shocked onlookers while he kept screaming and attempting to free his hand from her grip.

At last she released him and, enunciating each word distinctly, said, "I said, don't touch me."

By this time the other patrons were slack-jawed with fascination at the scene unfolding in front of them. Even Flabby Sidekick had backed away and was just watching, unsure what to do. Zakaya didn't see any of them except peripherally. She never took her eyes from those of Big Ugly.

He was livid. "I will touch you, you Black bitch! I will—"

She saw it coming for two whole seconds. His eyes telegraphed his clumsy move unmistakably. He was nothing but a huge bully. Untrained. Undisciplined. The instant he lunged she deftly stepped aside, catching his left foot with her right, sending the unchecked momentum of his full weight careening into the edge of the bar counter with such force that, when his head struck, it knocked him out cold. He doubled up, unconscious, on the floor.

She stepped over him and calmly slid back onto her bar stool.

"How much do I owe you?" she asked the bartender as though nothing at all had transpired.

He laughed. "It's on the house, Miss."

"Thanks." She smiled at him. A genuine smile. As she slid off the stool and started for the door she again noticed the lone drinker at the far end of the bar to her left. Good-looking guy. Maybe thirty-five. Maybe slightly older. He was watching her. He seemed amused by the whole scene. She took mental note, but kept going.

8

There was an opposing tug as she reached out to pull Brassy's push-pull swinging entrance door. A huge, dark figure was pulling it from the other side. A cop. A big, burly, Black cop. Her first instinct warned her she was in trouble. Then her jaw dropped.

"Oh my god! JJ?" She took a step back and looked at him expectantly.

"In the flesh," he said automatically, and had already walked past her a couple of steps when recognition hit. He turned back and stared. "Zakaya?"

She nodded. He stared. They both exploded with laughter at the same time and threw their arms around each other. The patrons were still awe-struck. Apparently, the show wasn't over. The two of them took one of the tables along the wall of windows opposite the bar, two down from the glued-together couple.

"Bartender call you?" she asked him.

"No. Should he have?"

She nodded toward the bar where Big Ugly was still laid flat-out on the floor but slowly regaining consciousness. He was groaning and holding his head in his hands. Flabby Sidekick was hovering over him.

JJ's brow furrowed. "Hmmm. What happened?"

"Wandering hands. I objected."

"Hang tight. I'll be right back."

JJ got up from the table and walked over to Ugly. He looked down at him, then looked around. "Anybody with this guy?"

Flabby Sidekick looked up and nodded.

"Get him out of here before I take his ass to jail."

He came back to the table and smiled at Z.

She said, "Aren't you going to arrest me?"

"Nope. That dude won't press charges. First of all, he was in the wrong. And second of all, nobody's going to report you. No one, especially an oversized bully, wants the world to know that a little five-and-a-half-foot tall Black woman whipped his tail."

"Five-three." She corrected him.

"My goodness, girl! It's been a long time. Where have you been? What have you been up to?"

She shook her head and smiled back at him. "Twelve years. But never mind me. What have *you* been up to? Jarron Heywood-Jones! Still JJ, though, right?"

He nodded.

"You ever get married?"

"Yep. Married my high school sweetheart. How many guys can say that for real?"

"Got any kids?" She gave him an impish smile.

"Sure do. Three. All girls." He laughed. "What can you do?"

"Lot of mouths to feed, for sure. Is that why you became a police officer?"

"Pretty much. Had to have somethin' steady, you know?"

"How did you get the job? I mean, I thought Blacks were the red-headed step-children of the U.S.A. Last in. First out."

"Most of the country is still like that, but some progress is being made in a few places. Like this one. I'm handy to have around, it seems. Go places the white officers don't want to go. Do jobs they feel are beneath them. You know how it goes."

She nodded and changed the subject. "You were the best tight end Alabama ever had."

He broke out laughing. "And how in the world would you know that?"

"Oh, I keep up. I know Alabama football. Always did. And you were the best. Put on a few pounds since then, though, haven't you?" She didn't even try to suppress an impish smile.

"Ouch!" He nodded at the truth of her observation and gave a gentle pat to his midsection.

"I remember that famous fourth and four with six seconds left in the game. Bama was down by three and they decided a tie just wouldn't do. Olson took the ball from center and faked to the running back. Who was he? I forget. Anyway, you held back while the defense piled onto the back as he faked having the ball and plowed through the line. Olson passed a quick little side-arm to you, and you thundered over those four yards into the end zone, knocking their safety to the ground in the process. The clock ticked to zero and the game was over. Bama won 27 to 24. Gutsy call by the coach, I thought. Never forgot it."

JJ shook his head and laughed. "How in hell do you remember that?"

She grinned at him. "Some things are unforgettable, JJ. So what have you been doing? Enough crime here to keep you busy?"

"More than you might think. Lately we've had our fair share, for sure."

"What do you mean?" Z was particularly interested in any local crime due to Zeena's abduction which had initially taken place in this area.

"People disappearing. Some found dead. Strange situations. Hard to explain."

"Hard to explain to me? Or just hard to explain?"

"Hard to explain the situations. But that's not a fun subject. What about you, Z?"

"It's a long story. Bad things happened." She saw him nod. Maybe he knew. Or guessed. So she wasn't going to spell it out. She just skipped right to the heart of the matter. "After high school, and…the things that happened to me, I made my way to the Cascadian border and was rescued—in the truest sense of the word—by one of the finest men I've ever known. He arranged for me to stay. He took me home, adopted me, and raised me up with his own daughter. If you can call it raising. After all, Alex was twenty and I was eighteen by then. Anyway…." She looked around cautiously, but no one seemed to be paying any attention to them. She lowered her voice just the same. "He was CIMA. A Mission Agent for the Cascadian Intelligence Bureau. Kinda like your CIA. At least Alex and I had each other after he was killed on a mission. So I've been pretty happy there in Cascadia."

He nodded his understanding and then quietly asked, "You CIMA now, too?"

She looked at him seriously. "JJ…I'm just a friend of yours who used to live here. You don't have any idea what I do for a living, right?"

"Right." Then he changed the subject. "Your mama must be really proud of you. And happy to have you home. You staying long?"

She frowned slightly. "You know my mama?"

JJ chuckled and looked away. Then he looked back directly at her and shook his head. "Miss Z, *everybody* knows your mama."

She tilted her head and looked at him quizzically.

He explained. "After you left, that woman became a force to be reckoned with. She took on the powers-that-be and never flinched. When she saw unfairness, discrimination, hate, you-name-it, she was in those corrupt faces like stink on shit. Pardon the expression. A lot of us here in town worried for her safety, but she had that figured out, too. She made herself such a well-known figure that the uproar would have been deafening—and dangerous—if anything had happened to her."

Zakaya was as fascinated at this as the patrons had been when she was putting Big Ugly on the floor. She said, "I was just here five years ago. How come I didn't know all this?"

"She probably didn't want to talk about all that. Just wanted to see you. That was all that mattered. She was really just getting started at that time, anyway. And you didn't stay long on that visit, did you?"

"No. I couldn't. I had planned to, but I got called away."

"Oh yeah? What for?"

She smiled. "Can't tell you. Or—"

"—You'd have to kill me, right?"

"Something like that."

They both laughed.

JJ said, "I guess you noticed all the changes around here when you drove in?"

"I did. I was downright amazed."

"That was your mama's doing."

Z told him, "My Aunt Juanita said something to that effect. But you know Aunt Juanita. No telling what she will say next."

JJ laughed. "Yeah, I do. The Black Tornado of Doom."

Z nodded in agreement. "So tell me about Mama. What did she do, exactly?"

"She rallied this town into a hurricane of pride and activity. She preached from the pulpit of her church, too, while the Reverend Johnson sat down and nodded his approval and shouted more than a few Amens. She got everybody so riled up they started believing they didn't have to live like second- and third-class citizens just because the government didn't seem to care about them anymore. Not that it ever much did, of course. She told them they could be somebody. They could live in clean, safe communities. But they couldn't wait for the government to clean it up for them. They had to do it for themselves and for each other. There was a chorus of Amens and Praise God's. She had 'em. They listened. And then the craziest thing happened."

"What?" Z was fascinated.

"They did it. They turned this whole area into something to be proud of. The way it used to be. Better than it used to be. The way Greenwood Avenue was in Tulsa way back in history before the whites bombed it and burned it to the ground. The gangs here were shut down and the members given purpose within the community. People watched out for each other, and they began to take a special pride in their homes and property. It's a showplace now according to International Magazine. They did a piece last summer about Selma and how the businesses here are flourishing."

Zakaya just shook her head as she listened. Her mother had always been a force. At least she had thought so. She was that strong woman that every other woman strived to be. Kind, yet powerful in her own way. Somebody.

She remembered the "Selma Blues" card in her pocket and took it out.

"What do you know about this?" She slid the card across the table to JJ.

"Oh! The Selma Blues. I see you had an introduction." He laughed and then continued. "They were the gang members I mentioned that were given something useful to do besides intimidate people."

"Well, I found them pretty intimidating when I got here."

"The town pays them. They are kind of like an unofficial police force. They have no authority to keep people out, but they will put the fear of God into anyone who seems like they might be here to cause trouble."

"Authority or not, slinging rifles made them pretty scary."

JJ nodded. "That's one thing that's never changed. The gun laws. No matter how many people get killed, it's still legal to walk around with guns in this country."

Z frowned. "They kept them on me until I told them who I was. Then you'd think I had won the lottery and they wanted to be my best friends."

JJ laughed and asked her, "You want somethin' to eat? I was gonna have a sandwich and a cup of coffee. Gordon," he nodded toward the bartender, "Makes the best subs in town."

"No. Thanks anyway, but I guess I should be getting back. I only left because Aunt Juanita was showing her tail."

JJ laughed so hard he nearly knocked over the little condiments stand. "Your Aunt Nita. A disaster walking around looking for a place to happen. And almost always finds one."

"Truer words were never spoken. As they say. By the way," she said, "we are having a barbecue next week. Come."

"I might just do that."

"Good. See you then. You know the address, right?" She got up and squeezed his shoulder.

He nodded. "See you later, Z."

"You, too, JJ."

Her training always just beneath the surface, she looked back once and noticed Big Ugly and his flabby sidekick had gone.

And there was an empty stool at the bar where the lone drinker had been.

ഗരൽ

Inside a gray-painted office in the J. Edgar Hoover building in Washington, D.C., the phone rang. A rather fit man in a dark suit laid his cigar into a thick glass ashtray, reached across his mahogany desk, and picked up the receiver of a special land-line telephone.

"It's possible she could be who we think she is, but I'm not sure at this point." the voice on the other end said matter-of-factly. "I don't think there's a need to rush on this. I will keep on it and—"

He was cut off by Dark Suit. "I will decide whether or not there is a rush here. But I think you could be right to let it play out until we see exactly what she's doing here. Just make sure you don't let her too far out of sight. She's the only one who fits our profile so under no circumstances let her leave the country."

"Yes, sir."

The phone clicked to silence and Dark Suit looked at the receiver as though it was, itself, impertinent. Then he dropped it back with a clack into its cradle on the body of the phone, reclaimed his cigar, leaned back in his chair, and expelled a stinking cloud of blue smoke into the confined office space.

9

Not more than six blocks from Brassy's, in a suburb of old Southern homes, stood a peeling, white two-story with a torn screen door that squeaked when opened and slammed shut with a *whap* when released.

This morning, hours before Z's plane had touched down in Montgomery, he was upstairs in his mother's room opening the window to let in some fresh air. He hated the musty stink of the closed room and inhaled deeply as a light breeze caught at the ancient, yellowed lace curtains lifting and billowing them into the room in a slow, wave-like motion. The sun was already casting shadows on the wall through the purple crepe myrtle that grew a short distance beyond the window.

He looked back at her.

There she was, propped up in the bed all regal and comfy, like a queen. Ignoring him like always. She wouldn't even look at him. She just kept staring at the portrait of his father on the wall opposite the bed. He disliked the portrait almost as much as he disliked her. He backed out of the room into the hallway, his chubby-fingered left hand resting on the doorknob and her breakfast tray gripped firmly in his right. He closed his eyes, then opened and rolled them heavenward.

"I'll be back to check on you later. Don't forget to take your pills."

You old witch.

He closed the door and sighed. He had always tried to make things better. Even for her. And even though she didn't deserve it. It's what he was all about. It's all he had ever tried to do. Ever since he was old enough to do anything. He was sure of that. And it hadn't been easy. She, of all people, should be able to recognize that. But sometimes it just wasn't possible to make things better. Sometimes the opportunity didn't present itself. And he was sorry about that. He really was.

He was about nine years old when he first made things better for someone. That someone was Joanie Crowder. She was about nine years old then, too. He knew that because they were in the same grade at school. She had blue eyes and long straw-colored braids that hung down over her shoulders. Little ribbons were tied into a bow at the end of each one. Every day there were different colored ribbons. He thought she was pretty. Even though she had freckles. When he first heard her name he had laughed and laughed. Just like the other kids. He'd always wanted to fit in with the other kids and they all called her "Crowder peas" and teased her. But he didn't tease. He felt sorry for her even though he did think her name was funny. He could tell she wasn't happy and he had thought long and hard about how to fix that. And then one day he did it. And you should have seen her. She looked so peaceful and happy in her pink satin casket. Everybody said so. After that, he decided his mission in life would be to make things better for people who were not happy. And there were so many of them. It had kept him quite busy over the years.

Right now he had to go to work. He would be late if he didn't get a move on. He liked his job even though he didn't really need it. The inheritance from his Uncle

Robert had set him up for life. Not a very plush life to be sure, but still an independent one. His job, though, gave him the opportunity to get out of the house. Away from *her*. At least for a while. Best of all, it gave him a chance to see other people once in a while and help them out when their situations called for it.

He went downstairs quietly—just as she had always demanded of him—and took the tray into the kitchen where he scraped everything off into the trash and then washed up the teacups and plates, dried them thoroughly, and put them back into the cupboard—the handles of the cups facing to the right.

They must always face to the right. Stupid boy. Do you want your knuckles whacked again?

In the privacy of his own bedroom, he dressed for work. He liked that his bedroom was downstairs—away from hers. He liked the privacy. He liked that the windows faced the street and he could look out and watch the people as they passed by. He liked the blue sky and white clouds he had painted on the ceiling. And the picture of a little boy wearing a straw hat and overalls, fishing in a creek. And he liked his uniform. It was blue and he liked blue. He especially liked his name embroidered in red thread on the white oval patch on the left-hand side—just where a breast pocket would have been if the uniform had had one: *Billy*. It made him feel important. Like somebody. And that's all he had ever really wanted. He hummed and then sang quietly:

> *"Can she bake a cherry pie,*
> *Billy boy, Billy boy?*
> *Can she bake a cherry pie,*
> *Charming, Billy?"*

He liked the "Charming" part. He liked being charming. Yes. Even though some people didn't seem to think so. What did they know?

> *"Did she ask you to come in,*
> *Billy Boy, Billy Boy?*
> *Did she ask you to come in,*
> *Charming Billy?"*

What he didn't like about the job was that the company wouldn't allow him to drive. Never mind that he could never pass the driver's test and had no license. It was always some other guy at work who got to drive the big, lumbering truck while he had to get out and get his nice uniform all dirty and stinky. But that was part of the job and, after all, he did have a washing machine. And nice, thick gloves to keep his hands clean.

He smoothed out and folded his pajama top and bottoms into precise rectangles and placed them into the second drawer of his bureau. On the right-hand side. Nice and neat.

He admired himself in the mirror. Not too bad, he thought. But nothing special. He knew he was nothing special. *She* had told him so often enough. He disliked the scars from the acne he had suffered as an adolescent. And he knew he was too pudgy—fat even. But he liked chocolate cake and candy bars. *She* would disapprove, but she was upstairs, unable to come down anymore, so she couldn't see him. Indulging himself. Getting fat. So she could just keep her bossy mouth to herself.

Still, when he smiled he thought he looked quite nice. And people liked you when you looked nice.

And they trusted you.

He checked to be sure his room was tidy with everything in its place. Then he smiled at his reflection.

Maybe today he would find someone sad. Someone he could make better. Happier. He began to whistle.
  Charming Billy.

10

It was seven o'clock by the time Z got back to her mother's house. Her Aunt Juanita had, mercifully, gone home and taken her negativity with her. Her mother and Zeena were sitting at the kitchen table when she came in. It was the same table she remembered. The same cook stove still sat in the corner beyond the sink. Perched on the windowsill above the sink was a glass of water containing a sweet potato suspended by three toothpicks and from which grew a decorative vine of greenery—one of dozens her mother had grown over the years. The smell of fresh-baked biscuits filled the room.

"Z! Come in and sit down." Her mother motioned her into the room and patted the seat of the chair to her left in welcome. "You want a cup of coffee?"

"That would be heavenly, Mama."

"How about a syrup biscuit?"

Z noticed Zeena was happily munching away on one of her mother's syrup biscuits and a flood of childhood memories washed over her. Syrup biscuits were a favorite when she was a girl.

"Mama, that would be just the thing."

She watched as her mother picked up one of her huge biscuits from the pan of freshly-baked and, with her index finger, poked a hole into the side of it—deep into its middle. Then she poured syrup from the bottle directly into the hole and handed it to Z.

"Thanks, Mama." She looked over at Zeena. "You like syrup biscuits?"

Zeena silently nodded her approval as she continued to eat.

"Yum! Alex should be here. She eats like a horse and never gains an ounce." Z laughed, then added, "But you would have to cook an extra pan of biscuits if she were."

Her mother laughed. "I would be glad to. I'd love to meet her one of these days. And the extra pan of biscuits would be no trouble at all, Z. No trouble at all."

The coffee was really good and just what she needed. At last she was relaxing. She remembered the legacy brooch in her bag and held up a finger. She swallowed her bite of biscuit and said, "I'll be right back. I have something for you, Mama."

Mrs. Kalu watched her go into the front room and come back with her bag. Z dug around in it until her hand located the soft velvet of the small case and she brought it out and handed it to her mother.

"What is it?"

"Open it!"

Her mother looked at the faded rose of the velvet and could tell it was quite old. It had obviously been handled many times before it came into her hands. She opened the box to find the blue-stoned brooch nestled in the age-yellowed white satin.

"It's lovely, Zakaya. What kind of stones are these?"

"I don't know, Mama. This was my legacy. It was in the legacy box I chose on my birthday. There was a note with it, too."

She told her mother the story of the brooch and how it had belonged to someone who was very much loved. Then she explained that her mother was also very much loved and so she wanted her to have it.

"It will look wonderful on one of your church hats. Maybe the dark blue one. Do you still have it? Those light blue stones will look really fine on that dark blue."

"I believe it will, too. Thank you, Z." She looked up from the brooch. "You say you got this in one of the legacy boxes on your birthday? Tell me how that works again?"

Her mother was somewhat familiar with how things in Cascadia worked, but she apparently loved to hear Z tell it just the same and Z was happy to oblige her. She described the custom in Cascadia of citizens leaving a "legacy" for people who would come long enough after them that they would never know who would receive it. Something small. But something nice. Sort of a gift of friendship from an older generation to a younger one. All kinds of things were left, after being approved by the Sage of the Legacy Library, of course, and then the legacy boxes were sealed and a seventy-year timer began counting down. When the seventy years were up, the boxes automatically unlocked, and their contents were available for someone to claim.

"Of course no one can claim the contents of a legacy box unless they're Cascadian—and until they have reached their thirtieth birthday. From that day they are eligible to choose a box. But only one. And just one time. No second chances." Zakaya laughed. "Then, after they receive one, they are encouraged to leave something for someone else who will come along seventy years in the future."

"Did you leave anything?" her mother asked without looking up from the stones as she turned the brooch this way and that, catching the light on the many facets.

"No, ma'am. Not yet. I don't have any idea what I would leave. But I have plenty of time to decide."

"What are the boxes like? How big are they?"

"Do you remember the old post office boxes here with glass doors on them? They are pretty much like those except they are a bit larger and have two doors instead of just one. The outside door is made of glass and has a number printed on it. The Sage can lock and unlock that one with her master key. But the inside door is solid metal and hides the contents of the box. After the legacy gift is placed inside, the interior metal door is closed and the Sage depresses a button key. That key locks the door securely and starts the timer counting down seventy years before it automatically unlocks. Once the metal door is locked, not even the Sage can open it again. After that inner door is locked, the Sage closes and locks the outer glass door with her master key."

"How can you tell which boxes are unlocked so you can choose one for your legacy?"

"There's a tiny light that glows between the two doors. If the light is glowing red, the inside door is still locked. But if the light is green, the timer on the inner door has counted down to zero and the lock is released. There were eleven boxes with green lights when I visited the Hall on my birthday."

"How on earth did you figure out which one to choose?" Her mother kept admiring the brooch as she talked.

"I just chose the first one I saw that was right there in my face. Seemed logical to me. There was no way I could know what was in any of them, so it didn't really matter which one I chose. I'm glad I chose the one I did, though. This brooch is just perfect for you. And I really like that it belonged to someone who was loved. Now it does again." She leaned over and gave her mother a hug.

Her mother looked at the brooch for several moments more then closed the box and placed it on the table in front of her. She looked at Zakaya. "Now. Tell me about your

life in Cascadia. Tell me about the people you work with."
She waved her hand. "I know! I know! I know I've heard
it all before but tell me again."

Zakaya started laughing. "Where on earth shall I start?"

"Tell me about your team."

"Well, first, there is Viking. His name is Erik Larsen,
but no one dares call him that. Everyone always calls him
Viking. He's the team leader. He's big, tall, and fierce.
Long, dark blonde hair. Beard. Blue eyes. Dangerous
looking. But kind. And a great team leader."

Her mother smiled and nodded, waiting for more.

"Then there is my partner, Gray Hawk. He's Native
American. He's the one you saw in the photo with Alex.
He's very quiet. Doesn't talk much. But he's very
observant and he has an uncanny ability to read people."

"He is a handsome thing, that's for sure."

Zeena stopped munching the syrup biscuit and broke
into a big smile at that and nodded her approval. "He's
beautiful!" she said.

"Uh huh." Z reached over and rubbed her head. "Too
old for you, though, Miss."

Zeena giggled.

Mrs. Kalu asked about Alex's partner.

"That's Parker. Parker West. He's good-looking, too,
right Zeena?"

Zeena nodded her approval again.

"He's a good guy to have on your side, too. He's got a
crazy sense of humor. Sometimes he seems more boy than
man, but he's a very conscientious team partner. He's
smart. And brave. Alex is lucky to have him."

"Isn't there another member of the team? I seem to
remember another."

"Oh. Yes. Budgie. He's the computer expert. He's
super-intelligent, but very socially awkward. He never

goes on missions. He's a bit autistic. And he has a huge crush on Alex."

Mrs. Kalu finally asked the question Z had been hoping to avoid having to answer.

"Didn't Alex turn thirty a couple of years ago? What did she get for her legacy?"

"Long story, Mama. Let's go sit on the sofa."

They retired to the comfort of the small living room where Z told her mother the story of Alex's legacy and how it had turned out to be the fascinating journal of a young American woman named Rachael. She explained how Rachael's scientist father had accidentally created an extremely deadly chemical that the U.S. Government wanted to turn into a weapon.

"Long story short," Z said, "he destroyed the formula and then hid the chemical itself. Then he encoded messages in Rachael's journal that tangentially revealed the chemical's location so it could be recovered and destroyed by the Cascadian government. He sent Rachael to Cascadia to deliver the journal to the Sage at Legacy Hall, in Santa Rosa. Apparently, he and the Sage were old friends who had worked together in the States some time earlier. Unfortunately, there was a man—American CIA or FBI—we never really knew which—who had been tasked with recovering the journal for the United States because the U.S. Military believed it contained the formula for the chemical. Anyway, the girl, Rachael, was accidentally shot outside the Legacy Library in Santa Rosa. She died in the Sage's arms just after the Sage stuffed the journal into an empty legacy box and locked it to keep it safe from the man. Then, seventy years later, when Alex visited Legacy Hall on her thirtieth birthday and chose that very legacy box, she found the journal, deciphered the messages, and the CIMA-2 team geared up to recover the deadly chemical before the Americans could find it. There were indications they were still after it, and we believed they wanted to turn it into a weapon of war."

She stopped talking. She deliberately left out the part about being wounded, but she had the nagging feeling she had already said too much just the same.

She looked into her mother's eyes. "This is all confidential, Mama. My safety here depends on no one knowing I had anything to do with any of that."

"Any of what?" the very wise Mrs. Kalu asked innocently.

Zakaya, trying to look deadly serious, could not suppress a smile. "Thank you, Mama. But the best part of that whole mission was finding Miss Cute Thing here." Z hugged Zeena close.

"That was the best part for me, too," Zeena said.

"Yes, that was a very good thing," her mother said. "But so dangerous, Zakaya. I worry about you."

"I know, Mama. But that's my job. I really wouldn't want any other."

11

Z lay awake early next morning, taking in her old room. The walls were still painted a light robin's egg blue and the curtains were still white eyelet—touches of femininity she didn't often show outwardly these days, but they felt somehow appropriate here in this house and on this morning. The covers on the bed were new, however. A sunshiny yellow and blue quilt. And the sheets were snowy white and soft.

She stared up at the ceiling. The old crack was still there and she smiled at her memories of lying in bed as a girl, imagining various images that seemed to appear along the curves and lines of the crack. If she closed one eye, the jagged lines of the crack became a butterfly. If she closed the other, they became a dragon. When the dragon morphed into Uncle Bo, she closed both eyes and turned her face away.

She stretched slowly to avoid waking Zeena. The girl was facing away from her, sleeping with legs drawn halfway to her chin. Her face was peaceful and calm. Delicate. Z had come to love her very much. She wasn't sure why. She had never once felt the desire to be a mother yet the girl had stirred something within her. She was thin. Fragile. Much like she, herself, had been at that age. But there was something more. There was a vulnerability that

Z had recognized instantly. And the bond had formed almost as quickly.

She laughed silently as she remembered how Zeena had announced she wanted to be a CIMA agent, like herself and Alex. That was on a Friday. By the following Monday she had decided she wanted to be a fashion designer. Z was particularly protective of her because of everything she had been through. But even more than that, because she was somehow so very young for fifteen. Most girls at fifteen these days were rather worldly, but Zeena—as far as Z could ascertain—hadn't had the experiences of growing up among friends with whom to banter back and forth about dreams and ideas. Further, she was small for her age and did not appear anywhere near fifteen years old. Z had taken her to a physician after the rescue two years earlier and learned the girl had, mercifully, not been sexually abused. Her virginity would have been a bonus to her traffickers and that is probably the only thing that had temporarily saved her.

Money. It always came down to money with that kind of filth.

She reached out and placed her hand on Zeena's head. The cushion of her hair felt soft beneath her fingers. The girl stirred.

"Good morning, Sleepyhead." Z sat up now and propped herself on a couple of pillows.

Zeena rubbed her eyes and yawned. "Morning."

Her eyes. Z loved Zeena's eyes. They were green. Her father must have been from the islands. Or her mother. She had never said and Z did not ask.

"You ready for our big grocery shopping trip?"

Zeena yawned again and stretched out her arms. "How much fun can going to a grocery store be?"

"You never know. They may have some exotic and wonderful new kind of peanut butter or something." Zeena laughed and Z smacked her good-naturedly with a pillow. "Better get up and get dressed."

A knock on their door. Mrs. Kalu stuck her head in. "You girls want some breakfast?"

Pancakes! Zeena loved pancakes. With peanut butter. And maple syrup. Z settled for just the syrup and a little butter. And a nice, hot cup of coffee.

After breakfast, Mrs. Kalu supplied them with the list of items she wanted for the BBQ and they headed out for the store not long after the dishes had been cleared, washed, and put away.

On the way to the grocers, Z decided to broach the subject of Zeena's mother with her. The girl was politely non-receptive.

"She doesn't want me, Miss Z."

"Why do you say that, Baby?"

"Because it's true. And I don't want to go back. I want to stay with you. You won't let her take me away from you, will you?" Zeena's voice was quietly steady but her eyes pleaded.

"What makes you think she would try? Didn't you just say she doesn't want you?"

Zeena was visibly concerned. She was torn and confused and not ready to deal with Z's logic. "I know, but—"

"Let's just wait and see what happens, okay? Try not to worry about it. I want you to stay with me, too. But you do have a mother. And it's been two years. It's only right that we go to see her. You know. To see how she really feels. Maybe she misses you terribly. I know I would."

Zeena gave Z a half smile but then frowned, turned her head away, and looked out the window. She said nothing more.

Z sighed.

What a mess! I should have left her in Cascadia. But…

એ૭એ૭

Z decided to surprise Zeena with a small gift. Something to take her mind off her worries. At least for a little while. She pulled into a parking space in front of an art supply store in a shopping center and they went inside.

"How about some supplies for your designing projects?"

Zeena was still down emotionally but couldn't hide her pleasure at this. "Miss Z! Do you mean it?"

"Of course. Let's see what they suggest for a budding young fashion designer."

Z was relieved to see the girl perk up. This seemed to be just the thing. At least for the moment. Twenty minutes later, drawing supplies and pads of paper purchased, they piled into the car and headed for the grocery store.

Mrs. Kalu had tasked them with a long list. Everything from charcoal briquettes—the old-fashioned way of cooking out, but still the best as far as she was concerned—to condiments for the ribs and burgers. Z directed Zeena over to the condiments aisle to gather the mustard and pickles while she pondered the selection in the meat department.

This domestic stuff was harder, she decided than many of the cases she had worked for the CIB. She frowned at the packaged selections in the meat department as though she had never before been to a grocery store. Of course she had been, but at home in Cascadia it seemed different somehow. Easier. She wasn't sure why. Maybe because she mostly ate fresh vegetables and fruit—a habit she had picked up as Gray Hawk's partner. Alex would eat almost anything you put in front of her, gobbling up her own last crumb and then taking yours, but Gray ate mostly vegetarian. She was wondering what Alex would choose when she heard someone speaking to her.

"Zakaya Kalu? Is that you?"

Z straightened up and turned to see a pleasant-looking, elderly woman.

"Miss Nana!" She pushed the grocery cart aside and wrapped herself around the woman.

She turned her loose and looked at her. "Is it really you?"

Nana was much older than she had been when she had taken care of Z as a child while her mother worked. Round eyeglasses perched halfway down her nose and a sweep of gray hair was pulled back in cornrows on each side and ended in a sort of bun at the back of her head.

"Yes. It's me. I'm still here, praise the Lord!" Nana pushed her glasses back up her nose.

Z was beaming. "It's so good to see you again. I should apologize for being such a handful when you were taking care of me."

Miss Nana laughed. "Child, I've had worse than you ever were. Five times over. That one right there!" She pointed down the aisle toward a little red-headed, freckle-faced boy who was examining everything on the shelves within his reach.

"He looks like a handful, all right. How long—" Long. The word "long." She suddenly felt a wave of fear sweep over her. Zeena had been gone too long.

She stopped talking, dropped the shopping list, and began to run the length of the store punching up Zeena on her wrist-mounted tele-communicator as she ran. With the t-com Z could see Zeena's location. The display indicated she was very close.

"Zeena!" She called the girl's name as she ran but there was no answering call. She dashed quickly from aisle to aisle, peering down each one, continuing to call out for the girl. Her fear grew with each empty aisle. When she reached the condiment's aisle she saw yellow and tomatoey-red goo splattered in fingers across the floor where mustard jars and ketchup bottles had landed and broken when they had fallen from the shelves—or from the hands of someone frightened—or taken. Z's fear gripped at her throat, cutting off her breath. Zeena was not there.

She ran quickly, searching each empty aisle until, at last, she came to the final possibility and saw no one. In the middle of the aisle, boxes of cereal had been tossed about as though thrown hurriedly and without concern.

Everything began to spin. "Zeena!" she shouted.

But there was no answer. She told herself to breathe as she began walking slowly down the aisle checking the t-com display. The display indicated she and Zeena were closer and closer until they appeared as connected dots. But there was no one in the aisle.

Without warning she felt a soft touch at her ankle. A small, dark arm and hand reached out from the lowest shelf between skewed boxes of cereal. A flood of relief swept over her. She fell to the floor, took the hand, and dragged Zeena from behind the tall boxes of cereal she had used in an attempt to conceal herself.

"Zeena! What's the matter? What are you doing there? What's wrong?"

"I saw them."

"Who, Baby?"

"The men."

"What men?"

"The men that took me before." Zeena was shaking. Her face wet with tears.

"What is it, Miss Z?" Nana had followed her.

"Nana! Take her hand and don't let it go!"

Z released the girl to Nana and ran to the front of the store and out the door. She looked in every direction but saw nothing out of the ordinary. A couple was casually loading groceries into the back seat of their car and several people were walking toward the store on their way in. On the road beyond, she saw only regular traffic and a single police car cruising past. A large garbage truck was pulling out of the parking lot. She noticed everything yet came up with nothing. There was nothing to be done. Not right now. Nothing except to get Zeena home again.

And then, taking a risk she had hoped to avoid, she would go to the police.

Maybe.

First, she would call Alex in Cascadia.

12

Driver glanced at his partner in the passenger seat. "Damn! How did that girl get loose? I'm positive she recognized us. Do you think she remembers? Do you think she recognized us?"

Partner shrugged his shoulders. "Of course she recognized us. Why else would she panic and drop the stuff all over the floor? Who cares? She's a kid. Nobody believes anything kids say. Besides, she's Black. Nobody will care double. Don't worry about it. We never hurt her, did we? Go around this block and come back up facing the store. Park over to the side. We'll wait for her to come out again. Then we'll follow."

"Why should we follow? We should just get the hell out of here."

"Because she saw us. We need to get her back before she causes major amounts of trouble."

Driver sighed and looked back at the road. He turned off the main road into the residential area opposite the shopping district. He drove around the block emerging again on the side road facing the grocery store, then parked at the curb.

"I don't know," he said. "If she can identify us…"

"Why are you so worried? Even if she can, who is going to believe her? She's a skinny little kid with a vivid imagination. We look like somebody she saw once. That's all. Nothing to worry about. We'll get her back and that will be the end of it."

"Maybe." Driver sounded not at all convinced.

"So stop worrying. Besides, we have to concentrate on the upcoming transfer. Too much money is at stake to be panicking over some little 'ninny' who's afraid of her own shadow. We'll take her, put her with the rest, and that will be that. Stop worrying."

Driver sighed. "You're right, I guess. Still, it makes me uneasy. I never expect to see any of them again. And here one of them is. Right under our noses. How did she get loose? I thought she was long gone and I doubt the buyer just dumped her. It was a long time ago, too, wasn't it?"

"A while. Couple of years, I think. But once I do my part I don't know what happens to them."

"You don't care, either, do you?" Driver sounded impatient.

"No. And neither should you. Otherwise, find a different…occupation."

"Maybe. Maybe. But we shouldn't have dumped that last one like we did. What if she wasn't dead? What if somebody finds her and she tells?"

"She's dead. Stop worrying. I'm telling you. You worry too much."

"How do you know she's dead? What did you do?"

"She's dead. Stop worrying about it. Look! There she is." Partner nodded in the direction of the grocery store parking lot. Z and Zeena were heading to their car.

Driver frowned. "Who's that with her? Never seen her before."

"Don't know. Maybe a relative. For sure not that crack-head mother of hers. Worthless piece of humanity."

Driver looked from the two emerging from the grocery store to his partner beside him. "How are we different?"

"For Christ's sake! How did I get partnered with a schizophrenic? Will you just pack your conscience away for five minutes and follow those two?"

They watched as Z and Zeena got into their rental and pulled out of the parking lot. Driver started the Orca and eased back out onto the main highway, merging with the rest of the traffic a couple of vehicles behind them.

"Well, you didn't have to kill her. That last one."

"She wouldn't stop screaming. Why do you think Snitch called me to come get her? What was I supposed to do with her? Just turn her loose? Get real."

"Still…"

Partner pulled out his pocketknife and began cleaning beneath his fingernails. "Besides, Snitch had already ruined her. Damned guy can't keep his dick in his pants. Didn't really have a choice. So just shut up and drive, will you?"

Once they got past the Selma Blues at the city limits and determined that Zeena was staying on Levoy Avenue, they turned north again and headed back to Crimson City.

Partner was quiet for a while. Then said, "She did see us. That's certain. We have to get her back again."

Driver said nothing.

&&&

There was no denying the episode at the grocery store had left Zakaya shaken and, with Zeena safely home, she called Alex on her secure CIMA number. A sleepy voice came through the T-com.

"Hello? This is Alex."

"Alex! Z. Did I wake you?"

"Uh huh. What's up?"

Z could almost see Alex rubbing the sleep from her eyes. She checked her t-com. It was still early in Cascadia.

"Sorry. But Alex? I think I made a mistake bringing Zeena here."

"Oh yeah? How so?"

Z told of Zeena's general worried demeanor since they got off their flight. Then she described the incident in the grocery store that had sent her into a panic.

Alex let out a "Whew!" on the other end of the conversation. "She hid behind cereal boxes? What did you do?"

"There was nothing I could do. By then, whoever it was had fled the store. I ran up front but didn't see anyone or anything suspicious. I just have a really bad feeling about all this, Alex. I should go to the police, but I'm halfway afraid to."

"Why?"

"You know why, Dufus! That mission two years ago!"

Alex laughed at being called the old familiar name Z had tagged her with when she was being obtuse, then grew serious. "I don't think they could possibly know you were there. We entered the country under aliases. Very good ones, at that."

"Still…" Z was thoughtful. She said, "For all their bad decisions in governing, the Americans are not stupid. And they were really pissed off about losing that chemical. You know how warlike they are. They badly wanted to weaponize it. They're probably still fuming over that loss. Anyway, I think bringing Zeena here was a mistake. I'm close to deciding to just get on the next plane out of here and take her home. It's not safe here. I'm sure of that."

"But you just got there! Anyway, how did your mother like the brooch?"

"She loved it. I knew she would. So far the visit with her has been great except for my Aunt Juanita and if it weren't against the law I would have drowned her in the toilet. How are things there?"

Alex laughed. "Fine. Except the director has pulled Chuck Ball from CIMA-3 to pair up with Gray in your absence. I think Gray is on his last nerve with him and wishes you would come home. All Chuck does is moon around sighing that you're not here. And when he's not sighing, he talks. All the time. That just drives Gray crazy."

"Gah!" Z rolled her eyes. "Me and Chuck Ball? That's never going to happen, He's an okay guy but he's just not my type. Tell Gray I miss him, too."

"I will. So…what are you going to do?"

"Take a chance. Go to the police. At least that's my thinking right now. The only problem is that I have no concrete evidence for anything. And Zeena is no help. She's paralyzed with fear. Also, I can't even prove she was ever taken by traffickers in the first place. I'm toast if I reveal my part in freeing her during the mission. Even if they don't know who I am right now, they're bound to start putting two-and-two together if I get too explicit. And with Zeena here with me, I can't risk being arrested. Also, what if the authorities, whoever they are, decide to take her away from me and give her back to her mother. Zeena swears her mother doesn't want her and she lives in fear that I'll take her back there. Honestly, Alex, I don't know what to do. This is a situation where I'm damned if I do and damned if I don't."

This was an unusual quandary for Z. She had never been in any situation quite like it. She had been in many dangerous situations, but never when the alternatives were lose-lose.

There was silence on the other end. Z could imagine the wheels turning in Alex's head and she felt maybe she had burdened her with something she really could do nothing about. At least not at the moment. And she could almost hear what Alex was thinking.

First, there were the relations between the United States and Cascadia. So far, like competitive siblings, the two countries held each other at arm's length in a kind of suspicious truce. Yet sharing a history, and the same continent, it often worked to the advantage of both to cooperate. So the maintaining of good will was of sensitive importance. The CIB and her CIMA-2 team were very much a part of it all. Still, she had no doubt that if the Americans positively connected her to the mission two years ago, they would arrest her and exact retribution from her country. What that retribution might entail was anyone's guess, but Zakaya's instincts were to avoid it if at all possible.

Secondly, she was positive there were many other girls at risk besides Zeena. To be taken by some strange man who would put his hands on your body and force you to do things—horrible things—against your will was something most people could not fathom. Yet it happened to young girls all over the world every day. Zakaya was all too familiar with it and her strongest instincts were to stop it. She could not turn away.

Two instincts. Save herself and her country's reputation? Or save Zeena and some small number of the young girls facing a life of slavery and abject misery? If she went to the police there was a chance she could do one at the peril of the other. And a greater chance she could do neither.

Finally, Alex spoke. "Well, Z, I've never known you to run away from a challenge. Or from a fight if it came to it. You will figure this out and you'll know what you have to do." She paused and then asked, "So when are you going to the police?"

Z laughed in spite of herself. Alex knew her too well. She said, "I don't know. Honestly I'm just not sure. My mother has planned a barbecue especially for me this week. Everybody and his fifth cousin is invited. I don't want to mess that up by getting myself in hot water. Still, I may have to take that chance. By the way, Mama says you should comb your hair."

Alex laughed. "Whatever you do, be careful. And keep us updated here. If you need this team, all you have to do is signal."

"I know. I will. I love you Alex."

"I love you, too."

Zakaya ended the conversation with a click.

She needed to think.

13

Z stewed over the dilemma and had come up with no answer until this morning when she dragged herself to the kitchen table with an early-morning cup of coffee and the day's newspaper. The story on the front page had given her the seed of an idea.

Apparently, a body had been found in one of the local cemeteries. Jokes would probably be made about that all over town. She could see them already circling in her head like swirling newspaper headlines in some old black and white movie: **Police Baffled at Finding Dead Body in Graveyard!** And **Body in Cemetery Confounds Police!** She chuckled at the irony and shook her head, then read the article more thoroughly.

The paper described the strange scene discovered by a ten-year-old boy taking a shortcut to the ballpark in the next block over from the cemetery. The boy said the dead man was smiling and looked weird "like a fake dummy in the movies." The body was lying on the granite slab above the burial site of a Mrs. Joseph Cunningham, but there was, as far as could be ascertained, no relation between the two. The man was easily identified as Jake Conway, a local man known by many and who had recently become homeless due to his late wife's medical bills. She'd had cancer and her treatment had bled the couple of every cent they had. A small bottle containing a flower, and a small amount of water—to keep it fresh, it was guessed—had been carefully placed in his hands. The flower, apparently, had been pilfered from one of the nearby graves. Mr. Conway's throat had been cut from carotid to carotid with a sharp instrument. Though no weapon had been found, it was thought to be something razor-sharp, like a scalpel. Police were asking for help from anyone who may have seen or heard anything unusual in the area over the past two days.

Headline jokes aside, this was no laughing matter. Or maybe it was. Whatever it was, it was damned strange. According to the police report, which quoted the medical examiner, the smile appeared to have been "pushed" into position on the victim's face after death, rendering the whole scene grotesque. Because of the gentle way the body had been treated, the police had dubbed the unknown suspect the "Kind Killer." The case was ongoing, and the police were investigating.

The police were investigating.

She read on. The article described the frustration of the public with the police who had, as yet, no suspect in this current case, and had also been unable to find a young girl who had gone missing back in May. She had been shopping in a local dress shop with a friend when she just seemed to disappear without a trace. Now, with this new homicide, it was feared the police might just shelve that case since they now had their hands full with this new one.

The words sang out to her as she sipped her coffee a little slower. She was thinking. This could be an opening for her. A way to legitimately investigate the traffickers. It would be much easier to do it from inside the police department as a temporary deputy or detective than out here on her own.

Somehow she had to get involved with this. If nothing else, she should alert the police to human trafficking in the area. The traffickers who had taken Zeena were still out there, close by, and that hit a nerve deep within her. This was personal. If the local LEOs would accept her help, she could work from inside the police department, in some capacity. On the inside, she would have access to information she would be hard-pressed to get any other way. But how to get on the inside?

She decided she could offer her services as a visiting "officer"—a police detective from her own country. It would be dangerous, depending on how savvy the local police were, but it could work given that they were pretty small potatoes compared to the Feds. Then, after her mother's barbecue, she would put Zeena on a plane for Cascadia. With Zeena safely out of the way, she could devote herself to finding those scumbags and ending their vile activities forever.

And if the police said no? They might well do that. Still, she had to try. Her mother had told her many times when she was little and struggling with something difficult: nothing beats a try but a failure.

Even though it was all tentative, she had to contact the team in Cascadia to make arrangements. They would have to be involved since she would need an ID and weapons. She would also need permission since, by definition, her vacation would have morphed into an international covert mission hunting human traffickers—even if that mission was not under the "official" sanction of the CIB.

She took her coffee into the backyard, away from other ears, and punched up Viking, the CIMA-2 team leader, on her t-com. She explained the situation and he agreed to run it by Tillerman, the head of the CIB, and get back to her as soon as he had an answer.

She waited nearly three hours for the call to come through. Permission had been given. With caveats. First, she would have to present herself as an ordinary police detective with no connection to the CIB. Secondly, if the police agree and somehow manage to find her out, she would basically be on her own since, under the circumstances, there would be little the CIB could do to help her. Even hitting the red emergency call button on the inside of her t-com couldn't be guaranteed to bring the help she would need.

She understood.

"We have an operative somewhere in this area, right?" She fidgeted with the handle on the coffee cup as she spoke.

Viking acknowledged the presence of the operative. "He works undercover. I'm not sure exactly where he is or who he is. But, yes. We have someone there."

"I will need several things," she told Viking. "I'll need a weapon and boots. Also, a boot knife. You know my sizes and preferences. And, of course, I will need identification as the regular police detective I'm being demoted to." She was silent for a moment. Then, "How long will it take?"

Viking sighed. "Z, are you sure about this? If anything happens to you, Alex will be devastated—not to mention the rest of us. You're vital to this team and we don't want to lose you to some hoo-ha yokels no matter how bad they need apprehending."

"I know. But I'm sure. At least I'm sure about going to the police. Maybe they won't even accept me. I just want to be prepared in case they do. If it turns out there is nothing I can do, I'll call and make arrangements to return everything to the operative and come home. But Viking?"

"What?"

"These traffickers are here. Zeena saw them. Scared the living you-know-what out of her. She's a mental wreck over it. These people are the scum of the planet, and someone needs to take them down. And if I do somehow get on this case, I promise not to hit Em-Call unless it's absolutely necessary. This is exactly what you would do, and you know it, don't you?"

Viking sighed. "Yeah."

"So how long?"

"You'll have everything by tomorrow at the latest. You'll be contacted with the time and place. Just sit tight. You'll be getting a pizza delivery later today. Make sure you are the one to open the box. And Z?"

"Yes?"

"You're determined aren't you? I mean, you would have gone ahead with all this even without permission, wouldn't you?"

Z was silent for a long moment. Then, "Yes. You know me, Viking. I can't let something like this go. True, not my country any longer. But still my problem. Zeena's problem. The whole freaking world's problem with garbage like this. Somebody has to do something. I'm here. They're here…"

Viking interrupted. "If you need assistance from the team…"

"I know. I won't signal unless it's absolutely necessary. And Viking?"

"What?"

"See if you can relieve Gray of Chuck Ball, will you? I understand the guy is driving him crazy."

Viking laughed. "Take care, Z."

"I will."

"I mean it."

"I know. I will."

Zakaya clicked off. Nothing to do now but wait. And think about how to approach the police.

14

In Cascadia, Viking pushed his huge hulk back from his desk in the CIMA-2 office and looked around. Budgie was busy on his computers, buried beneath headphones and intent upon something he was tracking down. Alex, whose desk was side-by-side with his own save for a three-foot walkway between the two, was busy with paperwork.

He looked from Alex to Parker who had just arrived for work and was standing while opening and shutting his desk drawers, apparently stowing something or looking for something.

Beyond Parker's desk were the desks of Gray Hawk and Zakaya. Viking watched as Gray stoically turned away from Chuck Ball who had been occupying Z's desk and talking non-stop since she had gone to the United States. He knew Gray was becoming more than weary of Chuck and his infatuation with Z. It was difficult to work under the circumstances. Chuck was an incessant talker while Gray was an extremely quiet and thoughtful person. Not a good match.

He would have to speak with Tillerman about getting Chuck transferred back to CIMA-3. An extra person wasn't really needed here at CIMA-2 in any event. And he needed to talk to the team without Chuck Ball listening in. He tapped Tillerman on his t-com and sent the message.

Two hours later, Chuck was moved back to CIMA-3 and Viking called the team together to fill them in on Z's tentative plans.

"She's determined, and you know what that means," he said. "Right now she just plans to go to the police there and offer her services as a Cascadian detective. I've already arranged for her to get the supplies she needs through our operative there. She says not to worry. She says maybe the police won't even want her help, but…"

"Yeah. Right." Alex was not convinced. "I doubt that will stop her. She knows those human traffickers are right there and I seriously doubt she will let it go. I think if the police give her the bum's rush she will just take it on by herself. What do you think?"

Viking sighed. "I don't know. But it's a precarious situation. If the American Feds somehow discover her connection to the mission two years ago…well…." He hesitated.

"They'll arrest her." Alex looked Viking dead-on. "Then what?"

"Then there won't be anything we can do except wait to see what would happen after that."

Gray said, softly, "I don't like it."

Parker spoke up. "Maybe we should just go in and bring her out whether she wants to leave or not."

Alex laughed, but her tone was serious. "Apparently you have never met Z."

Gray said, "That's why I don't like it. She could be in real danger there."

Viking looked up at Gray and then around at each of them. "I know. But she hasn't done anything yet. All she plans to do at the moment is go to the police and offer her services in helping to solve some local murders. She feels if she can get on the inside there, she will have the access she needs to track down the traffickers. So right now I think we just wait and see what develops. She will be in contact if she needs us. I just wanted you all to know what she's up to so you won't be surprised if we have to pick up and go at a minute's notice. And maybe it will all come to nothing."

"Maybe." Alex wasn't convinced. She knew her sister all too well. She should have discouraged her when she spoke with her earlier. But maybe Viking was right. Maybe the police there would just tell her to take her Cascadian ID and stuff it. Maybe she would forget the whole thing and bring Zeena home. Maybe. But every bone in her body was telling her Z would not give up that easily.

☙❧☙

For the past couple of days Z had made every attempt to hide her angst from her mother. An attempt that, as with most mothers, failed miserably. Mrs. Kalu finally pulled the basic story out of her and by the time Z had finished telling almost all of Zeena's story, Mrs. Kalu agreed she should go to the police. The "almost" part that didn't get mentioned, of course, was the danger she would face by going. There was no need to frighten her mother any more than necessary, and it was entirely possible the local police were more conceit than competence. Still, there was no way to know for sure until she actually confronted them.

At half-past three, a pizza delivery car parked in front of the house. The driver got out with a large pizza box and rang the doorbell. Zeena ran ahead of Z and answered the door.

"Pizza for Miss Kalu," the driver said. "It's twenty-four seventy-five, please."

Zeena turned and yelled loudly to Zakaya who was, by this time, standing right behind her and so close that Zeena laughed at yelling.

"How much, again?" Z asked. She looked up from Zeena to the delivery man for the first time. This was the man who had stopped her at the bridge when she first tried to enter Selma. Eli McClain. Surely he couldn't be the operative. Could he? Yet there was something there in his eyes. Her curiosity was piqued.

"Taking a day off from guarding the bridge?" she asked him.

"I sometimes take odd jobs," he said. Then, dimples showing, "There's more to me than meets the eye."

With a tilt of the head, she eyed him for a moment. "Uh huh." She couldn't decide if he was serious in his comment or just flirting with her.

"Twenty-four seventy-five, Ma'am." He flashed that brilliant smile she remembered and it was a few seconds before she tore herself away in order to dig about in her bag to come up with a twenty and a ten.

She handed the money to him. "Thanks."

He nodded and held the box out to her.

She took it, closed the door without waiting for the change, and turned her back to Zeena as she opened the lid.

"Just need to check and see if they got it right," she said. "Ah! Here's the receipt. Better keep it for my records."

She took the slip of paper taped to the underside of the box lid, read it, and shoved it into her pocket.

Printed on the receipt under "Toppings" was the message: **Tomorrow late. Sam's Package Pickup & Shipping. Locker 42.**

A small key had been taped to the receipt beneath the message.

Tomorrow. She wondered how it was possible for the operative to work so fast given that the request had to go up the chain of command in Cascadia until it reached the person who knew the operative's identity, then to the operative him- or herself, items secured, flawless identification made and everything passed along to her. But none of that was her end of the problem to work. She would trust those whose job it was and, tomorrow, she would visit Sam's Package Pickup. Right now, she would eat pizza.

"You like pizza, don't you, Button?" Zakaya smiled at Zeena who nodded enthusiastically. "Well, I know it's early, but let's just eat it anyway. What do you say? Let's call my mom in to join us!"

Anyone peering in the dining room window of the Kalu home would have seen the three generations of women laughing and talking, enjoying each other's company, and the huge gooey pizza lying in its box, table center, between them.

An ordinary scene of three not-so-ordinary women.

15

Z needed to pick up the package before Sam's closed for the day, and she needed to do it without Zeena. But breaking away from her posed problems. It wouldn't do for the girl to be present when she made the pickup and examined the contents of the locker. Z needed to find an excuse to leave her behind. She wasn't used to dealing with this kind of thing but she finally came up with something she thought would work.

She told Zeena she had to run out to the drugstore for something she had seen and wanted it to be a surprise. Zeena would stay home with Mrs. Kalu and practice her fashion designing. After all, it wouldn't be much of a surprise if she was right there with her, would it? Excited to get a surprise, Zeena was happy to agree. Besides, Mrs. Kalu treated her like a much-loved granddaughter—something she had never before experienced.

It was already half past five when Z got into the car and headed out. She made a quick stop at the drugstore where she examined the nail polishes and lipsticks, finally settling on what she thought was a pretty shade of pink and appropriate for a young girl. She made the purchase and hoped Zeena would be pleased. She wasn't very good at this sort of thing and felt completely inadequate. Alex would have been much better at it. She laughed inwardly at the memory of Alex trying on lipstick colors and smooching up her lips in the mirror. Any color would have looked good on Alex, while she, herself, stuck with one color and was done with it.

What she *was* good at was her next stop.

She pulled into the long strip mall that housed Sam's Package Pickup near the far end. She parked the rental and cut the engine. Looking around, she saw nothing out of the ordinary so she got out and walked to the bakery storefront two doors down from Sam's. She peered in the window at the goodies without really seeing them, focusing instead on the images behind her that were reflected in the glass, checking to be sure she was not being followed. She lingered a moment longer then turned and strolled casually down the walk to the package pickup store where she entered and surveyed the place with a single sweeping glance.

At the rear of the store was a long table for the wrapping and weighing of packages. On the left wall hung tape, paper, and all manner of assorted packaging supplies while the right wall held lockers that rose from the floor to about three feet from the ceiling—as high as a normal person could reasonably reach. There was another customer in the store so the employee behind the back table was busy with her. This afforded Z a moment to locate locker number forty-two without appearing unduly ignorant of the layout.

She slipped the key into the eye-level locker and gave it a turn. Inside she found a package wrapped in ordinary brown paper. It was addressed to her mother. Nice touch, she thought. She tugged the package out, nearly dropping it due to its unexpected weight. She wasn't sure what to do with the locker now that she had the package and didn't like to ask. So she closed and locked it, and pocketed the key.

Back in the car, she placed the package into the back seat and drove back in the direction of her mother's house by a circuitous route. She would open it and check the contents once she was a safe distance from the strip-mall and fairly certain she was not being followed.

⁊⁊⁊

In the J. Edgar Hoover building in Washington, D.C., the phone rang. Dark Suit picked up the receiver.

"Yes?"

"Forty-eight here. Still watching our girl. She came out of her mother's house rather late and went to the drugstore. Then she picked up a package—probably for her mother. All pretty ordinary stuff."

"Where is she now?"

"She got into her rental car and headed back to her mother's house."

Dark Suit was silent for a moment, then said, "Well, just keep an eye on her."

"I have to sleep sometime."

Dark Suit grunted into the receiver.

Forty-eight said, "Honestly, she hasn't done anything since she's been here except visit with her mother and take the girl she brought with her shopping. It does look like a vacation and nothing else."

Dark Suit scowled. "You keep an eye on her just the same. I don't trust her. We're still working on identifying her from this end. You just stay with her."

"Yes sir."

Dark Suit dropped the receiver back into its cradle with a clack and began prepping a new cigar.

Sometimes I think forty-eight tells me just enough to keep me off his ass.

⁊⁊⁊

Safely away from the strip-mall, and feeling fairly confident no one was following her, Z pulled the car into a church parking lot several blocks from her mother's house and opened the package.

Inside the box, she found a dun-colored t-shirt, a pair of camouflage cargo pants, and the high-rise boots she had requested. A special sheath was built into the leather to house boot knives. A KA-BAR boot knife had already been placed within each boot. The weapon, a SIG P340, three extra magazines, both a waistband holster and a shoulder holster, and two hundred rounds of ammunition were also included. No wonder the package was so heavy. She smiled and decided that somebody must think she's going into combat. The smile faded when it occurred to her they could be right.

A separate small box contained a Cascadian police officer's badge and a leather wallet with identification that included her photo. Viking was good. The local operative, whoever he was, was also good. And fast.

Z put the clothing, identification, and badge into her bag and the SIG, ammunition, holsters, and boots into the car's trunk and locked it. Then she drove slowly out of the church parking lot and back to her mother's.

She wasn't sure what would come of going to the police. Maybe getting the weapon and ID would all be for nothing. But if it wasn't, she was as ready as she was going to be. Tomorrow, she would go to the police.

16

What to wear was important. Z was so small in stature and youthful in appearance for all her thirty years, that it would be hard to convince of her abilities. She decided, finally, to wear the clothing that had been universal for well over two hundred years—blue jeans. She added a flannel shirt topped with a red sweater draped over her shoulders and a pair of running shoes.

As she looked herself over in the mirror she decided it would do. Neither too young nor too old, too rich nor too poor. Nothing in-your-face. Nothing shocking. Nothing to offend.

No hiding that mass of soft, twisted hair, but it wasn't as if they had never seen a Black woman before. They had likely seen more than she cared to think about, and in situations that, right now, she had no desire to imagine.

Leaving Zeena with her mother, she drove north through Selma and into Crimson City where she pulled into a space on the back edge of the police department's visitor parking area. She cut the ignition and waited as she mulled over her approach.

It was the end of October, but there was still plenty of foliage and the leaves were steadily falling like a light golden rain. The air had that crisp feel about it that promised winter. She watched as the tiniest of whirlwinds picked up and swirled several dozen red and yellow leaves in a vortex, then scattered them as it disrupted and disappeared as quickly as it had come. The swirl of leaves evoked a memory that swept over her like a chill, taking her back to a darker time.

She had been only thirteen when it had started. Just thirteen years old when her Uncle Bo had first touched her. To this day she had no idea why she had never told anyone and she wondered why she had assumed JJ knew when they met in Brassy's after all these years. Maybe she was just being paranoid. Was this sort of thing so usual an experience for young girls these days that it was a given? She shivered.

She watched for a while from inside the car as uniformed officers and ordinary citizens came and went from the building. She noticed an old red pickup truck and a brown car with a dented left rear fender parked at the far end of the parking lot. She was pretty sure she had never before seen the truck but felt she had seen the car at least once before. But she could not place it. It was probably nothing. After all Crimson City was a small town.

She took a deep breath, got out of the car, and went inside.

∽∾∽

The police station was better kept than most buildings in town though it stank of greasy take-out and cigarette smoke. The desk sergeant was watching television as Zakaya entered. He asked her what she wanted while distractedly looking her way and then back at the screen again.

"I need to see the chief."

He looked up and just as quickly looked back at the television screen. "What about?" he asked, not looking at her.

"Or, the officer in charge will do."

Her non-answer got his attention, and he finally looked her way.

"I said, what about?"

"It's private."

This answer clearly pissed this guy off and he started to yell at her when another officer came around the desk enclosure and announced, "I'll handle this, Mike. Miss? Come around and I'll take your statement."

He introduced himself as John Taylor, Captain, and led her through the half door and into the main open bullpen of desks littered with wadded pieces of paper, ashtrays, and general chaos. There were a few officers in the room. Some were at their desks and others mulled around at the end of the room refilling coffee cups. A pair of plainclothes officers came in from the backside door and when she looked their way they hesitated just a second too long. The hesitation didn't go unnoticed.

"Who are they?" Z asked.

"Who?"

"Those guys there." She inclined her head in their general direction.

"Oh. Just a couple of our detectives. Hadeon Cook and Donny Ray Swift. We call them the Fast Food Duo. Get it? Swift and Cook? Fast food?" He chuckled as though he had made an original joke, and added, "They are always leaving their Giant Burger wrappers and shake cups all over the place."

Z couldn't take her eyes off the pair. "Cute."

The officers turned their gaze elsewhere and went to their desks, but something about them nagged at her. Why their hesitation when they saw her? It was strange behavior for police detectives. She finally took her eyes from them and turned back to Captain Taylor.

"Have a seat here." Taylor motioned to a chair beside his desk and then seated himself. After taking her name and address and contact information he looked up and smiled.

"Now, what's the problem?"

Every worry she had had about this moment flashed through her head. What to do? How to act? What to say? She had to be careful.

"I think," she started, "there is human trafficking going on here."

He frowned. "What makes you think that?" He reached for his coffee cup, took a sip, and made a face. "Cold," he said and set the cup down again.

The coffee sip had given her a couple of seconds to think. "My young friend was taken and held captive but she managed to escape. I found her afterwards and I've been taking care of her. Then, several days ago, she saw the men who took her. We were in the grocery store and when she saw them she hid herself behind some boxes on the shelves. She was terrified."

"Several days ago?"

"Yes."

"So why are you just now reporting it?"

For all her careful and thoughtful consideration, this was one question Z had considered but was never quite sure how to answer. She quickly turned the question back on the police department. "I wasn't sure you would believe me. But I thought seriously about it and decided you would want to know."

"Did you see the men?"

"No. They were gone by the time I found her hidden from them."

"What did your friend say they looked like?"

"Both were white. One was tall. The other one was somewhat shorter and heavier."

"That's it? And you expect us to drop everything and go on some wild goose-hunt for two men that could be anyone in town? Have you seen the local paper? We have a smiling corpse on our hands. Smiling! Can you believe it? We've got some nut-job killer on the loose out there putting smiles on corpses! Can you believe it?" He repeated himself. "On top of that, we just got word a young girl's body was found in a ditch south of Selma, and for the last month we've had some crazy who's been streaking—naked as the day he was born—through residential neighborhoods in the northeast part of town. Woman, I have no time for this." He rose from his chair to indicate this nonsense was a waste of his time and he had heard enough.

Z was taken aback at this latest news. She remained seated, her brow furrowed in thought. She dismissed the crazy streaker as unimportant. Then she looked up at the captain and asked, "How old was the young woman you found in the ditch?"

Taylor sighed but answered the question. "The medical examiner says she was in her teens and we have hysterical parents demanding justice and exactly zero leads. So you can see that we are very busy here. Please go home."

"Maybe her body can lead to the traffickers. Have you investigated that possibility?"

"Lady, traffickers don't kill and dump what they consider valuable merchandise. They make no money doing that. It was probably some disgruntled boyfriend who caught her looking at some other boy the wrong way. Go home." Taylor folded his arms indicating he was now closed to this whole conversation.

It was risky, but Z decided to push a bit further. This could be her opening. "Maybe I can help. I'm here visiting my mother, but I live in Cascadia and I'm a detective on the police force there. Maybe I can help you find the killers. I'm very good at what I do."

The Captain looked at her for a moment. He seemed to be considering. He finally sighed. "I think we can handle this. Go home, Detective…Lady…whoever you are." He turned then and shouted, "Mike! Escort this person out!"

Exasperated, Zakaya stared at the detective for long seconds. He stared back, unyielding.

"Tell me something, Captain," she said, at last. "The girl I read about. The one who disappeared while shopping back in May. Is this the only girl ever to go missing from around here?" The captain said nothing so Z asked again, "Is she? Aren't you even interested in catching the people who took her? Don't you want to find her?"

Taylor yelled out, "Mike!"

Still determined, Z offered, "If you are not interested in the trafficking going on right under your nose, maybe I can help you find this Kind Killer, as you are calling him."

The sergeant hustled into the bullpen and stood solidly beside Zakaya. "Let's go," he said.

With an exasperated roll of her eyes at the captain, Z took up her bag and followed the sergeant out of the bullpen and then out of the station.

Once back in her rental, she slammed the car door and banged her head on the steering wheel.

Damn it! There has to be a way. I can't just let this go!

She started the car and circled around to the parking area exit. The red truck was still parked at the edge of the lot, but the brown car with the dented fender was gone.

❦

Hadeon Cook and Donny Ray Swift faced each other across their back-to-back desks. When Z had boldly looked them over as they entered the building, Swift had broken out in a nervous sweat. Once the captain had the desk sergeant escort her out, he whispered across to Cook, "What was she doing here? More to the point, why was she staring at us?"

"Was she? I didn't notice." Cook was shuffling through papers on his desk.

"You know she was! But why?"

"It doesn't matter. She's never seen us before we came in here today. We saw her. She didn't see us. Maybe she thought we were good-looking. You need to get over this paranoia, Swift."

"Yeah, right." Donny Ray was still sweating. He lowered his head and rubbed his forehead as though he had a splitting headache, then he looked back up at Hadeon. "You know what? I'm done with this. I can't do this anymore."

Hadeon Cook put the papers down slowly. Calmly. "No. You're not. You are in this just as deep as I am and I will take you down if you do anything to jeopardize our operation or our freedom. You better give that some serious thought. And while you are at it, think about your wife and baby and the mortgage on that fancy house you bought last year."

Donny Ray stared after him silently as Hadeon got up and walked the length of the room to the coffee machine. His stomach churned.

17

Z found herself becoming angrier and angrier as she drove. It wouldn't do to go back to her mother's house or to have Zeena see her like this, so she turned in to the strip mall that housed Brassy's Bar and Grille and went inside.

The bartender remembered her and lifted his head in silent greeting. She slid, habit established now, onto the same barstool she had occupied on her earlier visit, ordered a whiskey sour, and looked around.

Not many people around. She was especially glad that Big Ugly and his sidekick were not present. She had had enough of that miserable excuse for a man the first time. When the drink came she sipped it and considered what she should do now that she had been rebuffed by the police. She could just give it up, of course, and go home. That would probably be the smartest thing to do. Let someone else worry about child trafficking here. After all, this was no longer her country. What did she care?

Except that argument never held water. She did care. She cared because of Zeena. She cared because it was her mother's country and the country of her birth. And she cared because she was a decent human being and a citizen of the world in which this horror was happening every day. In addition, she had the chops and the qualifications to do something about it. How can you just walk away from something so heinous knowing you could be the one to stop it? Could she live with herself if she did? Could anyone?

She had about halfway finished her drink when the lone drinker she had seen at the end of the bar last time came through the swinging doors. He passed behind her and took a seat at the end where he had sat before. He ordered "whatever-the-lady-is-having" and smiled at her.

She pretended to ignore him and ordered another whiskey sour.

Who the hell is this guy?

There was no help for it. She was suspicious. She had told herself over and over again that you can't live life suspicious of everyone, yet the very nature of her job demanded it. Also her own inner sense of caution and self-preservation.

Her drink came and she began digging around in her bag for a pen and paper. She wanted to write down everything she remembered about the visit to the police station before any of it slipped past her. While she was busy searching for a pen at the bottom of her bag, Big Ugly and his sidekick came swaggering through the door and spied her. In three or four quick and determined steps the big guy was looming over her, his fist raised to strike.

She looked up just in time to see the fist coming at her when another hand reached out, and with great force twisted the guy's arm behind him. The owner of the intervening hand physically walked the bully back, pushed him out the door, and told him to get lost and not come back. Scowling, he held the door for his sidekick to exit with him.

It was the good-looking lone drinker who had intervened. He waited a moment then turned and came back to speak with Z.

"Sorry, Miss." He smiled. "I don't know about you, but I've had about as much of that guy as I can stand."

"Thanks." Z dropped the pen back into her purse and forgot about taking notes.

"I'm Martin Blaze," he said. "Mind if I join you?"

"Sure. It's a free country, isn't it? Well, almost."

He slid onto the stool next to her. "What do you mean, 'almost?'"

"I take it you have never read much about Black history in this country."

"Ah. Touché."

At that, she couldn't help herself and offered up a small, closed-lip smile of her own.

"And you are?" he asked.

"Zakaya."

"Interesting name."

"Well, my mother thought so." She smiled again. "But my friends call me Z."

"Zee. Even more interesting."

She laughed out loud then. "A friend of my brother, in London, called me Zed. He thought it was a great joke."

"So what do you do, Zakaya-Zee? Besides beating up on barflies, that is."

She hesitated and looked him over. Then, "I'm a police detective. But not here. I'm Cascadian. Just here visiting my mother. How about you?"

He sipped his drink then set it down on the bar and reached into his pocket. He pulled out a business card and handed it to her. "I'm a sort of private investigator. Not official police or anything like that. Still, I manage to make a living."

"Much call for that sort of thing here?" She looked over the card and dropped it into her bag.

"A bit. Used to work over in Jackson, Mississippi. But a bad drug deal and a misunderstanding with the local police there and I kicked the Mississippi mud off my shoes and moved on. I was working over in Red Stick last."

Z laughed out loud. "Red Stick. I haven't heard Baton Rouge called that in years."

He smiled. "But I finally got tired of driving Louisiana roads and decided to give Alabama a try. Mostly chasing down errant wives and husbands and such. Lots of waiting around. Watching. You?"

"Just cases." She frowned. "What's wrong with the roads in Louisiana?"

"You ever tried to drive them?"

"No."

He laughed. "It's like driving on rocks. I don't think they have repaired them in…well, at least my lifetime. So what are you doing here? Besides visiting your mother, that is?"

She furrowed her brow again. Thinking.

"What's wrong?"

"Nothing."

"Must be something. You suddenly got all frownie."

She wondered what and how much to tell this man. Though halfway suspicious of him, she was still drawn to him for some odd reason and before she knew it, she was unloading on him.

"I got all 'frownie,' as you put it because I just left the police department. I'm positive there is human trafficking going on right here in Crimson City and Selma and the whole general area, but they didn't want to hear about it. I even offered my services to help them but was refused and all but tossed out the door. Was told to mind my own business and, in so many words, to go home, little girl." She rolled her eyes and sipped her drink.

"But you're not going to, are you?"

"Going to what?"

"Mind your own business."

"Actually, I consider crime my business. So yeah. I'm going to be minding it. Either that or I'm just going to put my girl and myself on the next plane home."

"Your girl?"

"My young friend. She's here with me."

"Oh." He seemed to be thinking for a moment, then said, "What makes you think so? The trafficking, I mean."

"Because my friend was taken from here, but...managed to escape. Then, several days ago when we were in the grocery store, she saw the men who took her. She was terrified and hid behind some boxes on the bottom grocery shelf. At first, I thought she had been taken again, but, luckily, I found her. Right now I'm so disgusted with this place that I'm thinking of taking her and going back to Cascadia. Seems not much point in staying. Especially with her so traumatized and a police department intent on ignoring the whole thing."

"Whew. Sorry to hear that."

"Yeah, well. Me, too." Z asked the bartender how much she owed, fished out the cash, laid it on the bar, and turned to Blaze. "Sorry to unload on you. Nice meeting you."

"Same here. You be coming back?"

"Probably not. Really thinking about going home."

"Well, I hope you decide to stay. For a while, anyway. After all, it's not every day I meet a self-confident, beautiful police detective." He smiled at her again. "And if you need help while you are here, you have my card. Call me."

She laughed. "See you."

"Hope so."

Z grabbed her bag and left thinking she would probably never see him again. Too bad, that. He was nice. And very good-looking. Not good-looking like her partner, Gray Hawk, but good-looking in a more rugged way. The kind of guy she could fall for if she wasn't careful. And she couldn't help but smile at the crinkle around his eyes and the way he tried to smother a smile when he called her Zakaya-Zee.

But she had a lot of things to think over right now. She needed to put Martin Blaze on the back burners.

18

Just as she stepped outside Brassy's swinging doors, Z found herself once again confronted by Big Ugly who had apparently been hanging around outside waiting for her. He was leaning on a old beat up truck parked in front and just to the side of Brassy's entrance. His sidekick was hanging back in the parking lot a short distance from him near the rear of the truck, watching.

When he saw her come out, Ugly straightened up, puffed up like an angry rooster, and stepped in her way. He drew a handgun from his hip holster and waved it at her.

"Excuse me," she said, deadly calm. "Let me pass."

He said nothing but stepped closer and raised the weapon to her face.

Z looked him steadily in the eye and then, glancing to the side, she looked over his shoulder and behind him. She did a double-take and her eyes widened. She dodged her head back and gasped.

He turned to see who was behind him and found no one. Sensing he had been tricked, he quickly turned back again, but he was too late. Z knocked the pistol from his hand, drove her fist into his throat, and kneed him in the oysters so quickly he never saw any of it coming.

He doubled over in agony, gasping for breath and retching with what little breath he did have.

She kicked the handgun behind her and watched as Sidekick backed off slowly, then turned and trotted across the street.

Laughter sounded behind her. She turned to see Blaze bent over, casually picking up the weapon.

"What the hell is so funny?" she asked, still pissed at having to deal with Big Ugly yet again, and truth to tell, a bit shaken from the whole encounter.

Blaze laughed out loud. "You."

Still laughing, he released the magazine from the pistol and pocketed it. Then he cycled the action to make sure there was no bullet chambered. There wasn't.

"I've never seen anyone this small move that fast or kick the shit out of someone over twice her size. I'm impressed."

Big Ugly was struggling to his feet. Blaze turned to him.

"Belligerent bastard. I swear if I ever see you here again I will personally kick the shit out of you myself. Now get lost."

Z asked, "What will you do with the handgun?"

"I'll take it to the police. He can pick it up there. If he dares." He gave Ugly a final get-the-hell-out-of-here glance then turned back to Z.

She dusted off her jeans, then smiled. "Well, goodbye again, Martin Blaze."

"Bye, Zakaya-Zee. Hope to see you around."

❦

In Washington, Dark Suit picked up the phone. "Yes?"

"Forty-eight here. I'm keeping a close eye on her, just as you ordered. Not much to report except I think she might be planning to take the girl she brought with her back to Cascadia very soon."

"Well, find a way to stop her. Do whatever you have to do but don't let her leave the country. At least not until we can determine if she was part of that little foray two years ago that cost us that weapon. Are you working on that? Or just stalling?"

"Well, I can't just walk up and ask her, can I? This kind of thing takes time. The only thing we know for sure is that she was here five years ago."

"Have you spoken to her?"

"Yes. But just once. And if she was here with that team two years ago, she certainly hasn't given any indication of it."

Dark Suit grunted. Then he cleared his throat. "Even the best of them will slip up, given enough time. She has to be pretty good to work for Cascadian Intelligence. What does she say she's doing here?"

"Visiting her mother. Just like five years ago when we know for sure she was here. From all I've seen so far, that's exactly what she's doing. Except…"

"Except what?"

"She went to the police."

"What for?"

"She suspects child trafficking here in the area. But they didn't want to hear about it, apparently. She even offered to help them with the investigation."

Dark Suit's ears perked up at this. "What kind of help did she offer?"

"She told them she's a police detective in Cascadia—same as she told me—and offered to help them here locally. But, from what she said, she was told to mind her own business and go home. She doesn't think there actually is an investigation. Not into the trafficking. According to the newspapers, they have their hands full down here with some kind of mental case who is killing people and putting smiles on their faces after they are dead. And, in truth, they might not have believed her about being a detective. She's Black. And in this country that doesn't buy you much. As we know."

Dark Suit grunted. "Interesting. Keep on her, Forty-eight. And find some way to keep her here while we work on it from this end. In the end, we might just have to detain her until we find out what really went down two years ago. And who was involved in it."

Dark Suit clicked off without waiting for a reply.

Martin Blaze sighed. Checking in with headquarters was beginning to be a right royal pain in the ass. But he could see no way to avoid it under his present circumstances.

He shook his head at this weird state of affairs. Here he was, working for the FBI, pretending to be a private investigator, with an undeniable crush on a very attractive CIB agent—he was sure of that—pretending to be an ordinary police detective. Could his life possibly get any weirder or more complicated?

He shut out the question. He had long ago learned never to ask what else can happen, because as surely as he did, something would. And it most likely would not be what he wanted.

Well, as the saying goes, you get what you get. Now he needed to devise something that would keep Miss Zakaya-Zee in the country for a while longer. His attraction to her was undeniable. And the trafficking of young girls was something he couldn't ignore any more than she seemed able to. It was important. And, for Blaze, it was personal. Z had opened a door he had long kept closed. Now that the door was open again, detaining her—somehow—could result in bringing down the scum that had caused him so much pain. At the same time, the operation, if successful, would be beneficial to the reputation of the FBI while offering continued cover for himself.

Yes. He needed to find a way to detain the lovely Miss Zakaya-Zee.

And he thought he might have a way to do just that.

∽∾

Big Ugly was livid. His face flushed with anger as he aggressively put the truck in gear and, after picking up his buddy across the street, headed out of town. Sidekick, in the passenger seat, had remained quiet for several minutes but then he shifted uneasily.

"I thought that gal was gonna kill you fer sure. And then the guy showed up to hep her out. Maybe we ought best just leave them alone."

Big Ugly turned scarlet. "She ain't gonna kill me. I'm gonna kill her. And I'm also gonna kill that son-of-a-bitch guy, too, if he gets in my way again."

Sidekick spoke softly, "I don't know, but I'm thinkin' that's a bad idea."

"Did I ask you what you thought? Did I?"

Sidekick shook his head, then said, "I just think we might ought not tangle with those two again. Don't want either of us gettin' hurt, that's all."

"I'm the one that's gonna do the hurtin' and you best believe it. We'll just bide our time. There's gonna come a time when she least suspects. And when it does, I'm gonna get that little Black bitch and when I'm done with her there won't be nothing left."

Sidekick sat quiet for a long while as Big Ugly drove the truck back to the weed-infested farm he had let go fallow. After a while he ventured to ask, "You gonna go to the police station to git your pistol back?"

Ugly grunted and spat a glob of tobacco out the open window. He never answered the question.

Sidekick did not ask again.

19

Charming Billy trudged dutifully down the stairs carrying his mother's breakfast tray, just as he did every morning about a half hour after taking it up to her. He placed the tray carefully on the kitchen sideboard and scraped the uneaten food from the plates into the garbage can near the back door.

Once he had finished cleaning up the breakfast dishes and putting everything neatly away in their precise places, he spread the several-day-old newspaper out on the kitchen table, carefully pressing the creases from it with his hands. He opened it to the story about the smiling corpse and folded the pages back until that story was on top. He had to go to work soon, but he wanted to read the story once again. It gave him an indescribable thrill and a sense of importance.

The police were calling him the Kind Killer because of the gentle way he had lain the body out on the grave slab, and he liked that. Sort of. He liked being called kind because that's what he was. Through and through. But no way was he a killer. That part was just plain wrong and it irritated him. He was simply helping unhappy people to not be unhappy anymore. And that was a good thing. That was a very good thing. The police were stupid. Only a stupid person could possibly think that he was bad. Like his mother. And only someone who didn't know him could possibly call him a killer.

He began humming his "Charming Billy" tune as he closed and folded the newspaper carefully and placed it neatly on the coffee table in the living room no one had ever once used for living. It would be safe there. Nothing was ever out of place in the living room. He wanted to read it again this evening when he returned home from work, after showering the stink of the job off himself, of course. Who cares if it was the dozenth time he had read it. Who would even know? No one ever came here. His mother would never allow it.

Coming out of the living room, he quietly closed the French doors and went across the foyer into his bedroom to check his appearance. Appearances were important. Had to look your best.

Wash your face! Brush your hair! Brush your teeth! Wear clean underwear!

Satisfied at last, he yelled up the stairs on his way out the door, "I'll be home regular time!"

Witch.

⁂

Billy wished the sanitation department would sometimes allow him to drive because this was the route he disliked the most and he would much rather just stay in the truck. Instead, he would have to get out and possibly run into the kind of people he would rather not have anything to do with.

The driver maneuvered the truck carefully and slowly down the road leading through the heavily wooded acreage because it was unpaved and in bad repair. The truck eased and bounced over ruts and cracks until they had driven a short distance from the last turnoff. Here, a rutted driveway overrun with weeds at the edges, and marked with a large KEEP OUT sign, led to a medium-sized two-story house with neglected and peeling blue paint. The once-white window and door framing showed rot on the exterior and some of the windowpanes were broken and covered with pieces of cardboard.

Billy didn't like coming to this house because the men who stayed here were always milling around outside. They were big and gruff and extremely unfriendly, and they carried rifles and handguns at their sides. To Billy they always appeared mean and dirty. Sometimes screams could be heard coming from an upstairs window followed by a lot of men yelling and the sounds of young girls crying.

These people were not happy. The driver never paid much attention, ignoring the whole place until he could turn the truck around and leave again. But Billy had to get out and get dirty collecting the garbage and was made extremely sad by the awful situation here. The screams and crying were always the voices of young girls and Billy truly wished he could help them. But the armed men seemed dangerous and kept a close eye on the sanitation team until they were headed back down the weedy driveway and had turned onto the old secondary road once again.

Today, the screams were not quite as loud as they were the last time. But there was much crying and whimpering coming from one of the upstairs windows.

He tried ignoring it since there was nothing he could do about it. He picked up the first of the trash cans put out in front of the house and dumped its contents into the back of the truck without ever looking in the direction of the two men with rifles standing outside the front door. Watching him.

Empty potato chip bags, greasy pizza boxes, and many empty beer cans tumbled out with a crackle and clang into the truck. Something soft caught on the handle when he upturned the can to get the last of its contents. He reached up to pull it loose and dump it, too, into the truck when he realized it was a lacy pair of pink girl's panties. He looked around quickly to be sure no one was watching, then tucked the soft garment inside his coverall pocket. He flushed with embarrassment. He had never in his life been intimate enough with a girl to see or touch her panties. It was shameful and exciting all at the same time. He patted his pocket several times to make sure the panties didn't make a noticeable lump, then he dumped the other two garbage cans and pulled himself back into the passenger seat of the truck as the driver backed away from the house, turned around, and headed back the way they had come.

At home, Billy pulled the soft, lacy panties from his pocket and laid them out on the kitchen table. He ran his finger over the lace and across the silky cloth then picked them up and smelled them. He was disappointed to find no smell save for the faint aroma of pizza from the garbage into which they had been tossed, but the fabric and lace were cool and sensuous against his cheek. He flushed as he imagined the girl who wore them, then took them into his room and placed them carefully beneath his pajamas in the bureau drawer.

He would visit them again. Often.

∾∾∾

Inside the blue house, the mattress on which Kit Deming lay was on the floor in the far corner of an upstairs bedroom. She had pushed it as far from the door as she could, taking the space recently vacated by the girl who had been taken away. She had waited several days, but the girl never returned and so she had claimed her space. She liked being as far from the guards as possible even though it was only several feet from the spot she had occupied before.

She had been given only a flat sheet, an old, thin blanket, and a pillow without a case over it for her comfort. With the weather now turning cooler, it was not nearly enough. She had banged loudly on the door and begged the guy outside for a blanket but he only grunted and said she wouldn't be here much longer. When she asked if they were taking her home, she was answered with silence.

Empty pizza boxes, cold-drink cups, and burger wrappers were piled near the door. The guards took the trash away every day or two. Until then, it just piled up.

The girl whose place she had taken had been in the room for only a few days but she cried and screamed all the time and was no company at all. It was a relief when she was taken elsewhere.

Over the past six months, Kit had seen nothing except the thick stand of trees outside and the rotting wood of the frames around the nailed-shut window just outside the fogging glass. She could tell the house was blue, or at least it had been once, but she could see nothing else. Every now and then she could hear a truck approach. She tried to keep track as best she could and decided the truck only came about once a week. She decided this place must be somewhere out of town where regular garbage pickup didn't happen all that often. How she knew it was a garbage truck was strictly guesswork. When the truck came she could hear the banging of what sounded like trashcans, but she never actually saw anything since the room she occupied was at the rear of the house.

When she first awakened in this room she was disoriented and very frightened. She cried for her mother and banged on the door to be let out when she found it locked. It had seemed to her, looking back on it now, that she had cried for days. She tried pushing up the windows but they were nailed shut so they would not open. The days had been long and boring. The worst of it was not knowing what had happened to her or why she was here. Or even where *here* actually was.

When the door opened for the first time, she ran to the person standing there and told him she wanted to go home. He had merely said it wouldn't be too long and handed her a bag containing a Giant Burger and some fries and a drink.

One guard had given her several paperback books to read, but it was hard to concentrate. Every little sound and every distant voice or car engine perked up her ears in an effort to hear what they were saying or what direction they were coming from. With each day that passed, she became more and more despondent.

She was bored to the point of suicide but had no way of harming herself. She had read the motorcycle magazines and clothing catalogs tossed into the room by one of the several guards so many times she had lost count. The paperbacks had long been read three times over. As with the guesswork about the garbage truck, she concluded it had to be months now since she was brought here because the leaves on the few deciduous trees outside the windows had turned yellow and red. Now they were almost gone, leaving the trees nearly bare.

When she was first brought here, it was spring. She had been trying on prom dresses with her friend Connie. *How she missed Connie!* And then, when Connie left the dressing room to find another dress, she must have blacked out. She couldn't remember leaving the dress shop and had no idea how she came to be in this horrible house with these horrible men who would not let her leave. Her screams and cries had been summarily ignored. At first, she thought she would die here, but then, as the days passed without incident, she began feeling somewhat safe, yet perplexed.

Being ignored was the strangest thing of all. She had feared she would be raped, but the men who guarded her never touched her. This had given her an odd sense of security. The men would bring food and take away containers. They made her get on a scale every few days and if she had lost weight they would bring her extra food and watch until she had eaten it. They even brought her a change of clothes once or twice. But they never talked with her or answered any of her questions.

At first she had been alone in this particular room, but she knew there were others in the house because she could hear their cries even though she had never seen anyone else. Recently, another girl was unceremoniously pushed into the room and the door was closed and locked once again. She did nothing but cry and scream and so she was taken away one day and didn't come back. Kit often wondered what had happened to her. She liked to believe the men took her back home, but they wouldn't say, and she didn't like to consider any other possibility.

She had no way of knowing when she would be taken home, but lately she had heard men talking outside the door. It was hard to hear through the solid wood of the doors in this old house, but she managed to pick up snippets of conversation here and there.

A few days earlier she heard one man complaining about being tired of this whole thing and would be glad when the van came. The other guy said something about it not being that much longer now and the big-shots would be on the yacht and they could take some time off. On hearing this, she had cheered slightly. Maybe they were going to take her home because they were going on vacation or something. She hated them and feared them, yet they had never harmed her. And that was probably the most puzzling and scariest thing of all.

She had missed the prom and she thought a lot about her friend, Connie, and also about her boyfriend. She had been in this place a long time. Maybe Andy had found a new girlfriend by this time.

She just wanted to go home. She wanted her mother.

20

Z began looking deeper into human trafficking. She researched everything she could find on the subject and uncovered some interesting facts. It seemed that trafficking occurred in every state in the U.S. Some, more than others. It was particularly prevalent in the south. Georgia, she learned, was a high-trafficked state, but Alabama had, of late, become on a par with it. One in three trafficking victims were children, taken for the purpose of sex, pornography, begging on the streets to enrich their "owners," and/or for forced labor. Victims, it seemed, often would not seek help due to fear of their traffickers, or fear of law enforcement.

Fear of law enforcement?

She could scarcely believe what she was reading.

There were often language barriers. If the "taken" spoke no English, it often kept them from seeking help even when presented with an opportunity.

Indicators of a trafficked victim were several: Appearing malnourished, injured, or other signs of physical abuse. Also, seeming to have no personal belongings, and avoiding eye contact with others, especially law enforcement.

The police again! Why?

This reported fear of the police bothered Z more than almost anything else she read. The police were supposed to help people in trouble. Save them. Not frighten them into silence. And yet, the police here weren't interested in trafficking, even though young girls had been disappearing, locally, for some time. And Zeena had seen her own traffickers! Two men, she had said. The same two who had taken her two years ago. They were still out there. Free! Doing God knows what. The whole concept disgusted Z beyond words.

Her decision was simple. Being Zakaya Kalu, with a streak of fairness-demanding-justice that ran all the way to the marrow of her bones, she had no choice. If the police wouldn't do their job, she would pursue these particular traffickers herself. Alex knew she would. Viking had known it, too. She would be careful, and if it didn't work out, she would go home to Cascadia knowing that she had, at least, tried. But if she was successful, the lives of many young girls would possibly be saved. That, alone, made it worth the risk.

With Zeena in her care, however, it wouldn't be possible to do the work she needed to do. Tomorrow, after the barbecue, she would take Zeena home to her mother. It was way past time to do it even though the girl clearly did not want to go. Z could not envision anything other than a mother enraptured at being reunited with her daughter after losing her for more than two years.

Yes. It was the right thing to do.

☙☙☙

At dinner, Z took a final bite of the fried okra her mother had prepared and quietly placed her fork across her plate.

Mrs. Kalu eyed her for a moment. "What's wrong, Z?"

Z looked from her mother to Zeena and back again. "I…have some things I have to do, Mama. I'm really sorry this came up during our visit, but it was totally unexpected, and some things just can't be helped."

"What kind of things?"

Z looked over at Zeena who had stopped eating and was watching her closely. She reached out for the girl's hand and then looked back at her mother. "It's work. And it's important. I'm really sorry."

Mrs. Kalu nodded and started clearing the plates from the table.

"And," Z turned back to Zeena, "I'm taking you home to your mother right after the barbecue tomorrow."

"But Miss Z!" Zeena's voice grew higher in pitch and she pulled her hand away from Z's grasp. Tears welled in her eyes. "I want to stay with you!"

"I'm sorry, Button. My work will make it too dangerous so I can't risk keeping you with me. Besides, your mother will be thrilled to see you again and you should be with her. She's your mother. It will be okay. You'll see."

"No, it won't!" Zeena was dejected. She put her own fork down and got up from the table.

Z added, "Besides, it's time you were in school." She also rose from the table and reached out for her.

Zeena, withdrawing into herself, became silent and hung her head.

Z put on a big smile and hugged the girl close.

Gad, I hope I'm doing the right thing!

∽∾

Z was up early the next morning and went into the kitchen to avoid waking Zeena who had slept fitfully. She perused the paper over a strong cup of coffee at the kitchen counter. The story of the young girl found in the ditch had made the front page. Her name was Tiki Jameson, and her parents were devastated. The girl had been dead for at least a week, the story said, although she had been missing for just over two weeks. Strangulation, the medical examiner had announced.

"Hey." Zeena was peeking around the kitchen doorway and spoke softly.

"Hey, Sleepyhead." Z quickly closed the newspaper and set it aside. "Are you ready for the barbecue today?" Z reached over and ruffed up her hair.

"I guess so."

Z could tell the girl had no enthusiasm for anything right now. But she tried with her just the same. "It'll be fun. Lots of good things to eat and maybe even horseshoes. Anyway, let's get you some breakfast. It's a few hours till the barbecue so you'll need some fuel! How about pancakes?"

She got the box of pancake mix from the cupboard and began mixing up the batter in the old, blue bowl the size of Texas she was certain her mother had had forever.

Zeena hung around the doorway drawing half-circles with her left foot. "Miss Z?"

"What, Baby?"

"I didn't exactly tell you the truth about those men that took me."

Z stopped mixing the pancake batter, the dripping spoon in mid-air. She plopped the spoon back into the bowl of batter and gave Zeena her full attention.

"What do you mean?"

"I didn't exactly tell the truth. I mean, those men I told you about were really the men who took me, but they didn't promise me I'd be in a movie or nothin' like that. I just made that up."

Z was quiet a moment as she digested this information. Then she said, "Can you tell me the truth now?"

"Promise you won't send me back to my mama?" Zeena's eyes were wide and worried. She looked at Zakaya as though eyeing the only life raft remaining on the Titanic. "I'm sorry I lied, but…"

"It's okay, Baby. Tell me what really did happen." She pulled out a chair at the kitchen table and sat down. She motioned Zeena to take the chair across from her.

Zeena slid into the chair and said, "Well, the men were the same as what I told you. They looked the same and everything. But I wasn't on my way home from school. That part was a lie. I made it up because…"

"What did happen?"

"I was already home, and they came to the house and knocked on the door. Mama let them in and then she sent me to the back bedroom, but I peeked through the crack in the door to see what they were doing. Mama got all puffed up and said, 'that's not enough!' and then she crossed her arms and gave them face. You know. Stuck her face right up to the tallest one."

Z nodded, waiting for the rest of the story.

Zeena bit her bottom lip, then said, "Then they handed her something. I think it was drugs because it was in a white package. Kind of like baking soda in a plastic bag. She was real happy about that, but she still gave them a hard look and held out her hand. Finally, the tallest man took his wallet out and counted out dollar bills of money into her hand. He stopped once and looked at her but she tilted her head at him and frowned so he kept counting. Then I heard him say, 'That's it. Take it or leave it. She's not even worth that much.'"

Z's eyes grew wide and she felt like her head was going to explode. "And then?"

"Then she called me to come out of the bedroom and made me go with the men."

"Where did they take you? Did you get into their car? Tell me what happened next!" The questions tumbled out in a flurry.

"I don't know, Miss Z. I just don't know. I don't remember getting into their car. They really did give me something to make me sleep, I think. That part was true because I don't remember being in a car. I just remember waking up in a room in a house somewhere. I couldn't see anything but trees and woods out the window so I don't know where."

Z got up from the table and went around to gather the girl into her arms.

"You won't take me back to my mama, will you? Please don't take me back! She doesn't want me!"

Shocked, Z stared at the girl for a moment. Then, "No, Button. I won't take you back. I won't ever take you back there. I promise. But…"

"But what, Miss Z? You just promised!" Zeena didn't like the direction that "but" was going even without knowing what it was.

Z took her by the shoulders and looked at her seriously. "Even though I won't take you back to your mother, I can't keep you here with me while I do this work I have to do."

"Where will I go?" Zeena was still clearly distressed.

"How about I send you back to Cascadia? You can stay with Alex until I get home. How does that sound? You like Alex, don't you?"

"Yes." The girl visibly brightened.

"And Alex can get you enrolled in school. It's really way past time. You should have already been in school instead of coming here with me. What do you say?"

"Okay. When will you come back?"

"Just as soon as I finish up the work here. I promise." She hugged Zeena close.

"When do I have to go?"

"I'll make arrangements after the barbecue this evening and send you home tomorrow. How does that sound? It will be an adventure, flying all by yourself. You can handle it. I know you can. And the people on Cascadian Air are very helpful so you will be fine."

Z hoped she was right about this. Even though Zeena was fifteen, she seemed awfully young for her age. Still, she had to risk it. Zeena would go home to Cascadia and she would stay and find the traffickers. And put the scum away.

That die had been cast the moment Zeena had seen them in the grocery store.

21

The morning of the barbecue found the fast-food duo, Cook and Swift, cruising Selma in the neighborhood of Levoy Ave. Their police credentials had gotten them past the Selma Blues with no trouble, the armed Black men acknowledging their authority and quickly parting to allow them through. Still, it grated on Cook having to answer to those he felt beneath him. Once inside the city limits, however, he forgot the whole grievance. He wasn't one to look back.

"Good thing Snitch called us about the barbecue. An outdoor party like a barbecue is pretty busy and distracting. There's a real chance we can get the girl back again before she sees us or tells more about us." Cook mused, as much to himself as to Donny Ray, as they drove slowly past the Kalu's house.

Donny Ray added, "Yeah. And there's an alley behind the house where the garbage cans are put out by all the residents between Levoy and the next street over. The alley is plenty wide enough for the sanitation department's trucks, so they just drive through and collect both sides at the same time."

Cook looked at Donny Ray impatiently. "Who the hell cares about city planning for garbage pickup? Get to the point!"

Swift ignored Cook's impatient outburst and continued. "He said he will send the girl out with trash from the cleanup. There's a high wooden privacy fence back there behind the Kalu's house so she will never see us and she'll come out the gate next to the cans. He'll call to let us know when she's on her way out."

Cook grunted. "I don't want to be waiting there all day for her. Call him back and tell him to call when the party is beginning to wind down. That will give me time to get into place behind the cans. Crouching down there for more than a few minutes is not my idea of a good time. Are you sure you got the stuff?"

"Yeah," Swift hesitated for a moment, then said, "but I could only get the old stuff again. Octoflurane. He doesn't have any of the newest stuff. But at least it's not chloroform or sevoflurane like we used to use. Those were way too slow."

Cook asked, "How do you always get him to give it to you?"

"I just go to him with a fake prescription, and he sells the stuff to me for ten bucks. He's an idiot."

"Well, he's a useful idiot. Treat him right."

Swift shifted uncomfortably in his seat.

Impatient with him, Cook said, "Suck it up, Swift. It's just a job."

Donny Ray looked away from him out the driver's side window, so Cook added, "No point in us hanging around here. People might get suspicious. The Orca looks too much like what it used to be. Let's go get something to eat. We can be back fast enough when Snitch calls. I'll call him from the diner and tell him to give us ten- or fifteen-minutes lead time on the girl."

Donny Ray sighed as Hadeon began casually cleaning his fingernails with his pocketknife.

❦

The calendar had rolled over into November, but the weather was still nice. At the barbecue that afternoon, everything seemed to be going well. Zeena had cheered considerably after learning she would not be taken back to her mother. This, along with the near perfect weather, had cheered Z as well.

As with anything her mother planned, there was a enough food for Pharaoh's army, and everybody down to the last cousin five times removed had been invited. All were excited at seeing Zakaya again for the first time in five years. And everyone was completely in love with the shy Zeena. Even the Selma Blues had been invited and Eli McClain, with a dazzling display of dimples and very white teeth flashed at Z, volunteered to man the grill. He was, she decided, one of the good ones and she couldn't help herself. She was definitely attracted.

A good hour into the soirée, JJ showed up in uniform. He was still on duty, he explained, and couldn't stay very long. However, Z insisted he stay at least long enough for a burger and something to drink. Also to meet Zeena.

After reading about trafficked children's reaction to law enforcement, she was most interested in seeing how Zeena would react to seeing her friend in his police uniform but the girl showed no discomfort at meeting him other than her usual shyness at meeting anyone.

JJ took the girl's relationship with Z as a matter of course. No questions asked. That was JJ. A true friend.

After everyone had said their hellos and exclaimed at how wonderful Z looked, she finally found a moment to take JJ aside and tell him of her visit to the police station and how they had rebuffed her.

"The captain practically tossed me out the door!" she told him, waving her arm for emphasis.

JJ shook his head. "The captain isn't a bad guy. Not really. He's just very overworked. There's been a lot going on lately and he's really frustrated. We're not really all that equipped here since we are a pretty small station, but he tries. It's hard on him because the chief isn't a lot of help. He's more interested in playing golf with the mayor than he is in the business of the department. That leaves the captain to manage everything and our detectives haven't been very successful at closing cases. Still, I'm sorry he brushed you off like that."

"Well, it's not going to stop me. If he doesn't want my help, I'll just do some investigating on my own. There is definitely human trafficking going on here whether he wants to admit it or not. And this is not just a local thing, JJ. It's world-wide. And world-wide includes me."

JJ was shaking his head in agreement with her when he turned away in an effort to suppress a laugh. He turned back to Z who was looking puzzled that JJ of all people could find human trafficking funny, and, partially covering his wide smile, said, "Here comes your Aunt Juanita! Visors down!"

Zakaya poked him in the ribs and bent over behind him with laughter, hiding her face from Juanita. When she had suppressed her laughter as much as she could, she turned to face her aunt. That's when she no longer needed to suppress it. Tagging along behind Juanita was her Uncle Bo. Her blood ran cold at the very sight of the man and any humor she had been feeling vanished along with her laughter.

Juanita began commenting on Zeena's skinny appearance. "You need to feed that girl something. She looks pathetic. All skin and bones."

"She's just fine, Aunt Nita. You don't need to worry about her. She's flying back to Cascadia soon to get enrolled in school."

"She? You not going with her? What if she gets lost or something?"

"She'll be fine," Z said, becoming exasperated as she always did with her aunt. "My sister, Alex, will be meeting her."

"Sister! Shuh!"

Zakaya Kalu never wanted to smack anyone so much as she wanted to smack her Aunt Juanita right this minute. Instead, she turned to JJ.

"I'm so glad you came, JJ. I'll see you out."

Always one to catch on quick, the good-natured JJ allowed her to escort him out the gate and to the front of the house where his squad car was parked about a half block down the street. When she returned, Z saw Uncle Bo with his right hand on Zeena's left shoulder. The girl was squirming under his touch and trying to back away from him.

"Zeena!" she shouted to the girl.

Uncle Bo looked her way and slowly smiled at her, making her skin crawl. He released the girl's shoulder and she ran to Z.

Z gathered her to her side and looked back at Bo. He was talking to someone on his t-com, waving his free hand and arm in useless agitated expression that the person on the other end of the conversation could not see.

There was something about him Z couldn't quite pin down. It seemed to her to be an air of security. Comfort. Yes, that was it. He seemed comfortable and unworried, as though he had nothing at all to fear. She continued eyeing him, trying to determine what it was when she noticed his shoes. Italian and very expensive. When he waved his arm, the hand of his shirt fabric lay soft and supple on his arm. She narrowed her eyes.

Where does a shiftless do-nothing get the kind of money for clothes like that?

He finished his conversation and turned back to Z, smiled at her one last time, and left the party through the back gate.

She shivered.

∽∾∽

Two streets over from the Kalu's barbecue, Cook and Swift sat impatiently in the Orca. Hadeon's t-com buzzed.

"What's going on?" He turned to Donny Ray and reported, "It's Snitch." Then, into the t-com, "You were supposed to call and let us know when to get over there. It's getting late. What's going on?"

Donny Ray was uneasy. It was obvious to anyone except Cook that he wanted to be anywhere else. He twitched nervously and waited for Hadeon to finish the call.

"Shit! Why not?" Hadeon was becoming agitated. "I thought there was a back gate where the trashcans are stored. I thought you said you would get her to go out with some trash so we could get her."

He listened for a moment, then said, "Well, now what do you suggest?" Then he listened again.

Finally, he rang off and turned to Donny Ray. "Snitch says the older gal we saw with her outside the grocery store—you know, the one who came into the station—is keeping a close eye on her and he just couldn't get close enough long enough. He almost did, but the other one came back too soon. Apparently the older one is his niece. But we still have a chance. He overheard her say she's putting the girl on a plane back to Cascadia—not sure when, but we can check."

Swift asked, "What good does that do us?"

Cook examined the nails on his left hand and smiled. "All God's planes got to go through Atlanta."

22

The barbecue over at last, and all the goodbyes and the ya'll-comebacks said for at least the third time—the Kalu family were experts at standing on the order of going—Zakaya helped with the cleanup and retired to her bedroom where she made the reservations for Zeena's flight to Cascadia. She felt, after seeing Uncle Bo's hands on the girl, she couldn't get her out of the United States and back to Cascadia fast enough.

Reservations made, she called Alex.

"Hi, you," she said when Alex answered.

"Z! What's up?"

"I'm staying here for a while. I went to the police and was unceremoniously shown the door. Apparently, they neither need nor want my help."

"So…why are you staying?"

"Because the men who took Zeena are still out there. Here. Somebody has to stop them."

"Damn it, Z! How do you always get yourself into these messes? Why does it have to be you?"

"Because. Besides, you knew I would, didn't you?"

Alex ignored the question. She whispered, "It's dangerous."

"I know. That's why I'm sending Zeena back to Cascadia. I need you to take care of her until I get back.

She needs to be in school, anyway. Will you do that for me?"

"What a nutty question. You know I will. I just wish you were coming home with her and leaving the police there to do their own dirty work. You think Zeena will be okay? Coming all by herself, I mean."

"Yeah. I think so. I know Zeena is young, and anything but worldly, but she can handle this. Flying alone is done by kids all the time. Cascadian Air will take good care of her and you'll be there when she gets there so I'm pretty much okay with it. I think she'll be fine. It's just too dangerous to leave her here mostly by herself while I'm off looking for the lowest of low scum on the planet. It's possible they could try to take her again. I can't let that happen."

At this point, Z hesitated. Thoughts of her Uncle Bo's hands on Zeena rushed into her head. She went silent.

"And?" Alex asked.

"And nothing. That's it. If I'm lucky, I won't be long." Z decided Alex didn't need to know anything about Uncle Bo, so she changed the subject. "How's everyone there?"

"Ummm…" Alex hesitated as though looking around the room. "Viking is doing paperwork with his feet on his desk."

"Ha!" Z laughed.

"Parker and Gray went to lunch together to get rid of Chuck for an hour or two of silence. Even though Viking managed to get Chuck transferred back to CIMA-3, he still drops by like a bad penny turning up. I was going to go but decided to stay and catch up on my own paperwork. And Budgie, of course, is glued to his computer screens researching something."

"Speaking of Budgie," Z cut in, "would you ask him to find out what he can about a guy here named Eli McClain?

I'm wondering if he could be the operative in this area. Ask him to find out who the operative is for me, will you?"

"Z, you know the identity of our operatives is one of our most closely-held secrets. I doubt he will be able to find out. I doubt even Tillerman knows. Do you suspect this Eli fellow?"

"It's just a feeling. But I'd really like to know. I'm in hostile territory here and it would be great to know who's on my side. And if anyone can find out, it's Budgie. Ask him to find out what he can, okay?"

"Okay, but I doubt he'll be able to."

Z changed the subject. "Let Viking know what I'm up to here, would you? And tell Gray I'll be home ASAP."

"Will do." Then Alex got serious. "Viking knows you almost as well as I do. He knows what you will be up to, Z. And we are all worried about you."

"I know. I'll be okay. Later." Z clicked off.

Well, that's that. I'll do what I can, as quick as I can, then get back to Cascadia myself.

ೞ

The drive to the airport was uneventful. Even quiet. Zeena seemed reflective but calm as the cotton field view scrolled past the window. This calm made Z a great deal more relaxed than she thought she would be.

As they neared the airport, Zeena turned to her and said, "Thank you for not taking me back to my mama. I wish—"

"You wish what, Button?"

"I wish you was my mama."

For one instant Z's constant vigilance of her surroundings relaxed in the warmth of the girl's feelings for her and she missed seeing the beat-up, brown car with the dented fender pulling into one of the spaces in the parking row behind them.

She pulled into an empty space and turned to Zeena. "I can't be your mama, Zeena."

"Why not?" The girl could not hide her disappointment.

"Because, Silly! I'm too young!" Z laughed and pushed Zeena's shoulder hard enough to make her laugh, too. "How about I be your big sister instead?"

"Okay." Zeena was all smiles at this. Z reached over and hugged her.

Down to business now, Z told her the flight she would be taking first was not Cascadian Air. She would change to the Cascadian Air flight in Atlanta.

"Be sure to ask the flight attendant to direct you to the correct gate when you get to Atlanta and wait close to the gate for the plane to board. Don't wander around. Just stay close to the gate and don't talk to any strangers. Keep your t-com turned on. Don't forget. This is very important. Okay?"

"Okay, I won't forget." Zeena held up her wrist to show Z the t-com was already on.

"Good girl. Okay, grab your things. Here we go."

As they entered the terminal, the old hand-painted black and white Orca pulled into one of the taxi spaces near the door where Hadeon Cook got out and followed them in, flashing his badge to guarantee the car would not be towed for parking in the loading zone.

He was just far enough behind them not to be noticed.

❧

With Zeena safely on the flight to Atlanta, Z turned to making plans for her lone investigation into the traffickers. Without the help and facilities of the police it would be difficult for her, but not impossible, and she had one tiny crack in the door for access to those police facilities: JJ. How much help he would be willing to provide, if any, was not known. She couldn't ask him to do anything he felt would risk his future there. He had a family to consider, and he needed his job.

She also had the newspapers. And the library. Perhaps even the local Sheriff though that could be a long shot since, if the authorities in the county were doing any investigating into trafficking the police would have told her about it when she went to the station. Maybe. Or maybe not. The whole thing was going to be a long shot.

Long shot or no, she decided to visit the Sheriff's office first. Maybe she would get lucky. If not, she could at least strike that avenue of inquiry off her list.

<h1 style="text-align:center">23</h1>

The Sheriff's office was housed in a small log cabin style building. Probably, Z decided, an ancillary office perhaps staffed only part time. There was no one present except the receptionist and a man she figured must be the Sheriff himself. He was just inside the half-open door to the office at the back. The door was open just enough that the angle prevented Z from reading the name stenciled onto the privacy glass in its upper portion.

The receptionist was a heavy-set woman with hair piled up into an enormous heap and pinned rather messily to the top of her head. She wore a t-shirt over some kind of long-sleeved garment and peered at Zakaya over her tortoise-shell glasses. "What do you want, Girl?"

"I need to see the Sheriff."

"What about?"

"Business."

"Well, he's busy so you had best run along now."

"He doesn't look busy." Z looked beyond the woman to the man in the office. He was leaning back in his large, wooden roller chair with his feet propped up on his desk.

"Well, he is," the woman snapped.

Z decided to raise her voice. "I'm not leaving until I see him."

The man in the office looked their way. He shouted from where he sat. "What the hell is going on out there, Edna?"

"This here colored gal is demanding to see you but I told her you was busy!" Edna shouted back.

"Oh, for the love of—let her in!"

Edna gave her a stony look and told her to go on into the office as Z was already passing her by without a backward glance.

"Hello." She said as she entered the office. "I'm detective Kalu and I'm trying to find out what I can about human trafficking going on in this area."

The Sheriff, elbow on the desk, inspected his fingernails. "I'm not aware we have any of that here." He looked from his fingernails to Z, stony-faced.

Where the hell has this man been? In a cave? Is everybody in this country deaf, dumb, and blind?

Z's voice held steady. "I assure you, there is. I know this, personally."

She watched him closely. His eyes narrowed and he seemed to be thinking. Finally, he spoke up. "I've never seen you at any of the local police departments in this county. You have some ID?"

"Of course." She pulled the ID wallet from her pocket and handed it over.

He looked her in the eyes as he took it. Then he looked down, opened it, and examined the badge and ID card. He looked back up. "Well, Special Investigator Kalu from Santa Rosa, California, Cascadia, you have no authority or jurisdiction here."

"Yes. I know. It's why I've come to you for help."

Make him feel important. Make him feel needed.

He chuckled. "Well, I appreciate the confidence, but there really isn't anything I can do for you."

"What about the girl who was found dead in a ditch here a day or two ago? Wasn't that discovery south of Selma? Out in the county? And wouldn't that be your jurisdiction?"

"Yes, but since the police have better facilities for that sort of thing and, since the girl had lived in Crimson City, we felt it would be best to turn the case over to them. But even so, we don't believe she was a victim of trafficking."

"How can you be so sure?"

He sighed. "Are you sure you're a police officer? You don't seem to know much about crime."

Z shifted from one foot to the other and waited patiently for an answer to her question.

"Because traffickers don't kill the people they take. They especially don't kill young girls. They are too valuable for…other uses."

Z could have sworn the sheriff blushed. She said, "Maybe something went wrong."

"Look," he said, "you are wasting your time here. And mine. I really was busy when you came in."

"Yeah." She laughed. "I could tell by the way your feet were propped up on your desk."

He ignored her and snapped his fingers at the door. "Edna will see you out. Edna!"

"I'm surprised she can find her own way out." Z was irritated, but not completely blind to her surroundings. She had noticed and memorized the sheriff's name prominently displayed on a plaque center-front of his desk: Wilbur Cook.

Cook. She knew that name. It lingered silently on her tongue like the sickening after-taste of castor oil. She looked back once on her way past the puffed-up Edna to see the sheriff pick up his old land-line phone. She heard him speak the name, Hadeon.

Outside again, she looked back at the office. The sheriff stood at his office window still speaking into the phone's receiver. Watching her.

She slid into her rental car and drove a half mile down the highway before pulling off to think. This Wilbur Cook guy must be related to the detective, Hadeon Cook, at the Crimson City police station. She remembered the detective's name to be Hadeon along with his partner, Donny somebody. Why was the sheriff calling him immediately after her visit? The sheriff seemed too young to be the other's father. Perhaps brother. Or uncle. It didn't matter. What mattered was that now the police in Crimson City knew she was out here messing about on her own.

This could mean trouble.

Well, whether trouble would come of her investigation or not, Z decided to pursue it as far as she could. The sheriff was definitely stonewalling her. But why? And what was the connection to the detective at the police station in Crimson City? And did that connection even matter? There were no answers to these questions. At least not right now.

She decided the library was a good place to start looking for information, so she put the old rental into gear and pulled back out onto the two-lane blacktop. For now, she would file the sheriff away in one of the dusty back drawers of her mind. She would haul him back out at some later date if it became necessary.

❧❧

The sheriff, phone to ear, watched Zakaya as she walked past Edna, out the office door, and down the steps to the parking lot. She walked proud. Unafraid. There was something unsettling about her. Something he didn't like.

"Hadeon!" he spoke into the receiver when the other person had answered his call. "What do you know about a Black gal who claims to be a police detective from Cascadia?"

"Why? How do you know her?" Hadeon sounded genuinely surprised at this unexpected information.

"She just left my office. She wanted to know about Tiki Jameson."

"Who?"

"The girl you——. The girl that was killed and left in the ditch. That's who. What the hell is going on here?" Sheriff Cook frowned at the phone's receiver as though at Hadeon himself.

"Oh. Her." Hadeon. Calm. "She came in here recently offering her help in finding traffickers. The captain told her we didn't have a trafficking problem here and she wasn't needed. He had her escorted out by the sergeant."

"Well, I guess that didn't stop her from doing a little personal investigating because she just left here after asking me a bunch of questions."

"But..." Hadeon's voice had a slight lilt to it.

"But what?" Sheriff Cook was losing patience.

"But there's more. She's got the little Black girl that was sold to that rich SOB in Florida. We don't know how she got her, but we recognized the kid several days ago in the grocery store. Scared the shit out of us. And the kid. We got the hell out of the store fast. This older gal never saw us, but we've been watching her. She put the kid on a plane for Cascadia less than an hour ago."

"So she's gone? The kid is gone?"

"Yes. But she knows who we are. At least she would recognize us if she saw us again. Since we are plain-clothes, she can't have connected us to the police. Still, she's a danger. But..." The lilt was in the voice again.

"But what?"

"The plane she's on has to stop in Atlanta. You have contacts in Atlanta, right?"

"Why?"

"Because maybe she doesn't make the connection to the flight back to Cascadia, that's why."

"What's her name?"

"Zeena. I don't know the last name. Zeena should be enough."

"Damned short notice, but I'll do what I can." Sheriff Cook hung up the phone and immediately dialed again.

24

The library was semi-warm, and semi-lighted as well. It seemed soft and welcoming unlike other libraries Zakaya had frequented with their harsh, overhead fluorescent lighting. It smelled of books and ink pads and, somehow, of lilacs. Perhaps someone had just sprayed a freshener among the tall, labyrinthine aisles of bookcases.

Refreshing as well, the woman at the desk seemed completely indifferent to the color of her skin. She had greeted her warmly and asked if she could be of any help.

"Could you please direct me to the old newspaper issues?" Z asked her.

The librarian hesitated for a moment. Then, "How far back are you interested in looking? I ask because we have a limited number of back issues here. I'm afraid we toss them after six months. Any earlier than that and you would need to visit the newspaper's own archives."

"I will just start with whatever you have here, thank you."

The librarian led her to a small room at the back where magazines and newspapers were stored and left her to her research.

Not sure how far back to begin, she decided to start at the earliest of the available newspaper issues and work her way through them. She began with the headlines of the

June issues. She found nothing of interest as she slowly browsed each edition and was beginning the August issues when a young man who had been working on the far side of the room passed by her pushing a cart loaded with magazines and newspapers.

She put out a hand to stop the cart. "Excuse me, please. Why do you have these newspapers on the cart? Are they new additions to the library?"

"No." He looked down at the disarray on the cart. "These are all old issues that are being discarded. At the end of each month we always discard the oldest issues of magazines and newspapers to make room for new ones. We're a few days late this month, though."

"Could I please bother you to allow me time to go through these newspapers before you discard them? I promise I won't take too long."

"Sure. I'll just get them later. Take your time. It's about my lunch break anyway."

Z gratefully grabbed the stack of newspapers from May and plopped them onto the table, pushing aside the August issues. After examining each page of nearly half the papers in the stack, she had found nothing of interest. Then, in the Sunday, May 22nd, edition she saw something.

A young girl, Kit Deming, had disappeared the day before. She had been shopping for prom dresses with her friend, Connie Latham, in a local dress shop when she, apparently, had just vanished without a trace. According to the article, she and Connie were best friends and both attended Mid-County High School. They were very excited about going to prom. Their respective dates had been questioned but the boys had no knowledge the girls were even shopping, much less that one of them was missing, and they were not, at this time, "persons of interest" according to the police. The girl's parents were absolutely destroyed, and the police were asking for any information leading to the discovery and safe return of Kit Deming. A hot-line number was given. And that was all the information available. But this had to be the missing girl that had been tangentially mentioned in the article she had read recently about the Kind Killer.

Excited at this discovery, Z said aloud to the empty room, "Ha! So the police don't think trafficking is a problem here."

She began flipping through page after page of the rest of the May newspapers, but found only a couple of small pleas, again, for anyone with information into the disappearance of the missing girl to please call the hotline. Then, nothing. The girl was just gone. And that was that. The paper had other news to report. The world spun with dependable indifference through new days and nights— and life moved on.

She returned to the later issue papers and found an article about the dead girl, Tiki Jameson. This girl, too, had just vanished without a trace. She was last seen leaving the school gym and walking home across the softball field that separated the school from the housing development where she lived. The police currently had no suspects and were as perplexed as everyone else about what could have happened to her. Then, of course, there was the story of the discovery of her body beneath the old, abandoned wheelbarrow.

Could anything possibly be more depressing? Or suspicious?

At least she had one thing. A name. The name of a girl who wasn't wanted, it seemed, by the traffickers.

She would visit Connie Latham.

⁗

Connie Latham's home was quite nice when compared against the poverty that had overtaken the United States for the last hundred years. While not a mansion by any means, the home was still a large brick rancher in the style of Frank Lloyd Wright—sprawling, yet tidy of landscaping and in good repair.

Z felt almost apologetic as she pulled the rather beat-up rental sedan into the driveway and cut the engine.

A young Black woman about Zakaya's own age answered the door. She was wearing a maid's uniform. When she saw Z she was taken aback for a moment.

"May I help you?" she asked, still holding onto the door as though the home might be invaded at any second.

"Yes, please. I'm here to speak with Miss Connie Latham. I'm a police detective and have some questions for her."

The maid looked surprised but stepped back, said, "Wait here, please," and closed the door again.

When the door next opened, an older woman Z took to be Mrs. Latham bid her come inside.

"What is this all about?" the woman asked.

"I'm trying to find out what happened to your daughter's friend, Kit Deming. You are Connie Latham's mother, correct?"

"Yes…but the police already questioned her. She really doesn't know any more than she told them." Mrs. Latham hesitated a moment and then added, "And, to be honest with you, they really didn't seem very interested in pursuing the matter further. It was all very upsetting to Connie."

"I can imagine it was, and I want you—and her—to know that I think it deserves a lot more attention than it was given, and I am very interested in pursuing the matter further."

This statement seemed to resonate with Mrs. Latham, and after giving a cursory once-over of Z's badge and credentials, she motioned her to come through to a living room thickly carpeted in rose-colored wool beneath white leather sofas. Lush greenery grew from an indoor planter and recessed lighting lit the room with a soft incandescent glow. Z felt her feet sink into the cushion of the carpet as she took in the room.

"I'll get Connie for you," she said.

"If it's all the same to you, Mrs. Latham, I'd like to talk with her in her own room. I want her to be in her own surroundings and as comfortable as she can be under the circumstances."

"Oh. All right then. Her room is just back here."

Mrs. Latham led Z down a hallway carpeted with a thick Persian runner then knocked on a closed door to her right, behind which a current popular song was playing.

The music was silenced and the door opened.

Mrs. Latham said, "Connie, this woman is a detective and wants to talk with you about Kit."

Connie looked around the door and around her mother at Z who stood off to one side. When she saw Zakaya her eyes grew large.

Z stepped up. "It's okay, Connie. I'm working on finding out what happened to your friend. Would it be okay if I came in and talked with you about her?"

Connie nodded and Mrs. Latham said, "I'll just leave you two to talk, then."

Z stepped inside the room and Connie closed the door.

"You can sit on the bed if you want," she told Z.

"Thanks. It's very pretty. Your whole room, I mean. Is blue your favorite color?"

"Uh huh." Connie was still a bit wary.

"Connie," Z began, "I'm going to record this interview, with your permission, because I don't want to forget anything later. Is that all right with you?"

"Yeah, I guess so." The girl looked a bit wary but seemed calm.

Z flipped up the top of her t-com and pressed a button. Then she closed the top once again and turned her attention to the girl. "Well, Connie, I just want you to tell me exactly what happened the day your friend, Kit, disappeared. Would you do that for me, please?"

"But I already told the police everything I know."

"Yes. I believe you. But you might be surprised at the little tiny things you forgot to mention or didn't remember at the time. They could be a big help in this investigation."

"Okay." Connie moved some books out of a beige leather chair a few feet from the bed and sat down. "We were just shopping for prom dresses at Glamour Girl in the mall. We looked through all the dresses to find some we liked and the saleslady took them back to a fitting room so we could try them on."

"Can you describe the fitting room for me?"

"Ummm. It's just a fitting room. You know. It has a door and mirrors and a place to hang stuff and all."

"Where was it located? I mean, some dressing rooms have cubicles on both sides of a small aisle. Was it like that?"

"No. I mean, yes, the dressing room is like that. It has small rooms on both sides, but the one she took us to was at the very end."

"I see. The door to the dressing room you used…was it solid? I mean, some dressing rooms have only a partial door that is open at the top and bottom. Was this dressing room door like that?"

"Oh. No. The door was flat. You know. No decorations on it like on my bedroom door here." Connie pointed to her door. "And it was wider and it went from the floor to the top where the wall came down. Like my door. But it was just flat. No decorations, like I said."

"So you wouldn't have been able to see under it or over it, right?"

"Yes. I mean no. You couldn't see anything when the door was closed."

"Okay. How about the inside of the dressing room? Was it all mirrors or just one mirror at the back?"

"Oh, it had mirrors all around except for the wall where the door was. You know. So you can see the clothes from all angles. So just mirrors on three sides."

"Were they small mirrors? Or big ones?"

"Really large. I think the whole wall was mirror. Maybe. I forget."

"That's okay. Tell me about the salesperson who helped you."

"Oh, her." Connie halfway rolled her eyes.

Z laughed. "You sound like you didn't much like her."

"Well, she's kinda creepy. At least I thought so. And when we came back from finding a new dress for me to try on she didn't seem to care much that Kit was gone. She just said maybe she got tired and left. But I know Kit wouldn't have left me. We're best friends." Connie frowned, then said rather sadly, "*Were* best friends."

"What do you mean when you say you came back from finding a new dress? Did you leave Kit alone in the dressing room for some of the time the two of you were shopping?"

Connie looked pained and began to cry. "I'm so sorry, Miss Officer. It was supposed to be a really fun day. We looked forward to it for weeks and weeks. And now, because of me—"

"It's okay, Connie. It's not your fault. Absolutely none of this is your fault." Z reached across and took her hands. "Just tell me what happened the best you can remember."

Connie wiped the tears from her eyes. "Well, we were trying on the dresses and the lady opened the door and told me she found another dress that would be really great for me so I got dressed again in my regular clothes. You know, my jeans and stuff. Then I went out into the store with her to get it. I wish I hadn't. I really miss Kit."

"It's okay. I promise you. I'm going to find Kit."

Connie sniffed and rubbed her eyes. "Do you think you can? Really? Do you think she's…still alive?"

"I don't know, Connie. But I'm going to do everything in my power to find out. And if she is, I'm going to find her and bring her home."

"I hope you find her." Connie looked at Z expectantly. "I really miss her."

"Before I go, can you tell me about the police officers who were here to question you when it happened?"

Connie nodded. "There were two of them. But they didn't wear police uniforms. They did have guns, though. And they showed Mother their badges."

"Do you remember their names?" Z was hopeful.

"No. Sorry."

"Maybe you remember what they looked like?"

"Yes, a little bit. One was taller than the other one. And better looking. He seemed really calm and looked around. But it was kinda like he wasn't really seeing anything. You know? Like he didn't really care much. He kept looking at his fingernails."

"And the other one?"

"He was shorter. And fatter. But he wasn't really fat fat. You know? Just a little chubby, maybe. He seemed kind of nervous. I don't know why a policeman would be nervous, though. He's the one with the gun."

Z liked this girl. She smiled at the comment.

"Did both officers question you or just one of them?"

"Just the tall one. The short one just stood around. But…"

"But what?"

"There was something about the taller one that made me kind of afraid."

"What was that, Connie?"

"He had black eyes. I mean the color, not like somebody punched him in the eye. But his eyes were really dark black and they looked mean."

"In what way did they look mean?"

"I don't really know how to say it. They were just very dark and seemed really cold and looked right through me. It was kind of scary."

"Well, they are not here now, so you have nothing to be afraid of. Were they Black officers? Like me?"

"No. They were just regular white guys like you see all the time."

"Did they ask you the same things I've asked you today?"

Connie frowned slightly and shook her head. "No. They didn't ask anything about the dress shop or dressing room. They just asked where it happened and that was all. They told Mother the girl probably ran off with her boyfriend or something. But that would just never happen. I don't know why they would say a thing like that. Maybe they were trying to make me feel better, but it didn't work."

"Well, Connie. I want to thank you for your help today. Would it be okay if I called you or came back again if I need to?"

"Sure. Here's my number." She held her t-com up and Z took note of the number.

"Thank you, again, Connie. I really enjoyed talking with you."

"I hope you find Kit. Please find her."

"I will certainly try my best. If I find her or have any news of her I will call you. I promise. And one last question. Do you happen to know the name of the saleslady who helped you that day?"

"No. Well, I'm not sure. She had one of those little plastic name tag things pinned on her shirt. But I never really paid much attention to it. I think it was something like Franny, or Frieda maybe? I think it started with an F but I really don't remember. I'm sorry."

"That's okay. You've been a big help. You really have."

25

At the same time Z pulled out of Connie Latham's driveway, in a wooded area not ten miles away Kit Deming was crying and pounding on the door of the room in which she had been kept for six months. The girl who had been in the room with her had been taken away days ago. No one had said why and Kit had been left with no one to talk to at all. She had grown hopeless in the silence and could think of nothing else to do except pound the door and beg to go home.

"I want my mother! I want to go home! Please! I want my mother!"

She had been pounding on the door for what seemed like hours, though it had, in fact, been only about twenty minutes. A gruff voice had, at first, yelled back at her to be quiet but then whoever owned the voice just let her yell and pound away.

She had awakened early this morning cold and shivery and pulled her one blanket snug around her shoulders and upper body in an effort to keep warm. There was a light layer of frost on the window where she wrote her name with her index finger. Close to abandoning all hope of ever seeing her mother again, she had railed and cried before becoming quiet once again and retreating to her mattress in the corner where she began thinking of all she had lost and wondering how it had happened. She missed her little black dog, Rocky. She missed her cousins and her friend Connie. She wondered if her boyfriend had found someone new. Her mind raced through memory after memory, each overtaking the other as though they were cool water and she was dying of thirst.

Her thoughts returned, as they often did now, to the day in the dress shop. She tried hard to remember what had happened. She remembered the saleswoman, whom she had found cold and unfriendly. And she remembered reaching for a prom dress hanging on a hook beside the dressing room door. Then nothing. Except…

She tried envisioning the room. The day. Connie. Everything. Then, something new popped into her head as she remembered hearing something else. It was a squeaking sound, like the sound thick, new leather makes when it is pushed or tugged. It sounded very much like her uncle's pistol holster when he dropped by to visit on his way home after his shift as night guard at a local warehouse had ended. But she had been alone in the dressing room. Connie had gone out to find another dress. She had reached for the next dress she wanted to try on and then, everything was blank. As hard as she tried, she could remember nothing else until she woke up in this horrible prison of a room where she had recently decided, she would die at her own hand. This was not life. This was torture and she was ready to end it. Yet she had no way of doing so. If only the guards would allow her to have a razor she would slit her wrists like people sometimes did in the movies. But no such item was ever given to her—as her hairy legs and armpits now attested. She was disgusted and despondent. She wanted it over.

Whatever *it* was.

෨෨෬

Even though she had seen them only once, Z was convinced Connie Latham had just described the two detectives she had seen at the police station. Connie's description fit them like a bespoke glove. Still, though Connie's answers to her questions were forthright, they left more questions than they had fully answered.

Why weren't those officers interested in finding out more about the disappearance? Why weren't they astute enough to ask more about the dress shop? Why tell a young girl her friend most likely just abandoned her in the middle of a fun outing to run off with a boyfriend? None of it made any sense.

Sense or not, she had to caution herself not to jump to conclusions just because she had taken an instant dislike to the two she had seen at the police station. Whether or not she liked them personally had nothing to do with this case. Yet the big question still lingered: why did they seem taken aback when they first saw her at the police station. She was fairly sure it wasn't because she was Black. After all, JJ worked out of this station. But what other reason could there have been? It was a puzzle. But a puzzle that would have to wait. Right now, she would go to the Glamour Girl dress shop and check it out for herself.

❦

Z drove around the mall twice, taking in the layout of the sprawling building. It was on two levels but she determined from this recon drive the Glamour Girl shop was on the lower level at the rear. Visible from the outside was only the employee's windowless back door to the store. There was no customer entrance there. Deliveries could be made through that door or from the customer entrance in the mall interior—depending upon how the shop did business with its vendors. There was nothing more to see from the backside so she found a parking space near one of the mall entrances, and went inside.

The customer entrance to the Glamour Girl looked much like all the other stores that sold clothing and were still in business. Many, it seemed, were boarded up and defunct.

Mannequins decked out in the store's fashions stood on small metal support stands behind the glass fronts. Racks of gowns lined the walls and were dotted about the main floor on carousels. Customers wound their way through them until they found what they wanted and either took them to the cashier at the rear for immediate purchase or tried the items on first in the dressing room located through a door to the side of the cashier's counter. There was a second door to the other side of the cashier that Z guessed led to the stockroom.

A rather tired-looking woman with graying hair approached her with a frown. "I don't think we have anything here for you, Miss. This is a high-end shop."

"I think you might have something you are not aware of." Z ignored the slight and whipped out her detective's badge and flashed it at her.

At the sight of the quite official police badge, the woman became visibly nervous, her hands fidgeting with each other.

"I'd like to see the dressing rooms, please."

The woman's eyes began to dart back and forth. She blinked rapidly. "What for?"

"Because I'm a police detective and I am working a case. Shall we go take a look, Miss..." Z leaned back to read the woman's name on her plastic tag. She finished, "...Francis?"

The woman followed Zakaya into the dressing room. "There isn't anything to see back here. These are just ordinary dressing rooms," she said.

Z looked along the aisle that separated the small cubicles on either side. She counted nine of them. The eight rooms to the left and right had doors that did not go all the way to the top or to the bottom of their opening. The ninth, however—the one at the very end of the aisle—had a door that completely covered the opening.

"There was a girl that disappeared from this store back in May," Z said casually, looking inside each of the partial door cubicles as she slowly moved along. She turned suddenly to the woman. "Do you remember that?"

"Yes. But I don't see how you can blame the store for that."

"I wasn't blaming anyone." Z had turned to look at her. "I was merely asking if you remembered the incident."

"Yes. But no one knows what happened. The girl just disappeared."

Z approached the dressing room at the end and put her hand on the doorknob to open it. She found it locked. "Why is this room locked?"

The woman, Francis, appeared as a cornered animal looking to avoid capture. She was clearly searching for an answer. "We, ah…we keep that one locked because it's one less to clean up at the end of the day when we are not busy."

"I'd like to see it just the same. Unlock it, please."

Francis took a key from her pocket and, her hands shaking, unlocked the door.

"Stand aside, please." Z motioned for Francis to move back from the doorway and she stepped inside the room and looked around. Small seats were set into the front wall on either side of the door and there were hooks for hanging the dresses. It was not much different, really, from the interiors of the other rooms with the exception of the mirrors. The mirrors in this dressing room were somehow different. Rather than pinned to the wall such that their edges could be felt with an inquisitive finger, these mirrors seemed to be tightly framed and extended, as Connie Latham had told her, from floor to ceiling. She ran her finger along the edge of one of the mirrors and turned abruptly to face Francis. The woman's face had drained of color.

"Are you not feeling well?" Z asked her.

"Actually, I am a little faint," she said. "I have no idea why."

"Oh, I'm so sorry. I will hurry then. Tell me, please, which room did the girl who disappeared in May use?"

"This one over here." Francis pointed to the second cubicle along the left side of the aisle.

Z looked the woman in the eye and thought for sure she was going to faint dead away. "Why is the dressing room there on the end different from this one and all the rest here?"

Francis, with deer-in-headlights expression, coughed. "Ummm. Well, it didn't use to be a dressing room. It was just storage when I bought this space. Sometimes during the year we are much busier than other times and so I decided it would be good to have an extra dressing room. There is plenty of storage in the back and my inventory is almost all out front anyway. That's why it looks a bit different." Her eyes were enormous and tiny beads of sweat appeared on her forehead.

Z kept her steady stare on the woman's face for a long moment. Then she gave the entire dressing area one last look around and said, "Well thank you for your time. I think I'm finished here."

Francis quietly nodded and locked the ninth dressing room once again, then turned and led Z back out into the shop where two customers complained they had been waiting forever for some service.

Before Z could exit the store, her t-com buzzed. She didn't recognize the caller but decided to answer it anyway.

"Zakaya Kalu," she said, flatly.

"Miss Kalu! I'm so glad I caught up with you. Perhaps you remember me. Captain Taylor of the local police." The Captain's voice sounded a lot friendlier than it had when she had gone to the station earlier. Even more than friendly, it sounded somewhat hopeful.

Puzzled at first that he knew how to contact her, she at last remembered giving her information when she visited the police station. "As if I could forget. What can I do for you, Captain?"

"I'd like you to come down to the station, if you will, please. I have a kind of job for you if you are willing to do it."

"What kind of job?" She was immediately suspicious. After all, this was the same guy who practically had her physically ejected from the station very recently. Now he sounded almost conciliatory.

"We can discuss it when you get here. Can you come now? Say, in fifteen or twenty minutes?"

"I don't know. This sounds rather odd, quite frankly."

"I assure you," he said, "it's nothing sinister. But if you would rather wait until later today or even tomorrow, that would be fine, too. At your own convenience. It's just that I have some time right now and there's someone here that—"

Z cut him off. "I'll be there." She clicked off before he could finish.

This was really odd and she didn't like odd. Not this kind of odd. Yet, this could give her the access she wanted to those police records without having to involve JJ. She would at least go in to see what this was all about.

26

At the police station, Z was once again greeted by the desk sergeant. This time he was a bit more receptive and escorted her through the half-door that separated his station from the open bullpen, and into a conference room near the coffee station. Captain Taylor was waiting for her. And he was not alone.

"Miss Kalu!" the captain got up from his chair and extended his hand. "Come in, please, and take a seat." He indicated the offered chair and then nodded to the other person in the room before turning back to her. "This is Martin Blaze. He's—"

Z stiffened and cut him off with a very clipped, "Yes. I know Mr. Blaze." She looked at Blaze and then back to the captain. "Why is he here?"

Blaze spoke up. "I'm here because I proposed to the captain that you be brought in to help investigate their current cases."

The captain nodded. "Mr. Blaze here sometimes works with us. He seems to think you would be really good at helping us find the Kind Killer and, in all honesty, we could use all the help we can get on this case."

"You didn't seem to want or need my help when I was here before," she snapped at him. "And just how would Mr. Blaze know whether I'm any good or not?"

The captain started to answer but Blaze held up his hand to stop him. "You told me you were a detective. And I've seen you in action."

The captain spoke up. "I'm sorry for the way you were treated before, Miss Kalu."

"That's Special Investigator Kalu, Captain."

"Sorry, SI Kalu, but truth is, I've been under a lot of strain here and I thought you were just another person looking to make herself feel important. I do apologize."

Z looked steadily at the captain for a long moment and then nodded an acceptance of the apology before turning her attention to Blaze.

"You saw me take down an out-of-shape, untrained bully. You have no idea what kind of detective I am." She watched as Blaze gave the captain a look.

"We are willing to take the chance that you are as good as Blaze here says. And, in spite of my bad attitude before, we really do need the help," Captain Taylor pleaded. He looked from Z to Blaze then back again to Z. "So what do you say?"

That old tingle again. Something wasn't right. She had a sneaking feeling it wasn't the captain who was in charge here and that made her nervous. She hesitated longer than they had, apparently, expected.

"Detective?" the captain asked, "Will you?"

Conflicted, Z hesitated while she mulled this over. It was exactly what she had wanted. Okay…it was a bit suspicious. But it gave her the access she needed to find the traffickers who had taken Zeena.

She finally let out a breath. "On one condition."

"Yes?"

"I want full access to all evidence. And you should know that I will be investigating the trafficking of young girls in this area as well as the Kind Killer case."

Captain Taylor looked at Blaze who nodded so slightly as to be nearly imperceptible. He said, "Well, all right then! You can have access to whatever you need. When can you get started?"

"Tomorrow." The word was clipped and she turned her back and left the room without looking back at either of them.

As she was making her way out of the station, past the desk sergeant, she heard Blaze behind her.

"Wait up, Zakaya-Zee!"

She ignored him and kept going.

"Come on! What's wrong?" He caught up and walked alongside her to the car. "I thought you wanted to work with the police."

"I did," she snapped. "I do."

"So what's wrong?"

"I was shown the door when I came here earlier. And now, all of a sudden, like magic, the police are practically begging me to come on board. I wonder why?" She gave him her best I-know-why look and reached for the car door.

"Wait, please," he said. "I really do sometimes work with the police here. After all, you can only sit around spying on wayward husbands and wives for so long before you go a bit daft. Helping the police gives me a chance for some real detective work."

She said nothing so Blaze kept trying.

"So after seeing you in action…." He smiled at her. "I just thought I might have a little influence with the captain to help you both out. He gets the help he needs and you get the inside access you want. Win-win."

He was still smiling and there was no denying it. It was infectious to the point that she couldn't hide a small smile of her own. Too, whatever influence he had with the captain, it had gotten her what she wanted. Don't look a gift horse and all that…

"How about I buy you a whiskey sour at Brassy's? I've also been hired to work the Kind Killer case. We can talk about it over drinks and a sandwich."

Z slid into the driver's seat and turned back to him nodding her head toward the passenger seat. "Get in."

ഌഌ

Hadeon Cook and Donny Ray Swift were at their desks when Blaze and Z emerged from the conference room. They had come in while the closed-door session with the captain had been taking place and hadn't seen Z enter the station. On seeing her emerge from the closed door of the conference room, Donny Ray began to sweat.

"What's she doing here again?" he whispered across his desk to Hadeon, sitting opposite.

"Dunno. Doesn't really matter, does it? You worry too much."

"I'm telling you this is not good, Had."

Cook slammed a sheaf of papers down on his desk and got up. He leaned over his desk toward Swift. "For the last time, stop pissing and moaning. She has never seen us outside this police station—not even once—and she doesn't know squat. And if she gets too close to finding out, there just might be an accident."

Donny Ray put his head in his right hand and stared down at his desk. He muttered, "This is trouble. I just know it."

Cook started to walk away but was stopped by the buzzing of his t-com.

"Cook." He was curt. Still irritated by Donny Ray's inconvenient—and incongruous—conscience.

The voice on the t-com was shrill and panicked, but Cook was too far from the desk now for Donny Ray to hear what was being said. Hadeon was certain he could hear only the one side of the conversation.

"What do you mean, she inspected the dressing room?"

Garble...

"When?"

Garble...

"She doesn't really know anything. She's just fishing. I'll take care of it."

Garble...

"I told you not to worry, damn it! Calm down. I'll take care of it." Cook clicked off and turned back to his desk. He leaned over close to Swift. "I'm thinking there's going to be an accident a lot sooner than we thought."

Donny Ray was wide-eyed and silent.

"Besides," Cook said, "when she finds out the kid is missing, she will probably go back to wherever she came from all on her own and we will be rid of her even without an accident."

As Cook walked away, Swift said aloud to no one but himself, "I don't think so."

27

Blaze held the swinging door open and Z stepped inside the dusky warmth of Brassy's. Apparently Gordon, the bartender, had put on a little heat since the weather outside was getting somewhat cooler. It felt snug and comfortable as she slid onto the barstool.

"I'll order for us," Blaze said, then quickly thought better of it. He added, "With your permission, of course." He smiled at her, eyebrows raised.

She laughed at him.

"Whiskey sour, right? With Jack Black?"

"Yes. Thanks."

"Go grab a table over there by the window, would you? It will be easier to talk, okay?"

Blaze put in the order for the drinks while Z slid back off the barstool and claimed a table against the wall of windows.

Blaze joined her. "Gordon will bring the drinks."

She nodded.

"Still mad at me?"

"Not mad. Only dogs go mad."

He laughed.

She added, "But I'm still irritated as all hell. Frankly, it was hard to tell back at the station who was in charge: you, or the captain."

"Ah! Then I'm a better actor than I thought I was. I assure you I am in no way in charge of the police. I'm just persuasive. Anyway, we'll be working the case together so what do you think?"

"Cases," she said, emphasizing the plural. "I think I want access to the evidence. *All* of the evidence. Nothing held back. I know how police are sometimes. And they are likely to be doubly cautious with me being from Cascadia and not licensed here for anything other than renting an old beat-up car."

"I'm sure they will be forthcoming with you. At least, I hope they will be." He paused, then added, "Why do you do it?"

"Do what?"

"Detective work. Take down bad guys. You know."

"Because I have to. Someone has to. And I'm good at it. Like you said." She gave him an impish smile.

Their conversation was temporarily interrupted as Gordon brought the drinks and set them on the table. When he left, Blaze sipped his beer, then asked, "Speaking of Cascadia, what can you tell me about how the police operate there?"

"Nothing." Was he playing with her? Or just sincerely curious?

"You don't know? Or won't say?"

"Take your pick."

He laughed. "You are a hard one to talk to, Miss Zakaya-Zee."

At hearing him call her the name he'd made up for her, she finally relaxed and laughed, too.

"I've never been, you know," he said.

"Been where?"

"Cascadia."

"You should come sometime. You might like it."

"I actually plan to." He paused, and then, "You don't use money there, do you?"

"Not tangible currency, no." She sipped the whiskey sour. "But we maintain an account of credits which are more easily spent than messing about with cards and cash as you do here. It makes life a lot easier on everyone."

He seemed to be thinking about that for a minute. Then he asked, "How about your schools, hospitals, and prisons?"

"What do you mean, how about them?"

"I understand they are not like those here in the States."

"True. They are all funded through taxes so no one has to forego an education or healthcare because they can't afford it."

Blaze nodded in agreement. "That's the way it ought to be, I think. Here, the people pay taxes but they never seem to get anything for them. Instead, the government gives the money to big businesses like pharmaceutical companies who turn around and charge people through the nose for whatever it is they are selling. So, really, the people pay twice for their healthcare. Sometimes they even die because they can't afford to pay the price of a drug they subsidized with their taxes in the first place. It's insane."

Z picked up her drink but set it back down. She said, "I'm amazed the citizens of this country put up with that because you are right. It truly is insane." She looked out the window, thinking, then turned back and asked, "What about the schools here? Are they still as bad as they were before I left twelve years ago?"

He sighed. "It's still the same old thing. They are still run by the individual states so education is not uniform across the country. The people pay taxes but get very little back in the way of education. The lower grades are public so the kids get to attend, but they are so poorly funded it's almost criminal. It's gotten so bad that organizations are created to lobby for charitable donations in order to pay for supplies. Underpaid teachers often spend from their own pockets for basic supplies. At the higher, university level, everyone is expected to pay. Those who can't, don't get the education unless they can somehow get a scholarship or a grant. Pretty shabby, huh?"

"I would say so," she agreed. "And you're right. Still much the same as when I was here."

"And what about the prisons in Cascadia?"

"What about them?"

"What are they like? How are they managed?"

"Our prisons concentrate on rehabilitation rather than punishment."

He nodded. "I heard something about that. They are not run for profit, are they?"

"Absolutely not. What a horrid idea." She shivered as though trying to rid herself of something nasty. "They're run like small towns where the prisoners live in tiny cottage-like houses and have jobs to go to every day. The recidivism rate is almost nonexistent so we must be doing something right."

"Hard to argue with that," he said. "How about your government?"

"Our government?"

He peered at her over the rim of his beer glass and nodded. "What's it like?"

"Blaze, I know you weren't born yesterday."

"True. But I'd like to hear it from an actual citizen of Cascadia rather than the propaganda we get taught here."

She nodded, then said, "It's vastly different from your government here. You asked about the police before. They are part of the government. Sort of. To be a police officer you have to have a university education and you undergo extensive background checks. We don't want anyone with that kind of power prejudiced against any particular race, gender, and so forth. Same with other government positions. Our 'governors,' meaning 'those who govern' and not the leader of a particular state like here, are selected at random from the pool of former university graduates. They serve for four years if they are able. It's considered an honor. They return to their regular occupation when the four years are up."

"No elections?"

"I should hope not! Nothing like the mess you contend with here. They represent the people only—not businesses and certainly not some particular political party. We don't have those."

"How many of these governors do you have?"

"It depends on the population. Right now the population of Cascadia is right at a hundred and ten million. So we have a hundred and ten governors. One for each million citizens. If and when the population changes, the number of governors changes with it."

"So what about your president? I know you have one. How does he, or she, get chosen?"

"The president is also selected randomly for a term of four years, but only from the group of outgoing governors who have had some experience. But you know the best part of our government?"

"What's that?" Blaze was either completely engrossed or the best actor on the planet.

"It's run on the 'Veil of Ignorance' philosophy. Well, not exactly. But as closely as possible. The governors are tasked with first asking the question: Is this legislation even necessary? If they get past that one, they have to ask: How will this benefit the vast majority of our citizens?" She laughed and added, "Often doing nothing is the best course of action."

Blaze set his beer on the table. "In other words, if it ain't broke, don't fix it."

"Exactly. And lastly, they have to ask–How would I feel if I were the poorest of the poor or a member of the smallest minority and this legislation passed."

Blaze said nothing to that so she continued. "But don't get the idea it's all lollipops and roses. It isn't. We have our share of murders, theft of property, blackmail, you name it. People being what they are."

"Yeah, I know."

"What do you mean, you know? I thought you just told me you had never been to Cascadia."

"I haven't. At least for all practical purposes." He fiddled with his beer, moving it back and forth on the cardboard coaster.

"What do you mean, *for all practical purposes*? Have you been to Cascadia or not?"

"Yes. And no. I was actually born there but left when I was seven. My father got into some serious trouble and they gave him a choice—go to prison or the United States. He was born in Georgia so he chose the U.S. and they deported him."

Z sat up straighter. "Deported him? For what?"

"Running drugs. He wasn't what you might call a very upstanding citizen."

"Sorry to hear that." She sipped her drink.

"But, at least my mother was somebody special."

She nodded and waited for more, but it wasn't forthcoming so she didn't press for details.

She finally asked, "You an only child, then? No siblings?"

His mood became solemn and pensive as he answered. "I had a sister." He paused. "She's gone."

"Oh. I'm sorry."

"No need." He looked out the window and sipped his beer. "It was a long time ago."

Z tried to break the mood by changing the subject. "So you're actually a dual citizen since you were born in Cascadia, right?" she asked.

"I guess so."

"That's rather noncommittal." She sipped her drink and watched him over the rim of the glass, but he only smiled at her.

She decided to leave it and said, finally, "We do have some drug problems back home, for sure. In addition to other crimes. Some small. Some not."

"Keeps you in business, then, doesn't it?" He smiled at her.

"Yep. I stay busy." She smiled back at him, then added, "But I wouldn't trade it for what you have here, believe me."

Blaze asked, "What brought you to the States? Besides visiting your mother, that is? You have a boyfriend here, maybe?"

Blaze seemed most comfortable when talking about something other than himself and he appeared to Z to be teasing her so she teased back, glad his mood had brightened. She answered his tease.

"Yes. A big, tall, handsome guy. Very muscular. A multi-millionaire with seven houses in Hawaii and five in the Caribbean. And a big boat. One of those…whaddya call 'em?" She snapped her fingers twice. "…Yachts! Can you believe it?" Her eyes grew wide in mock amazement.

Blaze spit-laughed into his beer. "No."

He laughed again. Then he got serious. "Really. Why did you come?"

"I told you. To see my mother. It's been five years since I came to visit her. I've missed her. I was born here. In Selma. But I left when I was eighteen. Made my way to Cascadia and the rest is history. As they say. Also, it was my thirtieth birthday a couple weeks ago so I claimed a legacy. It turned out to be something I would probably never use so I decided to give it to her. To my mother."

"Ah yes!" he said. "Those legacy things. Libraries. Whatever they are called. Sounds really interesting. Tell me about them."

"Please, Blaze. Enough questions. You're obviously an educated man. You can't have gotten through school here without ever hearing about how Cascadia came to exist and how it operates as a country. So why all the questions?"

"You'd be surprised what they teach and don't teach here these days, but yeah. I know about them. What they don't teach in schools, we can look up in libraries. We still have libraries here, you know. I looked it up once."

Z couldn't help smiling at that last. "Well, as I said before, it's not all lollipops and roses. Besides, you have good things and good people here, too."

"Like who, for instance?"

"My mother, for one." She paused, then said, "Maybe you." She suppressed a smile. "Haven't decided about you, yet."

Blaze laughed. "Anybody else?"

She became slightly serious. She paused but then decided to ask a question she had wondered about for days now. "I met a guy when I first arrived. His name is Eli McClain. You know him?"

Watching her, Blaze ran a thumb over his lower lip, then said, "Yeah. Met him once or twice. Big, good-looking dude."

"No kidding."

"Hey…"

"Gorgeous smile. But I have a job. Not looking for a man."

"What if one finds you?"

"What if the moon really is made of cheese?"

He laughed. "So what did you get?"

"What?"

"What did you get for the legacy thing?"

"Oh. A pin. Like you wear on your coat. A brooch, it's called. It has light blue stones in it—the color of a swimming pool. I gave it to my mother like I said."

"That's nice. Nice of you, and a nice custom."

"Yes." She became pensive. "Problem is, I have no idea what I will leave for someone else to claim when their turn comes in seventy years."

"You must have something." He watched her as he sipped his beer.

"No. Nothing. At least nothing anyone would want or be happy to get. I guess I really have no legacy to leave anyone. In a way that makes me kind of sad. It's like there's nothing really to me, after all."

He leaned a bit toward her, his arms supporting him on the table. "Of course there is. We, meaning you and me and everyone else that ever existed, might only be specks on a space-dot, but if we are insignificant then we are all equally insignificant from the king to the peasant, and from the CEO to the cleaning crew. And that, Miss Zakaya-Zee, also renders everyone equally significant. Equally important. Equally valuable. Not everything we leave behind is tangible, you know. Some things are so valuable they're beyond price. Some things so heinous they're beyond imagining. You might not be able to leave it as a Cascadian legacy—something to be put into a box— but, believe me, you will leave something. People may not think they do, but everyone leaves a legacy, Zakaya-Zee. *Everyone.*"

Z grew silent. Blaze's words had impact and she was so taken with his insight and intelligence that, for a few minutes, she could think of nothing to say.

Blaze seemed to be lost in thought as well until he looked up at her and asked, "Doesn't it bother you?"

"Doesn't what bother me?"

"Being here. In the States. You know…"

"You mean because I'm Black?"

He nodded.

"It used to. Not so much now. Now I live in a place where it doesn't seem to matter. Here, all they see are the differences. They see skin color. They notice that my hair is different from their own. It doesn't register that I have eyes and arms and legs, just like them. Or that I bleed just as red as they do. Or when I'm happy I laugh and when I'm sad, I sometimes cry. Just like them. Noticing the differences gives them something to hate. Someone to look down on so they won't have to look at their own failures. It's a tribal thing and they don't even realize it. And yet, trapped in a burning car or building, they wouldn't for a single second refuse a Black hand reaching in to save them. They don't realize that, either. So, yeah. It bothers me a little. But I know who I am and that doesn't depend on their opinion."

Blaze became quietly thoughtful at this and so Z decided to change the subject.

"I'm hungry. Let's get one of Gordon's famous sandwiches to take with us—famous according to my friend, JJ—and then let's go back to the station and start to work. I've got some traffickers to catch and the captain wants his Kind Killer caught as well. Maybe we'll get lucky. I doubt the captain will care if we start now rather than tomorrow."

Blaze pushed away from the table and reached over to assist with pulling out Z's chair. He said, "I don't know that we will find anything on the traffickers since the police aren't investigating them."

Z grabbed her bag and got up to join him. "Well, you never know what you will find until you start seriously looking."

28

It was very late afternoon by the time Z and Blaze got back to the police station and checked in with the captain, telling him they had decided to get a head start on the work. There were no objections on his part, so they began pulling evidence.

"I'm going to want all the evidence from three separate cases," Z told the captain. She held up three fingers for emphasis. "First, I want to look at the case of the body found in the cemetery. The smiling corpse you assigned to the Kind Killer. Next, I want everything on the young girl found in that ditch south of Selma. And last, I want everything you have on the disappearance of…" She turned to Blaze and then back to the captain. "What was her name?"

"Kit. Kit Deming." The captain appeared a little impatient with this. "We already looked into that case. The girl just disappeared one day. Sometimes girls do that. And right now I need this Kind Killer caught."

Z looked him in the eye and said, flatly, "You looked into the case."

No statement of fact could have been more accusing and the captain visibly flinched.

Z said it again, in a kinder voice. "You looked into the case, but you never solved it, did you?"

"No," the captain admitted.

"Well, I'd just like to take a look at it. If you don't mind."

Zakaya Kalu had long ago mastered the unblinking eye-to-eye stare and was locked in on the captain in an unrelenting stand-off.

Captain Taylor turned to the desk sergeant, "You heard the lady, Mike! Get those evidence boxes and take them into the conference room for these detectives."

The sergeant obliged and soon all three evidence boxes were on the conference room table.

The captain said he would leave them to it and followed the sergeant out, closing the door behind him.

Z watched the captain out and turned to Blaze. "Since the captain was kind enough to give me all the access I asked for, let's oblige him by starting with the body found in the cemetery. The smiling corpse. If that one proves too difficult we can move on to the cases I'm most interested in. But we might get lucky." She unwrapped one of the sandwiches they had brought with them from Brassy's and began munching on it. "But let's take a look at the physical evidence from all of them just the same."

"That's a strange one. The Kind Killer thing." Blaze began unloading the boxes and placing folders and evidence bags beside the box to which they belonged along the table.

Z picked up the first folder and began flipping the stapled pages over the top, ticking off bullet points as she digested the contents. "This man was middle-aged. Seriously broken both emotionally and financially by his wife's ordeal with cancer. Throat slit from carotid to carotid. A smile, according to the M.E. was pushed into his face after death." She stopped reading for a second. Then, "Yeah. A strange one, for sure." She looked up at Blaze. "What have we got in the bags?"

Blaze picked up the first one that contained the man's t-com and wallet. There were still several hundred dollars in the wallet. "Doesn't look like robbery was the motive here, does it?"

Z shook her head as she took another bite of her sandwich. With her mouth full of sandwich, she said, "Wha 'bout this one?" With her free hand she held up the bag that contained a small, brown bottle. She swallowed the bite of sandwich. "What do you make of this?"

"Looks like a medicine bottle to me. No label, though. The report said it had a flower in it and was placed in his hands."

"Was that it?"

Blaze looked through the evidence box. "Yes. That appears to be the extent of the physical evidence other than his clothes."

"Hmmmm. Let's keep everything separate but take a first look at the evidence from the girl found in the ditch." Z picked up the folder, and began reading as Blaze pushed the Kind Killer box and evidence to the far end of the table.

"Her name was Tiki Jameson, and according to this," Z said, "she was strangled. No other marks on her body. She was sexually molested, however, and was found without any underwear. No panties. Really pretty girl." She slid the large, color photo across to Blaze who looked it over, shaking his head.

Blaze laid the photo back down slowly. "No marks on her body. Odd. She didn't put up a fight."

"What's that?" Z said, nodding toward the evidence bag near Blaze's elbow.

Blaze picked up the bag and took a good look. "Appears to be another small bottle. Blue, this time. Looks like another medicine bottle. What do you think?" He passed the evidence bag to Zakaya.

"This is crazy. The report says the bottle contained traces of Octoflurane and was found some yards from the girl's body. Probably tossed out the window of a passing car. They have no way of connecting it to her. So it says." She looked up from the bottle to Blaze.

"You thinking what I'm thinking?" he asked her.

"Yep. It's just too, too much of a coincidence for me," she said. "There's a connection. Or, at the very least, a possible connection to the Kind Killer case. But the cases are so radically different." She thought for a moment. "Even so, I think it's worth checking into. You?"

"Yep." Blaze asked, "Was there any mention of Octoflurane in the brown bottle found with the smiling corpse?"

"Ummmm…" Z flipped through the report on the Kind Killer. "No. Nothing. Just a small amount of water. But I still don't think we can rule out a connection, do you?"

"No. Not yet." Blaze had been taking notes in a small notebook and added this bit of information to it.

"It could also explain why no marks on the girl's body. The Octoflurane, I mean. Maybe she—Miss Jameson—couldn't fight back."

"Maybe."

Z tossed the sandwich wrapping paper into the trash can near the door and said, "Let's move on to the missing girl. Kit Deming."

"You sure you want to take that one on, too?" Blaze asked.

"I'm sure."

Blaze dug out the report and handed it to her.

"Ha!" Z pushed her chair back slightly.

"What?"

"Just as I suspected. Those two detectives I saw when I first came here—the day I was nearly kicked back out the front door—were the ones who interviewed Connie

Latham, the missing girl's friend. Donny Ray Swift and Hadeon Cook." She grimaced and flipped a page over the top of the folder and then back again as she looked it over. She shook her head. "What mother would name her son Hadeon?"

Blaze laughed. "What brought that on? It's just a name."

"Do you know what it means?" she asked him.

He shook his head and raised his eyebrows awaiting enlightenment.

She laughed at his expression. "It means 'destroyer.' Helluva name to hang on your baby."

"True. Well, what did they find out?"

"Nothing." She tapped her fingers on the table as she tried to decide how much to tell him.

"What?" he asked.

She hesitated. Then, "I decided if the police weren't interested in investigating the possible trafficking going on around here, I would do it without them. So I went to Connie Latham's house this morning and interviewed her myself. Nice girl. Very upset about her friend."

"You're kidding."

"I don't kid."

"Well, what did you find out?"

"That the officers who came to interview her— apparently this precinct's very own Cook and Swift— didn't seem at all interested in the case. They did just as little as possible, then left. The question that nags at me is…why?"

"Good question. We should make a note to look into that."

"Yep." Z eyed Blaze's still-wrapped sandwich beside him on the table. "You gonna' eat your sandwich or just toss it?"

"You were the one who was hungry." He teased her. "You want it?"

She reached across the table and took it. "No sense letting it go to waste."

29

The door to the conference room opened and JJ stuck his head in. "Hey Z! I saw you through the window. What's going on?"

"JJ!" Z reached out to him then turned to Blaze. "Martin, this is my friend JJ. We've known each other since forever."

Blaze rose from his chair and came around the table to shake JJ's hand.

"What's up?" JJ shook and released Blaze's hand then turned back to Z.

"I guess you were right about the captain being a good guy," Z told him. "He's agreed for me and Martin here to work the Kind Killer case and has given me the freedom to look into the trafficking I'm sure is going on here as well. So we've teamed up for these three." She waved at the three evidence boxes on the table.

A thought occurred to her as she looked from JJ to Blaze. "Since Blaze sometimes works with the police, perhaps you already know each other?"

"No," JJ said, "I'm sorry. Haven't had the privilege."

"I keep a low profile." Blaze laughed.

JJ frowned and turned back to Z. "What about your little friend, Zeena?"

"I've sent her back to Cascadia for her own safety. I need to be free to work these cases without worrying about her."

JJ shook his head. "Zakaya Kalu! Are you ever going to have a decent visit with your mother?"

"I know. I know. I'm the worst daughter ever. But I think she understands there are much worse people out there doing much worse things. And maybe—just maybe—I can help stop them."

JJ nodded. "Well, what have you got? Anything I can help you with?"

"Not much, actually. The only thing that seems out of place is that a small bottle was found at the location of each of two of these cases. One blue. One brown. One contained traces of Octoflurane and the other contained only water."

"But," Blaze interjected, "both appear to be what I would call small medicine bottles."

Z turned to JJ. "And that's about it. Except…"

"Except what?"

"Except the detectives who interviewed the surviving girl on the third case were two from this department. Cook and Swift."

JJ rolled his eyes.

"What's wrong?" Blaze wanted to know.

"Those two." JJ shook his head. "Useless pieces of work."

"Why do you say that?" Z asked.

"I don't think they have ever closed a case since I've been here, yet they are always out and about as though they are beat officers. I don't know. I just don't care much for them. And the feeling is mutual if you understand me."

"How's that?" Blaze asked.

"Wrong skin color for them."

"I see."

"Well, let's eighty-six them for the moment. I just thought of something else." Z picked up the folder for the wheelbarrow girl and checked it again. "This case here. The girl found strangled and stuffed beneath an old wheelbarrow. That location was south of Selma. Way out of the jurisdiction for this department, yet the sheriff turned the case over to them here just the same. I thought that was a bit odd."

"How do you know that?" Blaze asked her.

"Because before I went to interview Connie Latham, the girl who survived the missing girl case, I stopped by the sheriff's office and he told me so. And you know what else?"

"What?"

"His name is Cook. Wilbur Cook. And as soon as I left his office, after learning nothing about the case except that 'traffickers don't kill their merchandise,' he immediately got on the landline and called someone. I just thought that was odd."

She looked from Blaze to JJ who said, "The sheriff is Cook's uncle."

"I guess that explains it. Anyway," she continued, "all we really have here are two very similar bottles from two cases that don't appear to have any connection to each other except for the bottles. But it's late. And I'm really tired. So here's what I'd like to do."

"What's that?" Blaze asked.

"Tomorrow, I'd like to visit the town's pharmacies to see what we can find out. They should have some record of who purchased Octoflurane in the last six months to a year. Don't you think?"

"Sounds good to me." Blaze reached for his jacket.

"JJ can you lock this conference room so the evidence stays in here untouched?"

"I'll get the captain to do it right now," JJ said, and headed out of the conference room and down the main bullpen toward the captain's office at the end.

Blaze allowed Z to exit the conference room first and watched as she passed the desk sergeant and headed out the main station door. He called out to her, "Bye, Zakaya-Zee. See you tomorrow."

She waved over her shoulder without looking back.

৩৩৩

Blaze was still watching the empty doorway after Z had exited the station when his t-com buzzed.

"Forty-eight! I have a way we can find out if our Miss Detective Kalu was with that team in Atlanta two years ago. I've spoken with the two agents who were holding Mr…er…Mr. Parker West when he was taken—we think by our Miss Kalu posing as one of the motel maids. They are pretty sure they will be able to identify her if they see her again so I'm going to send them down to Alabama to have a look. I had a helluva time chasing them down. One was on vacation in Paris with his wife and the other was on assignment in Wyoming. So now that I've got them it would be a good time to send them your way."

"Sir, I would advise holding off for the moment. We—"

Dark Suit cut him off. "Why? If she's who we think she is we want her in custody. The sooner the better."

"Thing is…Sir…I've arranged for both myself and her to work with the police here solving some outstanding murder cases. And, I think she's on to a human trafficking operation working out of this area. From what I've seen so far, she's really good. It wouldn't hurt to let us finish this case before we make a move to arrest her. She's not going anywhere right now and we could save the lives of any number of young girls if we just hold off for a bit. And it sure couldn't hurt our image any to take down a good chunk of an international human trafficking ring."

Blaze could hear Dark Suit breathing but he wasn't saying anything. He grimaced and continued with his reasoning.

"If you really feel like you have to send them now, they need to be instructed to observe her while camouflaged in some way. After all, if they can recognize her, she can recognize them—if she's the one we are looking for. And then…well…we might just lose her."

"I see." Dark Suit finally spoke. "I will think about it. I may send them now. Or I may wait. Either way, neither of you will ever know."

The t-com clicked dead. The silence was so loud it rang in his ears.

Blaze had been holding his breath and exhaled loudly. *Shit.*

30

Z's sleep was interrupted very early by the buzzing of her t-com. In that half-groggy state where nothing seems real, she plopped the pillow over her head but the buzzing didn't stop. Finally realizing what it was, she rolled over and grabbed the thing from the night table and pressed the button.

"Wha?"

"Z!" It was Alex.

"Wha? Must be middle of the night. 'Smatter?"

"Wake up! It's Alex! Zeena wasn't on the plane! I waited as long as I could. I waited for three more arrivals but she wasn't on any of them."

Z threw the covers off and leaped from the bed to her feet. She began pacing the room. "What do you mean? She was on that flight! I put her on the plane myself. Atlanta was the only stop. I told her to—" She gasped for breath. "I told her to keep her t-com turned on. Did you check it? Did Budgie check it?" She was literally screaming now and the room was spinning.

Mrs. Kalu threw open the bedroom door and yelled, "Zakaya Renée Kalu! Stop it! Calm down!"

Z stopped pacing and looked up at her mother. "Yes. Yes. You're right, Mama. I have to calm down. But Zeena is missing! She didn't make the flight in Atlanta!"

Mrs. Kalu's hand flew up and covered her mouth. Z continued to listen to the voice on her t-com.

"We checked, Z. The t-com was not on. It's still not on. We have no way of tracking her. I'm so sorry." Alex was nearly as distraught as Z herself.

Z sat down on the side of the bed and looked up at her mother who was still standing in the doorway. "They've taken her. They've taken her again! My god! What have I done?"

"Who knew you were putting her on that flight?" Alex yelled into the t-com to get Z's wandering attention.

"I don't know, Alex. I can't remember. Er…yes. My Aunt Juanita knew. I mean she knew I was sending her home but not which flight and, crazy as she is, she wouldn't harm anyone. And…who else? JJ! My old friend JJ was there when I told Juanita. He's a police officer. And…and…my Uncle Bo could have heard when I told Juanita. Oh my god!" The very thought of her Uncle Bo made her stomach turn.

"Anyone else?" Alex kept talking, trying to glean information but mostly to calm Zakaya down.

"I don't think so. Wait! Yes. Well, I told my current partner I'm working with for the police that I was thinking about sending Zeena home, but I never told him when. I just don't know how this could have happened. I should have flown to Atlanta with her and made sure she got on that Cascadian flight. She's just an abandoned puppy, Alex. A tossed-away little kitten. She's the least worldly teenager I've ever encountered. Alex, she's smart but uneducated. Even more than I was at her age. This is devastating."

"What do you mean, your current partner? What's going on?"

"The local police here want a case solved and even though they practically threw me out the door when I offered my services earlier, they changed their mind, apparently. They have offered me the opportunity to help out in exchange for access to evidence in the cases I'm positive are trafficking."

"They changed their minds? Sounds fishy to me."

"I think I know who nudged them into giving me this chance so I'm not arguing with it, but I'm not stupid. I know it's fishy. But it's a chance and I'm just going to take it. Especially now."

"What will you do now?"

"I don't know! I don't know! I'm…I'm going to find her and put those traffickers away for good. If I don't kill them myself first."

"Do you need the team?"

"No. At least not yet. I don't have enough information to do anything right now and the team would just draw attention. I'll work this. I'll do this. If I can find the traffickers, I'll find her. I'm sure of it. But…"

"But what?"

"Get Budgie to see if he can somehow locate Zeena. If anyone can find her, it's Budgie."

"I will. And I'll apprise Viking and Tillerman of the situation. Do what you have to do, Z. Just stay safe and find her!"

"I intend to."

Z clicked off without even saying goodbye. She couldn't think of that right now. Right now she could only think of Zeena and where she could be and what might be happening to her. None of the answers that came rapidly to her imagination were pleasant. And she had not even a single clue where to begin.

⁂

As soon as Z terminated the communication, Alex tapped Viking.

"Viking! It's Alex! Zeena never arrived and Z is on the rampage in Alabama. This is not good."

The person on the other end of the conversation groaned and mumbled and began to snore. Alex screamed louder.

"Viking! Wake up!"

At last Alex heard him speak. "What? What's the matter? Who is this?"

"It's Alex! Zeena never arrived and Z has about lost it. Are you awake?"

The voice came crisp now. "Yes. Tell me everything."

Alex described Z's panic over the missing Zeena and the fact that she was somehow working with a local partner to help the police solve a case in exchange for access to evidence involving human trafficking.

"A local partner? Who is it?"

"She didn't say, but I'm not sure she fully trusts him. Still, she's willing to work with him, so that says something."

"Working with someone she doesn't fully trust is compromising. I hope she knows what she's doing this time."

"You know Z, Viking. When she's determined, there is no limit to what she might do. And this time, she's not only determined, she's really, really angry. I'm worried."

"I hear you. I'll notify Tillerman. We're going to prepare for sending in the team. Except for you. You need to be here in case Zeena magically shows up. Also, you will need to liaison with Budgie here."

"But—"

"No buts. You're staying. No way I'm losing both of you." He paused, then quietly added, "If it comes to that."

Alex's t-com went silent. She stared at it as though it were some bug on her wrist.

The hardest job of all was waiting.

☙❧☙❧

Viking thundered into the office about a half hour early followed by Alex fifteen minutes later. To his surprise, the other team members were already at their desks. He went to the coffee machine and poured himself a cup then gathered the team and explained the situation.

"With Zeena missing and Z willing to do who-knows-what in Alabama, I'm not sure what's about to happen but we can't wait around much longer. We're going to have to go to Alabama ourselves. Except for Alex. She's staying here this time. I need her here to liaison with Budgie in managing everything from this end. And in case Zeena somehow shows up."

Parker asked, "When are we leaving?"

"Soon." Viking didn't want to be more specific just yet. He added, "Nothing has happened yet. As far as we can tell, she's just investigating a case for the police. But she's working with a partner Alex feels she doesn't fully trust, and she's also looking into human traffickers. Stepping on those toes could be extremely dangerous. There is a ton of money involved in that kind of thing and there's no way it's contained just in Alabama. Or the United States. If it's not international I'll eat my boots."

Parker spoke up. "Damn! Z risked her life to come and get me out of that dingy motel in Atlanta two years ago. Not that the rest of you didn't play a part, too, but it was Z who risked everything in that motel room."

Gray spoke quietly. "She's not afraid of anything. Or anybody. That's what worries me the most."

Viking said, "I know. I know. No telling what she will get herself into. But we need to remember one other thing. She's smart. She may be angry but I've never known her to be reckless."

At the talk of Z being in real danger where she was unable to help, Alex's eyes teared up and she turned away.

Gray reached out and placed his hand on her arm to calm her. He said, "She's also clever, Alex. She won't do anything without thinking it through. She won't jeopardize her safety, or Zeena's. I'm sure of that. And right now, Zeena's safety could depend on her own."

"She's a firecracker, though." Viking said. "And she won't appreciate the team's intrusion there unless she calls for us herself. Best she doesn't know until it's absolutely necessary. So the tentative plan is that we will gear up and go to Alabama, remaining out of sight until she needs us. When we get the call, we'll already be there. I don't want to take any chance on losing her."

Parker smiled. "I'm not losing her. You can put money on that. What would we do without her crazy old-fashioned sayings that make everyone do a brow-knitting double-take?"

"Just so," Viking said. "I still remember the first time she told me she was busier than a cat covering up guavas on a tin roof." He chuckled but quickly grew serious and looked around at the team. He added, "I'll make the arrangements. We'll leave soon."

31

Every head in the police station turned as Z came thundering through the door shouting for the captain. There was no one present who couldn't see that she was upset, including the so-called "fast food duo" of Cook and Swift. They watched her every move then turned to each other, Cook giving Swift a warning eye to stay calm and quiet.

Captain Taylor came out of his office. "What's the matter, Detective?"

"My young friend! I put her on a flight to Cascadia yesterday morning, but she never arrived. She had one stop in Atlanta and she never made the Cascadian flight! She's been taken! I told you there was trafficking going on here! I told you!" Z clenched her fists and stomped her foot for emphasis.

"Take it easy. Take it easy. We'll figure this out." The captain tried to calm her. "Blaze is already here in the conference room looking over those cases you pulled yesterday. He's waiting for you."

"Did you hear me?" Z shouted at him. "I just told you my friend has been taken. I told you there is trafficking going on here. Why won't you listen? Is everybody in this place dumb as a rock?"

The captain tried to calm her. "You don't know for sure it's trafficking. Maybe she just missed her flight? Have you considered that?"

"Of course I considered that. But I don't believe it for a second. I told her to keep her t-com turned on, but it's not on. It hasn't been on. The girl is young, but she's not stupid. She knows how to turn on a t-com. Now there is no way to track her! I'm telling you, she's been taken!"

The door to the conference room flew open and Blaze emerged. "If there is trafficking going on here, we will find it out. I promise you. And we will find your friend. I promise you that, too."

The captain spoke up. "I seriously don't think there is trafficking here, but I've already told you that you are cleared to work both that and the Kind Killer case. The KK case takes precedence, however. That guy has the whole city spooked and I want those killings stopped."

Z snapped at him. "If you don't think there is trafficking going on here it's because you choose not to see what's right under your nose. But I can promise you this: I'm going to solve the cases on that table in there," she nodded toward the open conference room door, "and when I do I'm going to see to it whoever is guilty fries for it."

She stopped talking and looked at each officer in the room in turn, her gaze at last falling on Cook and Swift who were, by this time, shuffling paperwork in pretense of ignoring her.

"Come on. Let's get to work," Blaze said. He placed his hand on the small of her back in an effort to get her moving into the conference room.

Z finally tore her eyes from Cook and Swift and followed Blaze into the room, closing the door with a decisive thud behind her.

"I can't concentrate on these cases with Zeena missing!" Z was frantic.

Blaze, by contrast, was calm. "Well, what do you propose? Going to Atlanta and wandering the airport is not going to get her back, is it? If she was taken by traffickers, the only way we are going to get her back is to solve these cases right here."

"How can I think about these cases? My mind is everywhere else!"

"I know. I know. But think about it for a minute. You said your friend saw the men who took her, so you know they are right here. They must have somehow determined you were sending her home to Cascadia. Maybe someone heard you say it and passed along the information. Maybe they even followed you to the airport when you put her on the plane. We don't really know. But if they've got her, then the connection is right here. If you want to get her back, we need to solve these cases. The captain is going to have a fit if we don't wrap up this Kind Killer case so we need to get on that one first. Besides, we already have a potential connection with trafficking through the medicine bottles found in two of the cases. I know it's a long shot. A bottle is pretty slim evidence to go on, but the Kind Killer case could lead us to the traffickers even if indirectly. What do you say?"

Z was aimlessly walking around the room, rubbing her forehead. "Yes. What you are saying makes sense. It's logical. Still…Zeena is somewhere in Atlanta and I'm here helpless to find her."

"You don't know she's still in Atlanta. She may have been brought back here for all we know."

Z kept pacing. To stop her, Blaze reached out and took her by the shoulders. "Listen to me, Zakaya-Zee. We will find her. I promise you we will find her. But to do that, we have to find the traffickers. And we stand the best chance of finding them by working to solve these cases right here on this table. It may not be a lot, but it's all we've got. What do you say?"

Z looked at him and then drove her hands up between his arms and forcefully pushed his hands off her shoulders. She thought for a moment. Then, "You're right. I have no other workable plan. I have nothing else. So where should we start?"

~∂∞∂~

The minute Zakaya and Blaze were behind the closed door of the conference room, Cook stepped out the station side door and punched up the sheriff on his t-com.

"Hey Wilbur! It's me, Hadeon. Congrats to your people in Atlanta. Being sheriff has its perks, right? Pays to know the right people. They got the girl! She might not be worth as much as—"

"Slow down, Had. I know lots of people. But I haven't heard back from the ones I know in Atlanta."

"What do you mean?" Cook's brow furrowed. "Her friend, the Black gal that came to see you yesterday just flew into the station here screaming her head off about her friend going missing and yelling 'Traffickers' at the top of her lungs. Your contacts must have gotten her because she seems to have disappeared."

"Maybe so, but I haven't heard anything yet."

Cook was decidedly not happy. He was somewhat relieved, but not completely. He didn't like being in the dark with things like this. He didn't like dangling ends. Especially when those ends could eventually form a noose around his own neck.

"Well, let me know when you hear. The woman is still here. And she's running around playing detective. The captain has put her on the force temporarily to see if she can help solve the Kind Killer case. But thing is...she only agreed to help if she could work the cases she thinks are trafficking."

"Well, you've been careful, haven't you? No fingerprints, right? Nothing to trace back to you?"

"I'm pretty sure."

"Well, you best think about it and make damned sure."

The sheriff clicked off leaving Cook staring at his t-com. He turned to Swift.

"They got the girl again, so we can stop worrying now."

"Who got her?"

"My uncle's people in Atlanta. At least I think they got her. Anyway, she's disappeared so we can stop worrying."

Donny Ray Swift just stared at his partner then lowered his head and pretended to work.

32

Blaze divided the conference table into thirds for the three separate cases they had begun looking into. Then he stood back and frowned at them.

"Well?" Z watched him, still agitated. "What are you thinking?"

"We have only one thing that possibly connects two of these cases," he said. "I think we should begin with the bottles. If there's a connection, we'll find it."

"Okay…" Z was making an effort to think. Her eyes darted from one evidence box to the next. "But the only thing they have in common is that they appear to be small medicine bottles. Not even the same color. Nor the same contents."

"Yes, but they do have two things in common."

"What's that?"

"They are the same size and shape, and they were found on or very near two of our bodies."

"True. So…" Z was making every effort to remain calm and get down to business.

"We need to find out where they came from."

"Yes. Good idea. I just need to calm down and start thinking clearly."

Blaze was encouraged now that Z seemed to be on board again. He added, "And more than that, we need to know who purchased Octoflurane recently. It's a controlled substance. That could narrow our search down a bit. So we stay on track with our plan from yesterday, okay?"

"Okay. Okay. But it's hard to concentrate. They've taken Zeena again and I have no way to find her, Blaze. And I want her back, now! It's hard to think."

"I know. But if we solve these cases, we find the traffickers. And if we find the traffickers, we find Zeena. I know you're worried, but unless you have a better plan, we need to start somewhere. Might as well start here."

Getting back into this investigation wasn't going to be easy. But Blaze was right. She really had no alternative. She took a deep breath, opened the conference room door, and yelled out for the desk sergeant to find her a phone directory. Then she turned back to Blaze. "They do still have phone books here, don't they?"

Blaze looked up and nodded at her, then turned back to dig into the evidence boxes to retrieve the bags containing the small bottles.

Within a couple of minutes they were poring over the names of all the local pharmacies. Z grew impatient and tore the pages from the book and said to Blaze, "Let's go!"

He grabbed his jacket and raced out the door behind her. "How many are there?"

"About a dozen," she called back over her shoulder.

Once outside, she stopped and turned back to Blaze. "Do you want to take my rental?"

"We can take my car," he said. "It's right here."

Even in her current state of urgency, it did not escape her that she had seen this brown car with the dented rear fender at least once or twice before and said as much.

Blaze laughed. "I expect you have seen it. We've been at Brassy's more than once at the same time and it's the only car I have. So yep. I would bet money you have seen it."

She filed that away in the recesses of her mind. "Okay, then. You drive and I'll read off the addresses."

They decided to work from the center of town to the outskirts in a somewhat circular pattern.

They covered about half of the pharmacies, questioning the pharmacists and/or managers of each one yet learned only that Octoflurane had either not been sold from that particular store for months or had only been sold to physicians and hospitals. Everything had been accounted for. There were no shortages in inventory.

They discussed whether or not the perp could be a doctor. Certainly possible. But not their first line of investigation even though they wouldn't discount it completely. After all, the body in the Kind Killer case had had his throat slit with what was probably a scalpel. But for now, they put the doctor possibility on the back burner.

They pushed on until they had visited every pharmacy listed in the pages Z had ripped from the phone book. They had no luck except for one small observance on the part of a cashier at one of the last places they had visited. She had looked at the bottles in the evidence bags and shook her head.

"We don't see many of these type bottles anymore," she said.

"How's that?" Z perked up. It might be small information, but it was still something.

"Well, these days everything that can come in plastic, does come in plastic. What was in these bottles?"

"There was only water in one of them, but the other contained traces of Octoflurane," Blaze told her.

"I see. Water wouldn't have been put in the bottle by a pharmacist, so that's a bit odd. But it's even odder that Octoflurane was found in this kind of bottle. Octoflurane today is packaged in aluminum with a special lining, not glass like this. It must have been dispensed into the bottle from its original container." She handed the evidence bag back to Blaze. "Sorry I can't be more help to you."

Back in Blaze's car, Z said, "So where does this leave us?"

"I'm not sure. We need to back up and consider what we learned here."

"Good God. I don't have time for all this. Zeena is missing!"

Blaze looked over at her. "And we're going to find her. Don't you worry about that."

Z gave him a withering look and turned away to look out the passenger window as they made their way toward the center of town back to the police station.

As they drove past an old shopping center, something caught her eye. "What is that?"

"What is what?"

"That place in that old mall back there. Turn around!"

Blaze maneuvered the car into the parking lot of the derelict shopping center. He pulled up and parked facing the boarded-up stores.

"So?" he said.

"So look at that." Z pointed to their left.

"Ha! Good eyes!"

It was an old pharmacy. Long closed by the looks of it. Brown paper covered the windows and the glass in the door had been whited out with paint on the inside. There was no point in trying to see in from the front so they drove around to the backside of the building to take a look. It proved no more helpful than the front since there were no windows on the back at all—even in the door.

They drove back around to the front once more and Z took a photo of the place. She turned to Blaze.

"There's a name that has been removed from above the door. Can you make it out?"

"Looks like the first letter was an 'A' and the last letters were 'n' and 's' with maybe an apostrophe between them. You?"

"Yeah. Me, too," Z agreed. "But looks like whoever took the name down did a messy job of it and ripped the bricks right out from under the rest. Still, it's enough." She began punching up numbers on her t-com.

"Who are you calling?"

"JJ."

"Your police officer friend at the station."

"Ye—Hi! JJ? Do you know of any pharmacies in this town that have shut down in the past few years?" She looked at Blaze as she listened, then shook her head.

Disappointed, she added, "How about one over here on—" she looked at Blaze, "What's the name of this street?"

"Duncan."

"Duncan Street," she said to JJ. "It's boarded up and the name has been partially obscured, but it looks like it started with an 'A' and ended with 'n' or 's' maybe. Like Anderson's or—" She stopped and listened, then smiled broadly.

"Thanks, JJ. I owe you one." She turned to Blaze. "It was Addison's. Been closed for a long time. JJ wasn't sure exactly how long. It belonged to a Robert Addison who owned it until he died. He left it to his nephew, but the nephew closed it up as soon as he inherited it and that was that."

"Who is the nephew?"

"William Addison. Goes by Billy. He lives just a few blocks from Brassy's."

33

Now that they had a definite lead on *something*, Z began to settle down with serious determination to solve the cases to which she had been given access. It was the only way she could see to save Zeena. True, the lead was thin as thread, but still—it was still something. It was a connection. And the only one they had. Who knew where it would take them?

They pulled to the curb in front of Billy Addison's house and parked.

"Looks like something out of a Faulkner novel," Z said.

"No kidding."

"Well, shall we?"

Blaze and Z opened their respective car doors at the same time, stepped out, and looked around. The neighborhood was fairly quiet except for local wildlife. Two gray squirrels were busily running barber pole circles around an oak next door while a blue jay screeched at them. A large, white cat watched from the home's lace-curtained window.

They returned their attention to Billy Addison's house and walked up the steps to the front door.

Z pointed to the hinges on the screen door. "Rust and rot. Not taking very good care of the place, is he?"

Blaze looked over at it but said nothing. He knocked loudly several times causing the screen door to *blap-blap-blap* into its facing with each knock.

After several minutes, just as they were about to give up, the door opened.

"What do you want?" Billy Addison held the door tightly with both hands.

"Hello, William," Z began.

"Billy," he said.

"Sorry. Billy. We are police detectives, and we want to ask you some questions about your pharmacy. The one that's closed and boarded up over on Duncan Street. Could we come in and talk with you about that?"

Billy's eyes darted nervously from Z to Blaze and back again. He held his hands up near his face and tapped his knuckles together several times like a nervous tic, then he took a step back. "Okay."

They entered the home directly into the tiny foyer beside the French doors to the living room on their right. The stairs were almost directly in front of them, and to their left was an open door to what appeared to be a bedroom. It was a stark contrast to the appearance of the exterior in that this home was as tidy and well-kept as any they had ever seen.

Billy moved back only a few feet and stood in front of the stairs tapping his knuckles together.

"Could we maybe go into the living room and sit down, Billy?"

"Okay."

Z noticed the newspaper folded open to the Kind Killer story. She gave Blaze a look but said nothing.

"We understand that you inherited the pharmacy from your uncle. Is that right?"

"Yeah. My Uncle Robert." *Tap, tap, tap.*

"How long ago was that, Billy?"

"I don't know."

"Can you tell us why you closed it after you inherited it?"

"Because." Billy pulled his head down into his shoulders and fidgeted with the crocheted doily on the arm of his chair.

Z and Blaze exchanged looks. This wasn't going to be easy. This man was obviously not all there, but they decided to press on to see what they could learn if anything.

"Wasn't the pharmacy doing a good business?" Z asked him. "Was it making money?"

"I don't know. I closed it. I don't know about that stuff."

"So how do you make a living now, Billy? Do you work?"

"Yes."

"I like your blue uniform. Is that for work?"

Z's comment brought a shy smile. "Yeah. I ride in the truck and empty the trash. But they won't let me drive."

"Well, it's an important job, Billy, that's for sure."

It was now or never. Blaze took the small evidence bags from his jacket pocket. "Billy, did these bottles come from Addison's pharmacy?"

Billy's smile faded. "No. And you can't prove I did anything."

Billy began humming a song Z thought she recognized, but she wasn't certain. This behavior was just very odd. She said, "Did what, Billy?"

"Nothing. I don't know about those things."

"What things, Billy?"

"Bottles and medicine and things. You can't prove it. I have to make lunch for my mother." *Tap, tap, tap, tap.*

Billy's eyes looked everywhere except at his two visitors, and he began singing softly:

"Oh where have you been,

Billy Boy, Billy Boy?
Oh where have you been,
Charming Billy?"
Z and Blaze exchanged looks.

Z interrupted his song. "Where is your mother, Billy? Is she here?"

"She's not well. You can't see her. You have to go away now.

Can she bake a cherry pie, Billy Boy, Billy Boy?" Tap, tap, tap.

Z and Blaze got up from the couch and started for the foyer. Blaze reached down to the newspaper and picked it up.

"You have to go away now." Billy was becoming extremely agitated. He took the paper from Blaze's hand and laid it back down on the coffee table, straightening it so that it was perfectly aligned with the table's edge, and began rubbing his knuckles together in lieu of tapping.

Blaze smiled at him and then said, "Well, thank you very much, Billy. We appreciate you talking with us."

Z headed to the stairs and put her hand on the railing. She looked up as though she might proceed up the steps.

Billy pushed in front of her. "You can't go up there! You have to go now!

Billy Boy, Billy Boy. Charming Billy." Tap, tap, tap.

თოთ

Back in the car, Z and Blaze were still for a moment. At last, Z turned to Blaze. "That guy is definitely a bubble and a half off level."

Blaze looked over and rolled wide eyes. "You think?"

"What now?"

Blaze started the car. "Warrant."

"Yep. He's definitely hiding something."

They drove silently for a few minutes before Z spoke. "Blaze…"

"What?"

"While we're waiting for the warrant, I want to go back to the dress shop where I believe Kit Deming was taken by traffickers."

"Go back? Have you been there already?"

"Yes. That's where I was when Captain Taylor called me to come in about taking on this investigation. *These* investigations." She corrected herself at the last.

"What were you doing there?"

"You remember I told you I had visited the girl who survived that…abduction? Connie Latham?"

Blaze nodded but kept his eyes on the road.

"Well, during the interview with her, she described the fitting room she and Kit Deming used that day—and the saleswoman who helped them. So I decided to take a look at the place myself. When I did, an interesting thing happened."

"What was that?"

"The saleswoman willingly showed me all the other fitting rooms, but very hesitantly showed me that one. It was kept locked and she had to use a key to let me in. She really didn't want to, either, but I insisted. When I was finished looking into all the fitting rooms, I casually asked her which room the girls had used, and she pointed out a completely different room along the wall rather than the one at the end I had just looked over—the one Connie Latham said they had used."

"What did you do?"

"Nothing. I accepted her answer without question. I didn't want to spook her. And that's when I got the call from the police station, anyway. But now…Now I want to go back and take a closer look and confront her. She was almost as nervous as Charming Billy and I want to find out why."

Blaze laughed at the Charming Billy reference, then said, "We should gather up all the information we can find on her before we go. And while we are at it, we should also get a warrant for the shop, as well, if we expect to be able to take a thorough look."

"Right." Z hesitated a moment, then added, "I'd really like to see the blueprints and floor plan of that particular part of the mall, as well."

"Good thinking."

34

At the courthouse, after requesting the search warrants for the Glamour Girl dress shop, Charming Billy's house, as well as the defunct pharmacy on Duncan, Z and Blaze did a little research into the history of the mall, which proved interesting.

"Looks like that mall was sold off piece by piece," Z said as she sifted through the county records at the courthouse.

Blaze looked up from the records he was thumbing. "Oh yeah? How so?"

"Appears the mall was bankrupt or something. It was sold off a couple of times. The last purchaser sold it store by store kind of like selling condos. I guess he wanted to take some profit and wash his hands of it."

"Who sold it?"

"Some guy in Colorado. Looks like he only had it long enough to sell it off."

"Who bought the dress shop?"

"Um…Francis Worsham." She looked up at Blaze. "Francis. That's the name of the nervous saleslady who pointed me to the wrong dressing room. Must be her store. Let's go!"

"Wait up, there, partner!"

"What's wrong?"

Blaze nodded toward the door of the records room. "Looks like we've got our warrants."

Z looked around to see the judge's clerk waving several sheets of paper at them.

Blaze turned back to her. "She's got a dress shop. She's not going anywhere. She'll keep. Let's re-visit Charming Billy. If he's been at work, he should be back home by now."

"Okay…" Z hesitated.

"Okay what?"

"I just want to print out the floor plan of the dress shop first so we can go over it later. It'll just take a couple minutes."

With the warrants in hand and the floor plan tucked into Z's bag, they headed back to Charming Billy Addison's.

∽✺∻

On their way back to Billy's house, Z suggested they stop at the boarded-up pharmacy first and give it a good once-over. They had the warrant, after all, and the place was on the way.

Blaze pulled the car up to the entrance and they got out and stepped up to the door.

"How do we get in?" Z was looking over the blanked-out window as she rattled the handle on the locked door.

Blaze took off his jacket and wrapped it around his fist. Then he punched through the glass in the upper portion of the door.

"Oops!" He smiled at Z and reached his hand in where he worked the lock until it clicked.

Inside, they found themselves on a trip back in time. Everything appeared as though it had been undisturbed for ages and was covered in dust. Cobwebs stretched across items here and there.

Z pushed a cobweb aside that spanned the space between the shelves to the left and right of aisle number three. She walked slowly down the aisle, taking in everything, while Blaze checked out the next aisle over. She began to laugh.

"Look at this, Blaze." She held up a large bottle with a green label. "Shampoo. I actually used this stuff once upon a time."

Blaze peered over the top of the shelving that separated the two aisles to see what she was holding up but said nothing.

"Looks like the ingredients have separated." She shook the bottle then put it back on the shelf. "And look at all these old face creams!"

Blaze pulled his attention from the next aisle and joined her. "Looks like Charming Billy just shut this place down without even trying to liquidate anything. This whole store is a gold mine of collectibles now. He could probably sell it all off for a pretty penny."

"From what we've seen of Billy," Z said, "I doubt he was sharp enough to handle it. I guess that's why he closed it in the first place."

They continued walking the aisles and looking over all the old drugstore items as they made their way to the back of the store. Once at the prescription counter, they pushed open the small swinging door and stepped up onto the elevated platform used by almost all pharmacists once upon a time. There was evidence this area had been used recently. Z pointed to shoe prints visible on the dusty floor and Blaze took photos.

Careful not to touch anything, Z carefully studied each short aisle containing the prescription drugs, now out of date. She saw something and stopped short, causing Blaze to bump into her.

"Look!" She pointed to her right. "No dust on this."

"What is it?" Blaze looked over her shoulder.

She pointed to what appeared to be a silvery can. "Octoflurane."

She smiled and turned to face him. "I think we're getting warm," she said.

Blaze backed out of the small aisle and peered down the next one. "Here!" he called to her.

"What is it?" Z tore her attention from the Octoflurane and joined him.

"Bottles. Little blue and brown bottles in open boxes."

"Let's take photos of everything and get somebody over here to cordon off this place with crime scene tape. We'll bag some of this stuff and get on over to Billy's house." Z was excited now. They were making progress. She was sure there was a real connection to the two cases where the bottles were found. The bottles here at this old pharmacy were identical to the brown one found in the Kind Killer case and to the blue bottle containing the traces of Octoflurane near Tiki Jameson's body. She was sure of that, too.

The evidence was coming together. If she and Blaze could solve the Kind Killer case, that alone would free her up to concentrate exclusively on the trafficking cases. And find Zeena. It was just a matter of time now before they connected all the loose ends. And they were both pretty sure those loose ends, somehow, lay with Charming Billy.

35

Blaze knocked on Billy Addison's screen door with an even louder *blap-blap-blap* than he had done earlier in the day, but the door remained closed.

"Billy! Open the door!" Blaze called out and turned to Z who was listening for any sounds coming from inside the house. She shook her head.

Blaze stepped to his left, out of the way, and motioned to Z. "You call him."

"Billy! You have to open the door! We need to ask you some more questions!" she yelled at the door.

"Go away!" Billy finally answered and pounded his fists on the inside of the door.

"Billy," Z reasoned with him, "you have to let us in. The judge has given us permission to talk to you and take a look at your house. We have a warrant."

"Go away! Go away! I don't like you!"

"Awwww, Billy. That's no way to treat people. You'll make us feel bad. Besides," Z kept trying, "if you don't let us in we will have to get the police here with guns and they will break down your door. You don't want that, do you?"

"Go away!"

"We are not going away, Billy. Open the door or we will get the police here with guns."

At last, the door opened a crack. Billy's fingers holding the door and his left eye and cheek were the only parts of him visible.

"I already talked to you. Go away!"

"We have more questions, Billy. We are trying to find a really bad person. Don't you want to help us with that?"

They waited while Billy thought this over. He finally responded.

"Okay…." He opened the door and stepped back and began tap-tap-tapping his knuckles together just beneath his chin.

Z and Blaze entered and did a quick look around. Nothing had changed since they were here earlier.

"Sounds like you don't like bad people, Billy," Blaze said as he nodded for Z to back away and search the house. "Can we go into your living room again so you can help us find a really bad one?"

"Okay…."

Blaze opened the French doors and followed Billy into the room.

"Why don't we sit in here and talk." Blaze suggested.

"Okay…." Billy sat in the chair across from Blaze on the sofa and continued tap-tapping his knuckles. His eyes darted from Blaze to the doors. "Where is the lady? She can't walk around in here."

"I think maybe she was looking for the bathroom. She'll be back very soon. Don't worry." Blaze picked up the newspaper still on the coffee table and said, "Tell me about the kind of bad guys you don't like, Billy. It could help us find them."

Billy nervously eyed the paper in Blaze's hand. "I don't like bad people," he said.

"Yes, I know. I don't like them, either." Blaze watched him closely as he spoke. "Do you know any bad guys, Billy?"

"Yeah…I've seen bad guys in the woods." Billy kept looking toward the French doors for a sight of Z, but Blaze kept distracting him with questions.

"What kind of bad guys, Billy?"

"Mean bad guys. They have guns. I don't like guns. You won't have the police here with guns, will you?"

"No. Not if you tell us what you know."

Blaze was digesting this bit of information about bad guys in the woods when Z came into the room, a pair of pink girl's panties swinging from her index finger.

"Look what I found." She looked at Billy. "What can you tell us about these, Billy?"

"Nothin'." Billy's face flushed crimson.

"They were in your dresser drawer, Billy. How did they get there?" Z asked.

"I don't know."

"Well, you must have put them there. Where did you get them?"

"I don't know. You have to go now." *Tap, tap, tap.*

"Billy…" Z smiled at him. "I know you don't wear pink panties. Do you?"

"No." He flushed red again and turned away.

"So where did you get them?"

"I don't know. Somebody threw them away. You have to go now." *Tap, tap, tap.*

"So you found them in the garbage that you were emptying one day?"

"I don't know." *Tap, tap, tap.*

"I'll just go and take another look. Maybe you have more panties here somewhere. Do you, Billy?"

"No! Ha ha!"

Z looked at Blaze and tried to suppress a smile. This boy—and he was definitely more boy than man—had not a mean bone in his body. Of that, she was fairly certain.

But he knew something. Something important. And of that, she was certain as well.

She handed the panties to Blaze who nodded his understanding of the unspoken task she was passing off to him to keep Billy talking while she stepped back out of the room to take a more thorough look about the house. He placed the panties into an evidence bag and sat back down to engage Billy.

Billy watched the panties as they slid into the evidence bag. He was upset.

"You can't take away my things. That's stealing!"

"We have to take them for now, Billy. We think they may have belonged to a girl who was treated very badly by some very bad people. Is that okay with you?"

"Yeah. I don't like bad people." *Tap, tap, tap.*

While Blaze continued to keep Billy engaged, Z went quickly down the hallway and found the kitchen. Neat as a pin. Every dish in place. Every cup handle facing to the right like obedient little soldiers. It was uncanny. A glance in the trash can told her someone here wasn't eating their breakfast and then she remembered Billy's mother who was an invalid and stayed upstairs. Odd, though, she had never heard a peep out of the woman. Perhaps she was sleeping.

Coming back down the hallway, she peeked through the glass of the French doors to be sure Blaze had Billy's attention. Then she quickly and quietly took to the stairs two at a time. At the upstairs landing, there were two doors. One was open. A bathroom. She stepped inside and looked around. Sparkling. She stepped back out and turned to the other door. It was closed.

She reached out a hand for the doorknob but thought better of it.

Better knock instead.

She tapped lightly with the knuckles of her left hand. "Mrs. Addison?" she half-whispered.

There was no answer so she tapped slightly louder.

Still no answer.

She reached for the doorknob and turned it. The door opened easily but it opened to reveal only the wall at her right unlike most doors that opened revealing the entirety of the room. She could see nothing but the portrait of an elderly gentleman hanging there. A strange, musty odor hit her full-on. She covered her nose and then called again, "Mrs. Addison?"

Once again, no reply. She opened the door and stepped into the room. She stopped. Stared. She backed out of the room, gagging. She called out to Blaze.

"Blaze! You need to come up here and see this!"

"No! No! She can't go up there! You have to go now!" At the sound of Z's voice coming from upstairs, Billy had leaped from his chair and was banging his head into the French doors. Blaze attempted to pull him away.

"Billy! Stop!" Blaze pushed Billy ahead of him as he made his way up the stairs. When he reached the top, Z grabbed his arm and pulled him into the room.

With Z standing beside him, Blaze released Billy and stared.

There, on the clean and tidy bedclothes, lay Billy's mother. All two hundred and six mummified bones of her. A gray wig sat slightly askew over her gaping skull. One "hand" was outside the coverlet, rings still on her "fingers." The unsettling death grin gaped just above the neck of a ruffled blue nightgown, its ribbon tied into a tidy bow just beneath the chin.

Z stepped back. "We need to call in Uniform for this. I'll call JJ."

Blaze, suddenly remembering he had let go of Billy's arm, tore himself away from the scene and turned to find

Billy on the floor at the far end of the hallway, rocking back and forth and hitting his head with his hands.

"Come on, Billy," he said, quietly. "Come on, now. It's okay. Let's go back downstairs."

👁️‍🗨️

At Z's insistence, JJ had taken Billy to the affiliate station where he would be detained and undergo a psychiatric evaluation until it could be ascertained what was to be done with him. Captain Taylor had been notified and forensics were currently going over every inch of the house.

Back in the car, Zakaya and Blaze made a concerted effort at normalcy.

Blaze gripped the steering wheel with both hands and finally broke their silence. "I have to say I never expected that."

"Me, neither." Z agreed. "I've seen some crazy stuff in this line of work, but nothing like that."

"So what do you think?" Blaze asked.

"Well, forensics will find out all they can, but I doubt there's any way they can determine whether or not he killed her."

"What about the case?"

"What about it?"

"There are a ton of questions that Charming Billy still needs to answer," Blaze said.

Z nodded. "I know. But we have the panties and the link to the Octoflurane and the colored bottles. I'm positive he's the Kind Killer. Whether or not he killed his mother is another story entirely."

"But he's not the trafficker," Blaze added. "I'm positive of that, too. I don't think he's capable of it. Too much cunning and planning involved. He's not our guy. Not for that. Our trafficker is still out there and he is one heartless, sociopathic son-of-a-bitch."

Z became contemplative. "Still, Billy had those panties. DNA will tell us if they belonged to Tiki Jameson. It's another possible link. First, the bottles. Now the panties. Somehow there's a connection there, Blaze. Even if he's not part of the trafficking, he's linked to it somehow. We just have to find out how."

"He knows where he got those panties, too," Blaze said. "I'm positive he knows. He mentioned something about mean bad guys in the woods. I don't know what that was all about, but we need to get a lot more information from him. And we need to get him to tell us what he was doing with the Octoflurane."

"You're right. And we need to do it now before anyone frightens our Charming Billy into complete silence."

Z punched up JJ on her t-com and told him to ask Captain Taylor to isolate Billy in an interrogation room until they got there.

Blaze started the car and pulled away from Charming Billy's house.

Neither of them looked back.

36

At the affiliate station they found Billy Addison pacing back and forth in the number three interrogation room, tapping his knuckles together in front of his chin and humming his old tune. Captain Taylor was there, listening, and watching him through the two-way mirror window.

Blaze spoke with the captain briefly, then he and Z entered the room to question Billy.

"Hello again, Billy!" Z said, in an effort to be cheerful and put him at ease.

Blaze pulled out a chair and sat down at the table with a notepad in front of him. "Why don't you have a seat, Billy?" He pointed to the chair on the opposite side of the table.

"I want to go home now." Billy continued pacing and began tapping his knuckles together again.

Z took one of his hands in hers and smiled at him. "You can't go back just yet, Billy. We need to talk to you for a bit first. Would you like something to drink? Maybe some water or a cold drink?"

Billy pulled his hand loose and began tapping his knuckles once again. "Okay…."

"What would you like?"

"I like grape soda. It's called knee-high."

"I'm not sure the drink machine has grape," Z told him, "but I will have someone check and bring you something good, okay? Why don't you take a seat here at the table while we wait for it?"

"Okay. I like knee-high." Billy took the chair across from Blaze. Still thinking of his drink, he said, "I measured it once but it wasn't really as high as my knee." *Tap, tap, tap.*

She smiled and gave Blaze an eye roll. He just chuckled softly then began to question Billy.

"Billy, do you remember the man in the newspaper? The one that was found in the cemetery with the big smile on his face?"

"Yes. He was sad."

"But he had a big smile, remember?"

"That was after."

"After what?"

"I don't know." *Tap, tap, tap.*

"After what, Billy?"

"I like to make people happy." *Tap, tap, tap.*

"Did you make Mr. Conway happy?"

"Who?"

"Mr. Jake Conway. The smiling man in the cemetery."

"Yeah. He was very unhappy. His wife died and he had to sleep outside."

"How terrible. No wonder he was unhappy." Blaze tried to be encouraging while Z studied Billy from the far end of the room.

"Yeah. He didn't want to be unhappy anymore."

"So did you make him happy?"

"Yeah." *Tap, tap, tap.*

"How did you make him happy, Billy?"

"I told him to look over there and then I…made him happy."

"Did you do anything to make him happy?"

"I want to go home now. I have to make dinner for my mother." *Tap, tap, tap.*

"Someone is there with your mother, Billy. You don't have to worry about her right now."

At this point, Z decided to ask some questions herself and approached the table.

She began with a soft question. "Billy...," she said. "It's not wrong to make people happy, is it?"

"No."

"Well, then. How did you make Mr. Conway happy? Did he know you were going to make him happy?"

"Yes. He was glad. He said he didn't want to live anymore because he was so unhappy. He said his wife died and the hospital took his house, but I don't know how they could do that. He didn't want to sleep outside anymore."

"So what did you do?"

"I had a knife from the pharmacy and he told me where to cut him. He said to press hard and cut."

"So you did?"

"Yes. Then I made him really happy. I made him smile." Billy smiled and put his hands on the table. He began making circles with them as he looked from Z to Blaze, smiling.

"Did you put the brown bottle in his hands?"

"Yeah. And a flower. Everybody likes flowers. It makes them happy."

Z, hopeful now, asked, "Have you ever made anyone else happy, Billy?"

Billy Addison smiled shyly. "Yeah. I like making people happy."

"Can you tell us the very first person you ever made happy, Billy?"

"Yeah. It was Joanie Crowder. She was in my class at school but the other kids made fun of her because she had a funny name. They called her Crowder Peas and she cried. So I made her happy."

Z and Blaze exchanged looks. Captain Taylor had his Kind Killer. But they still needed information on those panties and the Octoflurane link to the murder of Tiki Jameson as well as the missing Kit Deming.

Z sat down at the table beside Blaze.

"Billy, we found some medicine called Octoflurane at your closed-up pharmacy. What did you do with that?"

"I don't know." *Tap, tap, tap.*

"Of course you do. Did you give it to someone?"

"No! You're wrong! Ha ha!" Billy laughed and began sliding his hands back and forth on the table.

"You didn't give it to anyone at all?"

"No! Ha ha! I sold it for money! You don't know anything!"

"Well, that was pretty smart," Z said, smiling back at him. "How much did you get?"

"Ten whole dollars! So there!"

"Wow! So much?"

"Yes. And I hid it in the kitchen. So she couldn't find it."

"So who couldn't find it, Billy?"

"My mother." Billy began tapping his knuckles again and added quietly, "The old witch!"

"I see." Blaze and Z exchanged looks. She looked into the two-way mirror where she assumed Captain Taylor was watching, then turned back to Billy. "Who did you sell it to, Billy?"

"Sell what?"

"The Octoflurane."

"I don't know." Billy became agitated and began tapping his knuckles once again.

"Are you sure you don't know, Billy?"

"I don't know. You can't make me."

"Well, can you tell me why you won't tell me who?"

"They will hurt me."

Ha! Not "He" will hurt me, but "they" will hurt me. More than one.

"Okay, Billy. You don't have to tell us who they are. Can you describe them for us?"

Billy only stared at her, tapping his knuckles.

She tried again. "Can you tell us how many of them said they would hurt you?"

"Just one. He's mean."

"So the mean one is a man, right?"

"Yeah."

"How do you know he's mean, Billy?"

"He said he would hurt me if I told anyone. And he has very scary eyes."

"His eyes are scary? What makes them scary, Billy?"

"They are black and they stare at you. He's mean."

"What about the others? You said they would hurt you. How many gave you money for the medicine? What did they look like?"

"Just two. The tall one is mean. But the other one is nicer. He's the short and fat one, like me. He's nicer. But I'm not really fat, am I?"

"No, Billy. I wouldn't say you are fat. How were these men dressed? Did they wear uniforms like you wear?"

"No. They just look regular. But they wear jackets like they are going to church."

"Do they wear ties with the jackets?"

"Yeah. Ties. Ties and Jackets. Not like most people. And they have guns, too. They're mean."

"Did you ever sell any of the medicine to a woman, Billy?"

"No. Can I go home now? I want to go home." *Tap, tap, tap.*

"Billy, listen carefully. These men are very bad people and they make other people very unhappy. You don't like people to be unhappy, do you?"

"No. I like making people happy." *Tap, tap, tap.*

"Well, can you help us find these really bad men who make people unhappy?"

"I don't know! You can't make me! I don't know!" *Tap, tap, tap.*

"Okay, Billy. Let's forget about those really bad men for a minute. Let's talk about those pink panties you had in your house."

Billy bit his lip and blushed. "I found them."

"I know. You said they were in a garbage can, right?"

"Yes. They didn't fall out right away because they got stuck on the handle. But I pulled them loose." *Tap, tap, tap.* "Sorry."

"You have nothing to be sorry about, Billy. They were thrown away so nobody wanted them, right? It was okay for you to take them."

"Okay."

"What we need to know is what garbage can you found them in. Where was the garbage can? Do you remember the house?"

"Yes. I don't like that place." *Tap, tap, tap.*

"Why not, Billy?" Z was getting slightly excited now.

"Unhappy people are there. And very big men are outside."

"How do you know the people there are unhappy, Billy?"

"I can hear them screaming and crying sometimes when we go there to get the garbage."

"What do they sound like? The people who are crying?"

"Girls. They are really sad."

Z's heart leapt into her throat. "Oh dear. That must be very upsetting. What do you do about that? I know you like to make people happy so what do you do?"

"I'm sorry."

"Why are you sorry, Billy?"

"I can't help them."

"Why not?"

"The men have guns and they are always there at the door."

"I see." Z thought for a minute then asked, "Have you ever seen any of these unhappy girls?"

"No. I want to go home now."

"Billy, can you describe the house for me?"

"It's blue. But nobody paints it. It's a really old house. It's very ugly."

"Is it a big house? Are there windows upstairs like at your house?"

"Yes. But some are broken and have boxes in them."

"Boxes? Do you mean cardboard like boxes are made of?"

"Yes. In the broken windows."

Z took a deep breath and asked the question she hoped would lead her to solving the trafficking case and finding Zeena. "Billy…what day do you go to this blue house?"

"Wednesday. Maybe. Sometimes. I forget." *Tap, tap, tap.*

"Just sometimes?"

"It's a long way so the truck only goes there sometimes. Not every time."

"Do you know which direction the blue house is from here?"

Billy looked around. "I can't see out the window. I don't know."

She laughed. "Of course you can't. But when you go to the blue house on Wednesdays sometimes do you know if you are driving north or south? Do you know the direction?"

"No. I can't drive. They won't let me drive the truck. But I want to. It would be fun to drive."

"That's okay, Billy. You have been really helpful and for that, we are going to see that you have a really nice dinner, okay?"

"I like chicken." *Tap, tap, tap.*

Z looked up at the two-way mirror and said, "The nice people here will be sure you get a nice chicken dinner. That's a promise."

Blaze said, "Billy, just one more question before we go, okay?"

"Okay."

"Did you make your mother happy?"

Billy dropped his head into his shoulders and looked down at his hands on the table. "She was mean."

"That must have been very unpleasant. Did you try to change that? By making her happy, maybe?"

"That's two questions." *Tap, tap, tap.*

Blaze and Z looked at each other and silently chuckled.

Blaze said to Billy, "You're right. Sorry. We'll see you get your dinner now."

⌘

The interrogation of Billy Addison over, and the two of them back in Blaze's car, Z took a deep breath. "I think I have never seen a more pathetic human being in my life as our Charming Billy. That young man has probably never known a truly happy day in his life. It seems that not even his own mother loved him and he's most likely been mistreated and looking for love his whole life."

Blaze let her talk. Expressing her feelings seemed cathartic and he was loathe to interrupt.

She sat for long moments looking back at the building they had just exited, nervously bouncing her right leg up and down on her stationary toes. Her thoughts turned to Zeena, someone who, it seemed, also had been unloved and her eyes misted. She tried blinking them clear.

At last she sighed and turned to Blaze. "Right now I could use a break. How about a stop at Brassy's? We could both use a breather."

"You got it."

37

Big Ugly and Sidekick sat in the truck at the side of the parking lot in front of Brassy's.

"How long we gonna to do this, Will?" Sidekick asked Big Ugly.

"As long as we have to. There's gonna be an opportunity. I just know it. And then, Bobby, my old friend, I'm gonna take that little bitch down."

"We've been watching them for a while now, Will. Every day. We can't do this for the rest of our lives. Damn! I'd like to go fishin' sometimes."

"Well go, then! Go on! Get out!"

Bobby cringed and turned his head away from the agitated Will. He tried to change the subject.

"How's Alice?"

Big Ugly grunted. "How do you think? She still can't walk. Doctor says she'll never walk again."

"Yes, I know, Will. I was there, remember? Damned drunk driver. They should all rot in hell."

"Won't do Alice much good now, though, will it?" Big Ugly looked away and spat out the window.

"What do you mean?"

"If they all rot in hell."

His sidekick, Bobby, quietly asked, "You still takin' her and pickin' her up from school every day?"

"Well, who else is gonna do it? Her mama has to work all the time if we expect to eat anything but squirrel."

Bobby sat quietly for a few minutes. Then, "I hear the lumber mill might be hirin' again soon. I bet you could get your old job back over there. You and that foreman was pals. What was his name?"

"He moved to Nebraska. Ain't nobody got any work here."

Bobby nodded and turned to look out the passenger side window just in time to see Zakaya and Blaze pull up and go into Brassy's.

"There they are now. What you gonna do?"

"Nothin' right now. I'm just waitin' and watchin' for my chance. And then I'm gonna get 'em when they least expect it."

"What are you gon' do?"

"You'll find out, Bobby. You'll find out."

❧❧

Z and Blaze took a corner table in Brassy's and, over drinks and sandwiches, discussed the several cases.

"You were really good back there," Blaze told her.

"How so?"

"With Charming Billy, I mean. You were very good."

"Oh. That. I just try to size up the person being questioned and put them at ease. At least as much as possible."

"Well, you're pretty good at it."

"Thanks."

"And not an easy job, considering the subject."

"True. He's really messed up, but he's also the Kind Killer. There's no doubt in my mind about that. Even so, I can't believe he's a killer in any sense of the word that we are used to dealing with. He's a damaged soul and needs help. Not imprisonment."

"You're a kind person, Zakaya-Zee. And you have a point there. So…What do you think about what he said?"

"I'm still chewing on it. But we got way more information from him than I thought we would. What do you have in your notes?" Z raised her brows and pointed her chin in the direction of the notes lying on the table in front of him.

Blaze took up his clipboard and began leafing through his scrawling handwriting.

"More than one person is in the trafficking business, for sure. But we knew that was going to be the case from the get-go. It's not like one person can pull off something this big and organized without help from somewhere. Maybe from more than one somewhere. And we know Billy Boy sold Octoflurane to two men. This town may be sprawling, but it's still small as cities go. So he probably sold it to our local traffickers."

"Two men in jackets and ties." Z looked Blaze steadily in the eyes. "And they had guns."

"Right."

"Sound at all familiar to you?"

Blaze smiled at her. "Could be me."

"Be serious."

"I am. We don't have enough information yet to peg anyone. But we'll get there." Blaze took a bite of his sandwich.

"We have to get there. We have to find Zeena before…" Her eyes began to well up and she looked away.

Blaze looked over the top of the clipboard. "We will. You'll get her back. Don't worry about that. I promise you, you will get her back. We won't stop until you do."

Z turned back and gave him the interrogation stare. "You seem awfully damned sure of that, Blaze."

"I am. I'm just as determined as you are. As the saying goes: 'Underestimate me. That'll be fun.'"

She took a deep breath. "What else do we have?"

Blaze read off his notes. "A dilapidated two-story blue house with crying girls. Probably located in a remote area. Rural county. Guarded by thugs. And on Charming Billy's garbage pickup route." He looked up at her. "What does that tell us?"

"It tells us the girls—and Zeena—are still here. Still local. The delivery to final destination at the hands of these sub-human scum hasn't happened yet. But time is not on our side, Blaze. We have to move on this as quickly as we can."

There was no denying the worry in Z's face or voice and Blaze made another effort to ease her worry just a bit. He said, "We will. I promise you we will get them. And Zeena. First, we need to get the information on Billy's routes and follow them until we find that blue house."

"Shouldn't be hard to recognize once we find it. Given Billy's description."

"What else? You have something?" Blaze asked.

Z frowned. "We need the DNA report on those panties to see if they belonged to Tiki Jameson. If they did, we have an absolute connection between at least two of the cases in addition to the medicine bottles. Maybe there will be other DNA present, as well. Not counting Billy's, of course. I doubt that poor boy has ever been that close to a girl before in his life. I firmly believe all he did was find them and handle them."

She reached into her bag and pulled out the hardcopy of the dress shop floor plans. "And we have this," she said as she laid the paper out on the table sideways between them so they could both lean a bit and view it right-side-up. "We need to take a look at that place soon. How do we prioritize? Sanitation route to the blue house? Or dress shop floor plan?"

"Hmmmm…." Blaze leaned over and studied the plan. "Looks pretty ordinary and straightforward to me. I think it might keep until we check out the blue house."

"Maybe." Zakaya sounded pensive.

"Why maybe?"

"Well, I was thinking we need to do a background check on the owner of the shop. Soon. If we don't find anything on her, then we can move on. If she has no record and is really just a dress shop owner, then we can put her on the back burner. But…"

"But what?"

"I'm positive there's more. I would just like to find out why she was so nervous the day I visited the shop. And why she directed me to a completely different fitting room from the one where the girl—Kit Deming—was last seen. That wasn't just nerves. I seriously doubt she forgot and just got the dressing room wrong. She knows something. I'm sure of it."

Blaze thought for a moment, casually flipping through his notes.

"And there's something else we need to do." Z held up a finger for emphasis while she punched up JJ on her t-com.

"JJ? I need you to run a couple of background checks for me. First, see what you can find out about the owner of the Glamour Girl dress shop, will you? And then run a check on that big ugly dude that tried to manhandle me the day we first ran into each other. Remember? See what you can find out about him, will you? I've got the license number of his truck. That should give you what you need. Get everything you can on him, will you? Call me." She gave the license number for the truck then listened. "Thanks, JJ. I owe you one. Maybe two."

"Why now?" Blaze asked. "I thought you pretty much scared the crap out of him last time when he put a pistol in your face."

"He's been following me. Us. Haven't you noticed? He and his buddy were watching us when we got here today. Sitting out there in his truck. I just want to know what's up with that guy. So. Back to work. What do you think about the dress shop?"

"Here's what I think," he said. "First we go to the sanitation department and get Billy's route information. Then, we visit the dress shop to take a look before we head out of town. I'd like to see this Francis person myself. But it has to keep until tomorrow. It's been a long day. You need to get some rest. If we are really hot on the trail of these bastards, we need to be fresh. Go home. Spend the evening with your mother. We will start first thing tomorrow."

"Do you think we are that close?"

"I don't know yet. But if we are and everything begins to fall into place, I expect things will start popping fast. We need to be ready."

Z got up and set her drink on the table with a slight thud. "I was born ready for this."

38

Z tried to have a normal evening with her mother but worry about Zeena put a definite edge on it. She had slept, however fitfully, and this morning she was up and ready to get to work. If Blaze was right about things popping all at once, she would be ready.

She decided to call Viking in Cascadia and punched him up on her t-com.

"Viking." The clipped and deeply resonant voice came through so loud and clear it was almost like he was in the next room.

"Viking, it's me. Z."

"Talk to me."

"Alex probably filled you in on everything so I'll get right to it. We—my local partner and I—are close to putting this puzzle together and we think today, or tomorrow at the latest could be the day everything falls into place. Or falls apart. Not sure how this is going to go down yet, but it's possible I will need the team."

"They are already there, Z."

"They? Who? Where?"

"Parker and Gray have been on the coast waiting for orders. All you have to do is signal. Fill me in on what you have so far and don't leave anything out."

"Where's Alex?"

"She's staying behind. On orders from me. Just in case Zeena magically shows up there."

"I see." Z knew Alex well enough to know the only way she would have stayed behind was on orders. Knowing she was safe, at least, was one good thing out of a bunch of bad ones right now.

"Besides," Viking added, "if this doesn't go well, I don't want to lose you both. So talk to me."

Z recounted everything she could remember. Everyone she had met. Everywhere she had been. Every suspicion she was harboring. Charming Billy. The blue house. Big Ugly. She even threw her Aunt Juanita and Uncle Bo into the mix.

Viking listened without interruption. Z knew him well enough to know he was weighing every tone of her voice. Every nuance. Every sliver of information.

When she finished filling him in, he said, "I'm sending Gray and Parker on up there. I want them nearby in case you need them in a hurry. Buzz me when you have the location of the blue house. See you soon."

"Wait!" Z held him up before he could end the conversation. "You said, Parker and Gray. Where are you?"

"I'm on the coast. Making arrangements. Not to worry. Just send the location of that house when you have it."

"Will do. And, Viking?"

"Yeah?"

"Tell Parker and Gray to stay completely out of sight when they get here, okay? Otherwise, they will stand out like sore thumbs and they will be in just as much danger as I am by being here."

"You got it."

When she clicked off the t-com she pulled the cargo pants the team had sent via the local operative from the suitcase in the closet where she had stashed them the day she'd gotten the supplies. She tried them on to check the fit. She might look a bit military, but she wasn't messing around today. The SIG, extra magazines, boots, and ammunition all waited for her in the trunk of the rental. Content with the fit of the cargo pants she changed back into her regular jeans and would stash the cargos in the trunk with the rest of the supplies until they were needed.

There was no way of knowing how this would all go down—or when—but she was going to be ready, whatever happened.

∽∾∽

Blaze's t-com buzzed. It was Dark Suit.

"Forty-eight! The men I told you I was sending down there arrived several days ago. They saw the girl and recognized her. You need to arrest her now and bring her in."

"Sir, I just can't do that. Not yet. We are just about to blow this trafficking case wide open. I promise you, she's not going anywhere. She's convinced the traffickers have taken her young friend and there's no way she's leaving until she gets the girl back and takes those criminals down. I'm working really close with her and I doubt I've ever seen anyone more determined."

Silence. Then, "Make sure you don't let her get away or I'll personally see to it that you go from forty-eight to zero. And that's my promise to *you*!"

Blaze stared at the t-com as it went dead.

"Yeah," he said to no one, "I just bet you will."

∽∾∽

After meeting up with Blaze at the police station they filled the captain in on everything they had learned yesterday and how things might come to a head today or tomorrow at the latest.

"We are really close," she told Taylor. "You've got your Kind Killer and we are very close to solving the murder of Tiki Jameson and the disappearance of Kit Deming, too. By the way…" She looked the captain dead in the eyes. "That boy. Billy Addison. No way that boy goes to prison. I'm counting on you being the decent guy JJ tells me you are to make sure that boy gets help. Not punishment. I know he can't just go free. But he's not your normal killer. And you know it, too. He wouldn't survive a week in prison. No matter what he's done, he doesn't deserve that."

She stopped talking and waited.

Captain Taylor nodded. "I do know it. He'll be treated right, Miss—Detective. I promise."

Z's steady gaze held his eyes a moment longer. He did not look away. Satisfied, she nodded, then turned to Blaze. "You ready to follow up that lead at the sanitation department?"

"Yep."

"Let's go."

39

On showing their IDs at the sanitation department, they were directed to the garage at the rear of the building. There, they located the manager who further directed them to the woman who drew up the routes.

"The routes don't often change," she said. "But some of them are erratic."

"How so?" Z asked.

"Well, the ones out in the county on back roads, you know? Out in the rural area that you wanted to know about. Those don't always have the same day assigned for pickup. Folks out there are not happy about it, but it's the best we can do for them. Otherwise they have to manage for themselves."

"I see." Z considered this for a moment while Blaze referred to his notes.

Blaze broke in. "We are looking for a particular house out in the county. But we don't have the street or house number. What we do have is the name of one of your employees who services that route when…er…when it's scheduled."

"Which employee? Maybe I can help you pin it down."

"William Addison."

The woman laughed. "Billy! Now there's a case for you. Poor boy."

"Why do you say that?" Z asked.

"Well, he's just not quite right in the head, you know? But he's harmless."

Blaze and Z exchanged looks at that last.

Z turned back to the woman. "Can you tell us the routes he runs out in the county, please? Perhaps on Wednesdays."

"Let me check." The woman flipped through her schedule book to check the past several weeks. Then, "Yes. Last week he was sent out in the truck with Jenkins, the driver, on route twenty-two. That's one of the erratic routes. Sometimes we send them down there on Wednesdays, sometimes on Thursdays. It just depends on when we have the time and the truck available for the run."

"Let's see that on the map, there, if you don't mind," Blaze said, pointing to the large paper map of the area pinned to the wall behind her.

"Of course." She got up from her desk and began searching the map. "Here." She pointed to a red line that ran south of town. "It's mostly on the county road. That road has eight or nine branches, but they drive it straight, taking each branch in turn. At the end of the route, they just turn around and head back here without any further stops. Here, I'll make you a copy of that route." She unpinned a section of map from the bulletin board, slapped it onto the copy machine, and punched a couple of buttons.

With the copy of the sanitation route in hand, Z thanked the woman for her time and turned to leave. Then she turned back. "You might want to warn Jenkins that he may be called for questioning."

"What on earth for?"

"Nothing against him. Not to worry. He just might need to give some information to the police in the near future about this house we are looking for on his route. He's in no trouble. And you might want to hire a replacement for Billy Addison. Thanks again."

"Wha—" The woman was surprised into silence as she watched Z turn to leave.

As they headed out the door, Z's t-com buzzed. She fiddled with an earpiece so the conversation would not be heard by anyone other than herself then listened for several minutes. She clicked off and turned to Blaze. "The DNA on the panties was Tiki Jameson's. Also Billy Addison's. And there were two others not identified."

"Great." Blaze was not happy. "Those two others are the ones we want."

"We'll get them. If it's the last thing I ever do. I promise you that." Z gave him a look, then added, "And wait till you hear this."

"What now?"

"Francis Worsham. The owner of the dress shop."

"What about her?"

"She's Hadeon Cook's sister."

"You're shittin' me. Is everybody in this damned place related?"

"Nope. And, apparently, yep."

Blaze thought for a minute. Then, "Well, that opens up another whole bag of worms, doesn't it?"

"Yep." Z gave him a look. "But...I don't think we should let on that we know that when we go take a look over there. She may freak and we don't know how involved she is in this whole mess."

"True."

They had made it to the car and Blaze was reaching for the door handle when he stopped and said, "Let's put that on hold for the time being. As we already said, she's not going anywhere. Let's drive the sanitation route to see what we can find. Then we'll head back and give that dress shop a going over."

"Suits me."

Blaze took the driver's seat and Z opened the passenger side door and slid into the car just as her t-com buzzed. It was JJ again.

"JJ! Hey! Got something else for me?"

She listened carefully for several minutes then thanked him and turned to Blaze.

"It was JJ. He ran down the license plate of the big guy who keeps annoying me at Brassy's and found out a bunch of stuff about him."

"What did he find?"

"Ummm…he has a minor record for disorderly conduct. Making threats. That sort of thing. Couple of traffic tickets, but no real criminal record."

"Anything else?"

"His name is William Wilcox. Goes by Will. He's married to the same woman for nineteen years and they have a little girl, Alice. There was an accident a couple years back that left her paralyzed. Apparently a drunk driver ran a stoplight and plowed into the side of their car on the passenger side. The drunk driver was killed when his head went through the windshield and the little girl was pinned in the wreckage."

"Ouch. Tough." Blaze shook his head. "Anything else? Any work record or anything else of note?"

"He worked at the lumber mill until it laid off over half the workforce two years ago. Before that, he worked in construction. Left high school in the eleventh grade so he never graduated. As far as JJ could find, that's about it."

"Not exactly a glowing résumé, is it?"

"Not exactly." Z sighed and turned to watch the passing landscape.

"All that must have turned him very bitter, because he's still holding a grudge against you. Probably me, too."

She turned to Blaze. "How do you know that?"

"Because he's following us."

40

Dismissing Big Ugly in the truck some distance behind them as no immediate threat, Z quietly watched the passing landscape as it grew more wooded with scrubby oaks and pines with each passing mile. Blaze kept glancing over at her. Checking on her, surreptitiously he thought.

She sensed his concern. "I'm fine, Blaze."

He smiled. "Just checking. You're pretty quiet over there."

"Lots on my mind."

"Your young friend?"

"Yes. And other things."

"What other things?"

"People. And the damage they do."

"What do you mean?"

"I mean people are destructive. Take these woods, for example. They are beautiful in their natural state. Like mountains. Like the rivers and streams. Like the ocean. Then man comes along and blows up the sides of the mountains, pollutes the rivers and streams, and cuts down the forests. You know. Just destructive. No concern for the results of it at all. And they do even worse to each other, given the chance. Mostly for gain. Money. In the end, it's all about money, isn't it?"

Blaze nodded. "Can't argue with that. But we'll have to save the environment later. Right now we have some girls to worry about. Check that route map, will you?"

Z unfolded the sheet of paper the woman at the sanitation department had given them and noted a side road listed close by. They had passed it about thirty seconds ago. "We're on the right road, but we missed the first side road about a quarter mile back. We can check it on the way back if we don't find what we are looking for before then."

"Okay. What's the next one?"

"Looks like…Blackberry. Short road. Just up ahead on the left."

They turned onto Blackberry and ended up at a ROAD END sign half swallowed by weeds. "Nothing here," Blaze muttered as he maneuvered the car out of the overgrown ruts and back onto the two-lane. "Next?"

"On the right." Z squinted at the map. "Doesn't even seem to have a name."

Blaze slowed the car to a crawl so they could give it a good once over. "Doesn't look like a road at all to me. Could be just an erroneous mark on the map." He drove on.

Z checked the map again. "Next one is on the left. There should be a street sign. It says Forest Lane on the map."

Blaze almost drove past the unpaved, rutted "lane" before he spied the street sign lying on its side in the overgrown right-of-way. He slowed the car and began backing up until he could maneuver into the lane. The lack of pavement and the ruts worn deep caused the car to bounce as it progressed slowly forward. But there was no growth in or between the ruts. This told them the tiny road was used often enough to keep the weeds at bay.

They watched as Big Ugly, behind them, slowed down to take a look. Checking on what they were doing. Then he drove his truck on by as though he had no idea who they were. After giving each other a look, they dismissed him and returned to the task at hand.

"Looks like this street—lane—path, whatever it's called, is used fairly often. Something is down here, for sure."

"Slow down, Blaze! No telling what's down there." Z was holding onto the door grip to keep from sliding sideways in the seat with each bounce.

Blaze slowed the vehicle to a creep, inching forward now.

"Stop!" Z reached out and grabbed his arm. "I see blue! There! To the right. Through the trees." She pointed out the open window.

Just ahead they saw the driveway, as rutted as the "lane" they had just driven and just as clear of weeds. A large KEEP OUT sign stood boldly at the entrance by a battered mailbox that sported several bullet holes.

Z stared at the blue through the trees. There was something sinister about this place—about this whole scene—that chilled her bones as though a dark shadow had fallen over her. She couldn't quite place it. But there was something…

"What should we do?" Blaze was looking ahead toward the house and didn't notice the chill in Zakaya.

She made an effort to shake the strange feeling. "Not sure. Think we should try to drive up to the house? Maybe pretend to be lost? Ask for directions?"

Blaze laughed. "Somehow, I don't think they would buy that."

"Well, let's just pull into the driveway by a couple of car lengths just to see what we can see up there. You know…Like we are just lost and turning around here."

"Okay." Blaze threw the manual transmission into first gear and inched the vehicle forward until the house was fairly visible straight ahead and slightly to their left through the trees.

Z's thoughts went to Charming Billy's description of the place and she became animated. "Definitely blue. Needs paint. Cardboard in the upstairs window. Dude with a rifle on the front steps." She turned to Blaze. "This is it. It has to be."

"Yep. And here comes the dude with the rifle."

"Back up! Let's go!"

Blaze threw the car into reverse, temporarily spinning the wheels in the soft turf and slowing down their exit as the dude with the rifle quickly approached. He eased off the accelerator until the tires finally caught, then inched the car back until it found the firmer ground of Forest Lane. Once on the Lane, they headed back the way they had come.

Checking the side mirror as they pulled forward, they could see the guy with the rifle standing ominously by the KEEP OUT sign, feet firmly planted military-style.

"Well, that was close," Blaze said. "Did you manage to get the house number?"

"All I saw was a zero and a two. That should be enough. I'll see if JJ can find out who owns that place."

They drove in silence for several minutes before Z said, "The guy with the rifle tells me they haven't moved the girls yet. You don't need to stand around with guns when there's nothing to guard. They're still here, Blaze. Zeena is still here!"

"You can't be sure of that, Zakaya," he said, his voice soft. "But even if she is, we can't just rush off in there. We need a search warrant. And we will need backup. Uniformed officers. A lot of them. And armed."

This was the first time he had ever called her by just her given name and she was momentarily curious. But the events were overriding everything else right now. "You're right. It's just that…"

"I know," he said. "I know. Let's go for the warrant first. Then, while we wait for that, we'll check out the dress shop. What do you say?"

"Okay." Z was nervous. "How long for the warrant, do you think?"

"We'll plead an emergency. Should be able to get it later today."

❦

Big Ugly and Sidekick sat in the truck where they had pulled off onto a dirt side road that led off the main county road and watched under cover of trees and weeds as Z and Blaze passed them by on their way back to town.

Big Ugly muttered under his breath. "They are lookin' for something. But why down here? Nothin' down here but woods. What's going on?"

Sidekick scratched his head. "Not sure, Will. But there's always been something not right about that place back there where they turned in. Not sure what kind of family lives back up in there, but I'm not anxious to find out, either. Some people are best left alone."

"Well, I ain't worried about who lives there, Bobby. What I want to know is, why is that guy and that little Black witch interested in the place. Do you really think they just happened on it by accident?" Big Ugly spat out the driver's window.

"You prolly right, Will. It did look like they was searchin' for someplace, didn't it?"

"Yep. And I think they found it because they stopped lookin' after they left there, didn't they?"

"Yeah. They sure did, Will."

Big Ugly was smiling. He turned to Sidekick. "And you know what else I think, Bobby, old buddy? I think they will be back now that they've found whatever it was they were lookin' for. And when they come, I'm gonna be ready for 'em."

41

Once she and Blaze got back to the police station, Z took a private moment to tap Viking, giving him the coordinates of the Blue House but asking him to hold off sending Parker and Gray there until she was ready.

"Tell them not to approach the house but to stay close by and remain out of sight until I give the word."

"Will do."

"Do you have a way to get us all out of the country when we finally get the traffickers?"

"I'm working on that, Z. Just hang tight."

"Right." She clicked off. If she couldn't trust Viking, there was no human on this planet she could trust.

But what about Blaze?

That was a question that had nagged her more than once over the past few days. She still wasn't sure she could trust him, and no way would she jeopardize Parker and Gray. The team's identity must be kept away from everyone until the very last moment of the operation. Whatever the operation turned out to be. This whole thing was extremely touchy. And iffy. And who knew where it would end up? At the last, once she had Zeena—and the authorities had the traffickers—she would have to evade Blaze and escape with the team. For that, she would have to depend on Viking.

He had never failed them yet.

⌘

Once the call to Viking had been taken care of, Z couldn't sit still. She paced around while the captain contacted the judge's office for the warrant they needed. She made herself a cup of coffee, then set it down without drinking it while it went stone cold. Looking around the bullpen, she saw only uniformed officers and the desk sergeant. Cook and Swift were not at their desks. She eyed the empty desks for a long moment with narrowed eyes until she heard the door of the captain's office open and turned to see what was up.

The captain emerged with an apologetic look on his face.

"What now?" Z's impatience was impossible to hide.

Blaze stepped in, diplomatically. "What is it, Captain?"

"I'm sorry," Captain Taylor began, "but the judge has been on a two-day fishing trip with one of his lawyer buddies and isn't due back until sometime tomorrow morning. His wife thinks he will be home by ten or eleven. He's over at Eufaula. It's about a three-and-a-half-hour drive from there. So if he gets an early sta—"

"That's just great!" Z interrupted him.

"Come on, Zakaya-Zee." Blaze reached to place his hand on her shoulder. "This isn't anyone's fault. We'll get the warrant. We just need to wait a little longer for it. We need to do this thing all wrapped up and legal so we can put these people away for good."

Z shrugged away from his touch. "People? You mean animals, don't you? No! Animals are way above and beyond better than they are." She turned away in disgust, eyeing the empty desks of Cook and Swift in passing. "In fact, I can't think of anything low enough to call them."

"Anyway," Blaze continued, "we've already got the warrant for the dress shop and this short delay will give us plenty of time to thoroughly check it out. We've been on the go all morning. How about we get some lunch and then head over to the shop?"

Z looked from Blaze to the captain and back again. "I'm not hungry."

"Okay…" Blaze tried to placate her. "Let's go, then."

Before the two of them could exit the squad room, JJ turned from the FAX machine and called out to them.

"Z!" He was waving a sheet of paper.

They held up and Z said, "What's up JJ?"

"I've got the owner of the house you wanted to know about."

"Great, JJ! Who is it?"

JJ grimaced. "You are not going to like it, Z."

"What do you mean?"

JJ looked from Z to Blaze and back again as though searching for some way to soften to blow. "You're just not going to like it, that's all."

"Why not?"

"Because it's Beauregard Kalu. Your Uncle Bo."

Z stopped dead in her tracks and stared at JJ. She felt her head begin to spin and her stomach churn. She put her fist to her mouth and ran to the station side door and outside where she vomited onto the pavement. Visions spiraled through her head. Uncle Bo. The blue house. His smooth voice talking to her. His hands probing her young body. A dirty mattress…

She vomited again. And again until there was nothing left in her.

Blaze and JJ had followed her out the door, Blaze offering a handkerchief and JJ offering apologies.

"I'm so sorry, Z." JJ looked sadder than Z had ever seen him as she peered at him over the handkerchief she had taken from Blaze and was holding over her mouth.

"It's not your fault, JJ," she mumbled through the handkerchief. "You have nothing to be sorry for. I just…" She couldn't finish her sentence.

"Come on," Blaze said, putting his arm around her. "Let's go."

In Blaze's car, she was silent for a minute and then said, "It figures."

"What figures," he asked.

"My uncle. The bastard." Tears welled up and spilled over in an uncharacteristic fashion for Zakaya Kalu. She wiped them away and said, "That house. That gawd-awful blue house. I felt there was something about it when we saw it."

For reasons she did not understand, she began unloading on Blaze her memories of what had happened to her as a young girl at the hands of her uncle. The words tumbled out in a torrent—a veritable waterfall of fear and hate and disgust and shame.

Blaze reached out to her and held her. She had not expected this but she gave in to it. It was what she needed at this moment. This feeling of strength and safety and warmth. Then he kissed her and she gave in to that, as well, kissing him back just as eagerly before abruptly pushing him away.

The kiss was unexpected yet wanted. And unwanted. She was conflicted. She had never fully trusted Blaze since the day he was first present at the police station when she was offered the opportunity to assist the police after being denied the same. It just didn't add up. Why the sudden change of mind by the captain? How much influence had Blaze had with him? How did he come by it? So many questions. And now here she was, in the arms of this man and giving herself over to him as though she had never harbored the slightest doubt. Yet the doubt, undeniably, was there. This was a man she could easily love. But love requires a necessary vulnerability that she could not—would not—allow. Not now. Not yet.

Blaze actually blushed. "I'm sorry, Zakaya-Zee. I shouldn't have."

Z said nothing so he said, "The dress shop can wait one more night. We have futzed around all day and we are both tired. We need to rest. Let's go home and get some sleep. Tomorrow, we will go—first thing—to find out what our Miss Francis knows and how she is or isn't involved in this trafficking mess. By the time we're finished up there, the judge should be back and we'll have our warrant. Then we'll go get those girls. We need the time to fully prepare, anyway. What do you say?"

"Tomorrow. Not a day later. Tomorrow." The steel in her voice was unmistakable. "But..."

"But what?"

"But...In the meantime, somebody needs to be watching that house. Just in case."

Blaze thought for a moment. "I'll see if Captain Taylor can send somebody out there tonight. Then, tomorrow, when the judge gets back and we get our warrant, we will go arrest ourselves some criminals and get those girls."

"Sounds good to me."

ℰℐℰℐ

In the Blue House, Kit Deming stood at the window, listening. Something was going on. Voices had been shouting back and forth since early afternoon. Vehicles had been arriving and departing. She could hear the engines and car doors slamming even though she couldn't see them. Guards outside the room had been murmuring amongst themselves. There was laughter. Something was definitely going on.

Being in this sparse and uninviting place was anything but ideal. It was not home. But it had become, over the past few months, at least a place of stability and, yes, of safety. She had never once been harmed or treated badly in any way—even when she had screamed and pounded on the door. The worst treatment she had received, other than being held prisoner, was that of being ignored.

The effects on her of this confinement and isolation were, at first, fright and uncertainty. Those soon gave way to boredom and, finally, a sense of hopelessness. She felt she might never see her mother and father again. Or her best friend, Connie. Or Rocky, her adorable little black dog. She felt small. Helpless. Confused. Worst of all, she had no answer to her question: Why?

The morning had been crisp, but after lunch it had warmed up a bit and that's when all the commotion had begun.

She could hear the guards outside in the hallway talking louder now and, as she turned from the window to better hear what was happening, the door to her room opened and one of the guards came in bearing a brown paper bag.

"Here you go," he said as he handed the bag over to her. "Get yourself prettied up. Someone will come to get you later on. So be ready."

"Am I going home now?" Kit, cautiously excited, was beginning to feel a bit of hope, but the guard didn't answer. She tried again, "Please! Am I going home now?"

"Just clean up and make yourself pretty. Someone will be here for you after while." He gave her a last look and left the room, closing and locking the door behind him.

After so many months devoid of any kind of real stimulus, Kit was intrigued. She opened the bag and discovered cosmetics. Eye liner! Mascara! Lipstick! Nail polish! Perfume! Even a razor!

She stared at these things as though she had never before seen such riches. There was even a pretty t-shirt and a pair of shoes. She took the shoes from the bag and shoved her foot into one of them. Slightly big, but okay. The t-shirt felt lightweight but it was brightly patterned. A bright thing in this room almost made for sensory overload. She was becoming overwhelmed and sat down on the mattress on the floor.

Soon, she had spread everything out before her, touching, looking, admiring each item in turn. Then she showered, using the treasured safety razor with its feminine pink handle, and the floral soap that had been in the bag with the other things.

Cleaned up, she applied the makeup and got dressed. Same old jeans, but the t-shirt was cheerful.

At last, holding closed the bag of treasured cosmetics tightly in one hand, she sat down and waited.

42

Z had tried to get some rest as Blaze had ordered. She wanted to be fresh for whatever happened on this day, but sleep had been difficult to come by. She had tossed and turned and finally given it up altogether at around four o'clock. She got up and dressed and went into the kitchen for coffee. Her mother had apparently heard her bustling around and soon came in to see what was going on.

"Today is the day we believe we are going to make some arrests, Mama. I hope to find Zeena and take her back to Cascadia. I just want you to know that I'm sorry this trip has turned into such a disaster. And I want you to know that if anything happens to me—"

"Now you stop that right now, Z. You hear me?" Mrs. Kalu grabbed Z's hand away from the coffee pot and turned her around. "I mean it. You stop it."

"Mama…I just want you to know that I love you. I wish, just once, we could have time together uninterrupted by my work. But what we are going to be doing today is important. And it's dangerous. And you should know that."

"I do know it. But I still won't have you talking like that." Her mother's eyes flashed. "You are going to be okay. No matter what happens. You hear me?"

"Yes, Mama. I hear you." Z smiled, then, and embraced her mother. Of all the places in the world, the safest place she had ever known was in her mother's arms. She couldn't bring herself to tell her mother that her late husband's brother was involved in the trafficking of young girls and may even now have Zeena in his clutches. Even worse, she couldn't tell her what that man had done to her, personally. She would never tell her that. The thought sickened her anew and she hugged her mother tighter.

"Okay." Mrs. Kalu finally broke the embrace. "Now drink your coffee before it gets cold."

"Yes, Ma'am."

છ૭૯૦

While Z was having coffee with her mother, Kit Deming was staring at an elegant-looking boat docked on the water behind a beautiful home in Point Clear, Alabama. Fear flooded every cell of her body. She had no idea where she was, but there was no doubt now she was not going home.

Last night the guards had unlocked the door to her room and, along with eight other girls, she was taken outside and loaded into a windowless van. The doors were locked and the van rolled away from the house where she had been held captive since May. All the girls were quiet, looking each other over for something. Anything. Mostly assurance. Of what, none of them knew.

After a while, the girls began to talk among themselves. One was from Georgia. She had, she told them, been going home late from a basketball game when a car pulled alongside her. A friendly-looking woman asked her for directions when someone from behind had grabbed her and shoved her into their car. She was taken to some house and put into a room with two other girls and was never let out again until she was transported several weeks ago to the blue house where Kit had been held all these months. The other two girls weren't transported with her. She didn't know what had happened to them.

Another had been to a friend's party. She had driven her parent's car that evening and on the way home, one of the tires blew out. It was really dark out there on the county road and when she saw the headlights of a car coming, she waved it down. The driver was a guy. He looked okay and told her he would take her to a garage so she could get someone to come out and fix the tire. But he lied. He took her to his place and then handed her over to someone else who paid him a lot of money.

The stories of the others were much the same. All were terrified. One or two were too terrified even to speak to the rest of them. They held each other close and cried.

When they had arrived at this place by the water, they were taken from the van one at a time and escorted aboard the boat. When it was Kit's turn, one of the men grabbed her upper arm in a tight grip and turned her toward the boat.

"Let's go," he said.

"I want to go home!" she yelled at him.

"Be quiet or I will punch you so hard you won't wake up until tomorrow." The man was menacing and his breath was horrid.

She struggled, but it was no use. She was simply not strong enough to break his grip.

As she struggled she noticed a man in a suit hand a small stack of money to the driver of the van. Then he patted the man on the back. The man laughed, folded the bills, and shoved them into his pocket. Kit was pulled forward to the boat just as the man got back into the van and began backing away from the property.

As soon as all the girls were aboard, the boat immediately left the dock and headed out into the Gulf of Mexico. It was an hour or more before the sound of the engines died and the boat was quiet and still on the water, gently rocking back and forth on the small waves.

Kit didn't know where she was. She had no way to find out. No place to go. No way to get there. Even her bones trembled at the not knowing what was happening to her. Even worse, what was *going* to happen to her.

43

The Glamour Girl dress shop opened early on Saturdays and had been open only ten minutes when Z and Blaze pulled into the parking lot and parked the car near the closest entrance. As they got out of the car and began walking in, Z buzzed JJ.

"JJ? We're here."

"Okay. I'm here by the back door in case she panics and tries to bolt."

"Good. Do you have uniformed officers lined up in case we need them?"

"Yes. They are just waiting for the word. Forensics have been alerted, too, in case you find anything."

While they were going to be spending time going over the dress shop, Z was worried about what was going on at the blue house. She asked, "Have you heard anything from the officer Captain Taylor sent down to keep an eye on the house?"

"He called in after he arrived. Said he was staying out of sight, but we haven't heard anything since then. He would have called in if there had been any activity down there."

"Okay. Thanks." Z hoped JJ was right. In any event, she and Blaze would be down there soon enough. Right now she had Francis Worsham and this dress shop to worry about.

"Okay. We're inside the mall and approaching the shop doors. I'll call if we need you."

Z clicked off with JJ and turned to Blaze. "Do you know how to lock the big glass doors to these shops once we get inside?"

"Yeah. No problem."

"Well, here we go, then."

They stepped inside the shop and Blaze closed and locked the doors behind them.

Francis Worsham was at the register at the back assisting a woman who had a fluffy pile of pink in front of her on the counter. She momentarily froze when she looked up and saw the two detectives. It was obvious that she remembered Z from her earlier visit.

"Could you hurry up, please?" the customer asked. "I'm really in a hurry today because we have this weddin—"

"This shop is closed, Ma'am," Z said as she approached the woman from behind. "You will have to leave now."

"What do you mean, closed? It just opened and I have to get this bridesmaid's dress for my daughter! I need it today!"

"Sorry. You will have to leave. But I think it will be okay if you go ahead and take the dress." Z took her by the arm and guided her to the front of the store where Blaze temporarily unlocked the door and ushered her out, still complaining, but with the fluff of pink cascading from her arms.

They turned back toward the register counter to find no trace of Francis Worsham until JJ pushed her through the stockroom door ahead of him and back into the shop.

"You were right, Z. She tried to bolt."

"Thanks, JJ. Stay back there by the door, will you? I'll call if we need those others we discussed."

JJ nodded and headed back through the stockroom and out the back door to wait.

Blaze turned to Francis Worsham. "Where were you going, Miss Worsham?"

"Nowhere." She bit her lip and looked nervously from him to Z.

"Well," Z began, "we just need some more information from you about that missing girl. Remember? I came here before to talk with you a few days ago about it?"

"I don't know anything!" Francis Worsham was wringing her hands and looking wildly from one to the other of them.

"I'm pretty sure you know something about your shop, don't you?" Z tried to calm her slightly. "Let's go into the stockroom in the back and take a look, okay?"

Francis said nothing as Z headed for the stockroom door. Blaze made sure the woman followed, sandwiched between the two of them.

Once in the stockroom, Z walked toward the back door and then turned to face the storefront end of the building. She pulled the copy of the store's original blueprint from her bag and looked from the paper in her hand to the layout of the storeroom. The blueprint showed a straight-line wall with two doors in it. However, the actual layout included a protruding addition that began about ten feet to the right of the door they had just come through to enter the stockroom. This addition was about eight feet deep and maybe six feet wide. Z walked over to the addition and examined its eight-foot sidewall. She turned to Francis.

"This room isn't on the blueprint. When was this addition put in here?" she asked her.

"I don't know." The woman's face was white.

"Oh, of course you do. It wasn't here when you bought the shop, was it? You know we can obtain this information without you, don't you, Francis? So you might just as well tell us."

"I don't know exactly when it was put in. It was here when I opened the shop."

"Hmmmmm." Z walked around the eight-foot sidewall to the six-foot expanse that contained a door. She reached out for the doorknob. A groan from Francis stayed her hand. "Are you all right, Miss Worsham? Would you like some water?"

The woman looked as though she would faint dead away, but she shook her head in reply.

Z reached for the doorknob again and gave it a turn. The door was locked. She turned back to Francis. "Unlock this door, if you will, please."

"It's just a storeroom. Why do you need to go in there?" The panicked Francis was wringing her hands again.

"Just unlock the door, please." Z's voice was steady but firm.

Francis took keys from her pocket with shaking hands, found one, and reached to unlock the door. Z took the keys from her.

"Thank you. Stand back, please." Z slipped the key into the lock, turned it, opened the door and found—nothing.

The space was empty and dark. The inside of the tiny space had been painted with a dull, flat, extremely black paint. Even more strange, the space was only about three feet deep. What was behind it, Z wondered, in the rest of the eight-foot-deep addition.

"My God," Z said quietly. "It's like the Black Hole of Calcutta in here. There's not even a light switch. Nothing."

While there was nothing in the tiny black room, the light from the open door made visible another door straight ahead. Z leaned to one side so Blaze could see what she was seeing. Then she tried the door. It, too, was locked. Z stepped back out and asked Francis to open it.

"I can't," she said.

"Why not?" Z asked.

"I don't have a key for that door."

"Why not?" Z asked again.

"Because he won't let me have one!" Francis moaned and began to cry.

"Who won't let you have one, Francis?" Blaze asked her.

"My brother!"

"But you own the shop, don't you, Francis?"

"Yes. But just in name only. It was my brother's money."

"And who is your brother, Francis?"

The woman looked from Z to Blaze, but said nothing.

"Who is your brother, Francis?" Z asked her.

"I can't tell you!"

Francis began wailing and hitting her forehead with her fist so Blaze reached out for her attacking hand and sat her down on some boxes to calm her while Z went to the back door and called JJ inside again.

"Break it down, JJ," she said, pointing to the door inside the black room.

JJ laid his shoulder into it several times before it finally gave way. Then he stood back to allow Z and Blaze access while he guarded Francis Worsham.

Z stepped through the door and nearly gagged. Her right hand went to her throat. "My God. Those bastards. Those freaking low-life bastards."

Before her were three two-way mirror windows into the dressing room Connie Latham had used and described to her. The same dressing room she had, herself, examined recently. A chair had been installed behind the center mirror window where some scumbag could sit and watch as young girls undressed just inches away, unaware they were being watched and sized up like cattle at an auction.

Blaze was silent behind her, taking everything in.

Z said, "That black room right there." She pointed behind her to the three-foot space between the two doors. "A person could enter it and close the door. And when he opened the door to this…this…*viewing room*, no one would ever see a flash of light behind those mirrors. They could enter here, silently, undetected until…"

She turned and backed out into the storeroom and asked Francis, "A person could remain hidden in that room in there until what, Francis? How does he get access into the dressing room?"

"I don't know! Please stop! He'll kill me!"

"Who will kill you, Francis?"

"My brother!"

"Why will he kill you, Francis?"

"Because he said so!"

"If he threatened you, why didn't you call the police, Francis?" Z asked, voice calm.

"Because he *is* the police! Who would have believed me?"

"And his name?" Z, still calm.

"Hadeon Cook!" Francis collapsed onto the boxes and cried.

Z and Blaze exchanged a look. They had him. All that remained was for forensics to go over every inch of this place. His fingerprints and DNA had to be in here. Nobody is that careful all the time. They had him.

They ignored her distress and continued questioning Francis Worsham.

"How does he get into the dressing room, Francis?" Z continued asking.

"I really don't know. He never allowed me to go in there. I don't know how he did it."

"He couldn't have done all this on his own. Who worked with him on this?" Blaze asked her.

"His partner, Donny Ray Swift."

"Anybody else?"

"No. Nobody else that I ever saw or knew about."

"JJ, guard Miss Worsham," Z said. "I'm going around, Blaze. When I get inside the dressing room, see if you can figure out how to open the mirror wall for access."

Z demanded the key to the dressing room from Miss Worsham and headed back into the shop while Blaze donned rubber gloves to check out the viewing room.

Once in the dressing room, Z closed the door and looked around. She could see nothing but her own reflection in the three large mirrors. There was no indication anything—or anyone—was beyond those mirrors. As she continued to examine the mirrors, she heard a click and a muffled shout from behind them.

"Try the door!" Blaze shouted to her.

She reached out for the dressing room door to find it, somehow, locked. She was trapped inside.

"It's locked!" she shouted back.

"Okay! Try it now!" Blaze's muffled voice answered her.

She heard another click and when she tried the door again, it opened easily. She turned and nodded to the Blaze she could not see beyond the mirrors.

She was still examining the edge of the mirror to her left when the mirror to the right of the small dressing room opened and Blaze stepped inside.

"So that's how the monster did it."

"Looks like."

Z and Blaze backed out of the dressing room through the mirror wall, viewing room, blacked-out closet, and into the stockroom once again.

Z eyed Francis Worsham steadily. For all her effort she could not summon the slightest compassion for this woman. She turned to JJ. "Get forensics over here right away, JJ. And put up crime scene tape on the front and back of this store."

She turned back to Francis Worsham and asked, "You knew what he was doing, didn't you, Francis? You watched those young girls go into that dressing room knowing what was going on, didn't you? Knowing what was happening and going to happen to them, didn't you?"

"Yes," Francis whispered.

"Where is your brother now? I noticed he and his partner were not at the police station yesterday afternoon. Where is he?"

"I don't know."

"I swear to God if you don't tell me, I'm going to personally beat the shit out of you right here and now!" Z had raised her voice. This was uncharacteristic but she was livid and her patience was at an end.

"I really don't know." Francis pleaded. "He and Donny Ray take a vacation every year. No. Sorry. They take two vacations. One in early May and one in early November. I don't know where they go. He would never tell me and I was afraid to ask."

"They take vacations together? Have they already gone?" Z's voice was beginning to have a panicked edge of its own.

"Yes. They left last night."

"Oh my god, Blaze! We've missed them! We've missed them!"

Blaze tried to reassure her. "Maybe not. The man Captain Taylor sent down to keep watch never called in any problems. So we don't know that we've missed them. But if we have, we will find them. Someone knows where they are. We'll find them."

Z turned to Francis. "Francis Worsham, I'm arresting you on suspicion of aiding and abetting human trafficking out of this shop. If you cooperate in all matters, things will go much easier for you. But make no mistake, you are going to prison for this."

Z closed her eyes for a moment to steady herself. Then, "JJ, take her into custody and…read her her rights." There was no way to hide her disdain and disgust. She didn't even try.

⌘

Once forensics and uniforms arrived at the dress shop, Z and Blaze turned it over to them and hurriedly made their way back to the police station. In the car Z mused, "I don't think she really does know where they went, Blaze. I think she's truly terrified of her brother. How are we going to find them?"

"Don't worry. We'll find them. If it's the last thing I ever do. We'll find them."

They sat in the car for a few minutes without starting it, each digesting what had just been discovered.

Breaking the silence, Blaze chuckled.

"What's so funny?"

"The Black Hole of Calcutta." He laughed. "Where did you ever come up with that?"

"My grandma." She turned to Blaze. "It was a perfect fit, though."

"How's that?"

"The site of a tragedy. Look it up."

"I might just do that."

Z scratched her head and turned to Blaze. "Why would someone go to the expense of constructing such an elaborate room to capture girls for trafficking? Surely there are easier ways. Just snatching them off the street would be a lot easier."

"True," Blaze said, "but that place is one where they would never be seen. Even loading the unconscious girls into their transport vehicle—whatever it was—wouldn't be likely seen so close to the back door. Plus, it's just an ordinary place of business where people come and go all the time. And the cost of the renovation to turn the place into a trafficking den would be more than paid for by the taking of just one unsuspecting girl. Think how much they could make by taking several girls a year. It's probably more than most people can make here in ten years. But you know the most diabolical thing about it of all?"

"Yes. Their victims come to them."

"Exactly."

Z became pensive. "Have we missed them, Blaze? Have I missed Zeena?"

"We can't know yet. But no matter what, we will find them wherever they are, Zakaya-Zee. Don't you worry. We'll get them. And you will get Zeena back, too. I promise you."

She was silent then for a few minutes before speaking up. "That judge better be back and issue that warrant for those scum at that blue house or I'm going without it. And that," she added, "I promise you!"

44

Z's CIMA-2 team members, Parker West and Gray Hawk, had come into the country via Mexico as tourists. Once across the border into Texas, they had taken an air-taxi from Brownsville to a small, private airfield in the southern end of Crimson City. Viking, the team leader, stayed behind in Matamoros, Mexico, making arrangements to get the team out of harm's way and back to Cascadia once this mission was over.

Matamoros had been chosen because it gave them easy access to the border and was also closer to Cascadia than Merida, the rescue site of their mission two years ago. That closer distance would make the trip home a shorter one—something always to be desired. The problem was that Viking remained as in-the-dark as Zakaya was herself. He had no idea where this whole thing was going to lead, but he busied himself making contingent plans for every scenario he could imagine might actually come about. He just needed a final word from Z in order to narrow and nail everything down.

Gray's and Parker's flight on the small prop plane had been fairly smooth but loud. The pilot hadn't seemed to take much notice of their rather military appearance in their dun-colored cargoes and had asked no questions. The small plane touched down, uneventfully, about thirty minutes before Z and Blaze entered Francis Worsham's

Glamour Girl dress shop. From the airfield they hired a taxi to take them a short distance from the coordinates of the blue house that Z had given to Viking.

Hunkering down some distance from the house, they could see it well enough through the foliage of the dense woods yet remain hidden from any eyes searching the area in their own direction. They had watched for at least forty-five minutes but had neither seen nor heard anything unusual taking place there. As far as they could discern from their position, there was no movement at the house at all. They could see the rutted drive leading to the front of the house, but they did not have a view of the actual front door from their position. They considered making a move, but Gray advised against. While he could, himself, negotiate woods without making a sound, Parker could not. It was best, they decided, to wait and see what happened. And wait for word from Z before they moved.

Z entered the police station and flew into the captain's office like a threatening storm.

"I told you there was trafficking going on here! Why wouldn't you listen? Why are you people so hard-headed?"

"Whoa!" Captain Taylor held up his hands in surrender. "What has happened? What have you found out?"

"Everything! Everything your sorry fast-food detectives failed to find out—and why. We solved your Kind Killer case, and we are hot on the trail of human traffickers—and don't you dare tell me there's no trafficking going on here! They are right under your nose!"

"What do you mean?"

"It's no wonder you can't seem to solve cases. You've got criminals investigating their own crimes! Your good-for-nothing detectives are part and parcel of the trafficking going on here. We have the proof. Hadeon Cook's sister has been arrested for her part in the whole operation and we are going after Cook and Swift just as soon as we get that warrant from the judge who had damned well better be back from his crappy fishing vacation!" She paused and drew a breath. "Furthermore, you had better get your big-boy pants on and arrest Sheriff Cook, because I'm almost certain he's part of the whole thing as well. For crying out loud, man, check their bank accounts if you do nothing else! And, finally, it would be wise of you to collect every speck of DNA from Cook's and Swift's desks over there to compare with the DNA found on those pink panties that belonged to Tiki Jameson! Remember her? Dead girl tossed like garbage in a ditch after being sexually abused and then strangled to death? I think you will find a match and close that case as well!"

Captain Taylor turned and yelled. "Mike! Get some crime scene tape in here right now and cordon off Cook's and Swift's desks over there. Nobody! And I mean nobody," he shouted to the squad room, "had better touch anything on those desks or anywhere near them. Do you understand?" On getting wide-eyed and open-mouthed nods, he turned back into his office. "Miss…er…Detective…I can't thank you enough for all you have done here. This job is hard enough, but when your own commit crimes it becomes nearly impossible."

"The warrant?" Z asked, impatient and eager to be on her way.

"You've got it. Now what?"

"Now we are going to catch us some traffickers and, if we are able, save some young girls."

♥♥♥

Z left the police station in as big a whirl as she had entered it.

She opened the rental's trunk and grabbed her holstered SIG. She didn't want to take the time to change into the cargos or don her boots. She turned to Blaze as she strapped on the weapon. "I'm driving this time, Blaze. Get in!"

"Yes, Ma'am!"

The two of them got into her rental and she spun wheels leaving the police station parking lot.

"Easy! Easy!" Blaze cautioned. "We're in town here. People are shopping. Kids are playing. Slow down."

"Sorry."

She eased back on the accelerator until they reached the outskirts of downtown proper and then she began to speed up again until, glancing in the rearview mirror, she saw someone behind them she recognized. A couple of someones. A couple of someones that spelled trouble. And right now she had no time for trouble. She eased up on the speed to see what those someones would do. As she suspected, they eased up on their speed, too.

"What's wrong?" Blaze was suspicious.

"Nothing." She neither had the time nor inclination to explain anything to Blaze right now.

She drove on for about a mile until her patience with the tailgaters was at an end. Then, she deliberately increased speed. When the car behind increased speed to keep up, in one abrupt move, she hit hard on the brakes causing the car behind them to brake and swerve into the ditch that ran along the side of the road. The ditch was deep enough the car wouldn't be going anywhere until a tow truck had pulled it free. And that meant the occupants would be going nowhere as well.

She reduced speed back to normal and looked in the rearview mirror once more to see two men emerging from the vehicle and shaking their fists at her. The driver was punching up someone on his t-com.

"What the hell? Why did you do that?" Blaze asked while looking back at the two men standing in the road behind them.

"I didn't like their looks."

Blaze tried but could not suppress a laugh. Z looked over at him and laughed back.

"Aren't you even going to check on them?"

"They'll be all right." She couldn't keep from smiling at the thought of the two of them stuck back there, unable to exact their revenge on her for leaving them tied up in that Atlanta motel two years ago when the team extracted Parker from their grasp.

It wasn't two minutes later that she noticed Big Ugly's sidekick was also following them.

"Now what?" she asked aloud, the aggravation in her voice unmistakable.

"Now what, what?" Blaze wanted to know.

She pointed over her shoulder behind them.

"We have more company. This must just be our lucky day."

Blaze turned and looked behind them to see Sidekick talking on his t-com. He turned back around. "He's harmless. Doesn't even have his big ugly buddy with him."

Fewer than five minutes later, Blaze's own t-com buzzed. It was Dark Suit.

He clicked off without answering.

⌘

In the car behind Z's rental, Sidekick was talking to Big Ugly on his t-com.

"They're headin' your way, Will! I told you they was looking for something at that old house down there. I think that's exactly where they're headed. The Black woman is driving, and she just ran a car off the road a couple of minutes ago. Not sure what that was all about, but she definitely caused it to go into the ditch and she did it on purpose. Then she didn't even stop. Never seen anything like that in my life."

Big Ugly became excited. "How far are they from the farm here?"

"Maybe eight or ten minutes. Not exactly sure."

"That's enough time. You know what we planned. Just keep following them and be ready! I'm gettin' in my truck now. The old green one she's never seen before. I'll drive up the road about a mile and get everything set up."

"I just don't like this, Will. We gonna get into some serious trouble if we do this thing."

"Just keep watchin' her and do what we planned or so help me—"

"Okay! Okay!"

☙☙

Back at FBI headquarters, Dark Suit was pissed when Blaze refused to answer his t-com and so called in Dotty Hightower, Blaze's partner. She hadn't been needed in Alabama and had been working solo there in Washington while Blaze was off on his current assignment checking on the identity of Zakaya Kalu.

Hightower was the kind of woman who was all-business. She stood over six feet tall and had straight, bobbed blonde hair. She always looked as if she had just stepped out of a photoshoot. This appealed greatly to Dark Suit while Blaze had found it a bit pretentious and, quite frankly, unattractive.

"Dotty!" Dark Suit pushed papers aside and stood at his desk when she entered the room.

"Sir?"

"Blaze is down in Alabama working with our primary suspect in that Blue-7 case from two years ago. You might remember that one."

"Yes, sir. I remember it."

"Well, I can't tell if he's serious about nabbing her once they finish up with a human trafficking case they are working together—a long story, that—or not. We now know she's definitely one of the people from that Cascadian team we've been looking for. She just ran two of our agents off the road down there and, according to the agents, Blaze was in the car with her. I don't know what kind of game he's playing down there."

"He's always seemed straight-forward to me, Sir, but I couldn't say about this situation there. Has he been checking in?"

"Yes. That's the weird thing. I told him to find a way to keep her in the country until we were sure she was one of the people we are after and so he arranged for her to work with the local police there on a human trafficking case. Seems her little girl was taken and she's determined to find her. All that seemed real enough. But I'm beginning to wonder what else is going on down there so I'm thinking of sending you down to find out and to arrest her at the first opportunity. You up for that?"

"Yes, sir."

"Still…" Dark Suit paused in thought. "If they really can bring down a human trafficking operation, it will look damned good for the Bureau. Tell you what. You get on down there and see what you can find out and let me know. We'll see what to do then."

"Yes, sir."

45

Z never let her foot off the accelerator for miles until she headed into a blind curve and saw an old truck sideways on the pavement ahead, blocking the road. She slammed on the brakes nearly sending Blaze through the windshield.

"Holy shit!"

"Oh my god!"

A body lay face down in the road just to the side of the truck.

Z released her seatbelt and leaped from the rental to see what she could do to help while Blaze struggled and cursed at his own seatbelt that had stuck and would not release.

The truck's door on the driver's side was open but there didn't appear to have been an accident. This was concerning to the cautious Z. Perhaps the man had had a heart attack. She reached out slowly to the body. "Are you all right?" She jiggled his shoulder. "Sir?"

When no response was forthcoming, she pulled on the shoulder to turn the body face up. The man rolled slowly over.

It was Big Ugly. He was smiling and holding a pistol aimed directly at her head.

"It's fully loaded this time, Missy. And I will sure as hell shoot you right here in the road if you don't do exactly as I say."

A thump was heard behind her and she turned to see Blaze slumped over unconscious as Sidekick hit him on the back of the head with his own pistol before cutting the seatbelt and tossing him into the ditch along the shoulder of the road.

She turned back to Big Ugly who said, "I'll have your weapon."

Z handed over the SIG. He looked it over. "Nice!" He pocketed his own pistol and kept the SIG pointed at Z.

She looked away.

"Let's just get in your car. You will drive. Let's go!" He directed her back to her rental.

"Bobby!" he shouted to Sidekick. "Drive my truck back to the farm. We'll come back and pick up your car later. Then come on to the barn." He motioned Z toward the car.

Z slid into the driver's seat and started the car.

The only thing on her mind was that they were going to be late to rescue those girls. And Zeena. Everything in her screamed to be rid of this nasty, stupid man once and for all. But at the moment, he had her own loaded weapon trained on her, and Blaze was unconscious in a ditch. The odds didn't look good here.

He directed her to a small dirt road that led up to a farm but told her to turn before getting to the house and drive to a barn several hundred yards away that appeared all but derelict. There, they got out and he pushed her forward into the barn.

A chair had been placed in the center of the large open room. Big Ugly pointed to it and told Z to have a seat. He handcuffed her to it with a pair of old-fashioned keyed cuffs. He shoved the key into his pocket.

"Do you treat all your guests like this?" she asked him.

"Shut up," he said as he unfastened her t-com from her wrist and began fiddling with it.

Z looked around the building. Nothing to see. It was apparently never used. Dust motes floated on light rays coming through a window to her left. There was another window directly across the huge, empty room to her right. The light from both windows served to illuminate the agitated dust specks caused by the disturbance of the big guy's shoes as he stomped around.

He was examining her t-com. "This don't look like an ordinary t-com. Where'd you get it?"

"Cascadia."

"Right. And I'm from the moon." He spat on the floor. "What's this? The top opens?"

"Yes."

He fiddled around with it until he found the release and the top of the t-com flew open. "What's all this?"

"Just a record button there."

"Is that this red one?"

"No!" Z acted agitated and nervous. "Please don't press the red one!"

Come on...come on...press it!

"Why not?"

"Because."

He slapped her across the face. Hard. "I asked you a question."

"Because if you press the red button it will erase all the memory. Please don't."

He laughed and held it up to her face as he pushed the button down.

You stupid ass. You have just hung yourself.

It was all she could do to look upset.

"What say I just stomp this entire gadget into little pieces, hey?"

"Please don't." She looked at him with a tilted head. "I wonder what Alice would think of what you are doing right now."

That took him by surprise. "What do you know about my Alice?" he demanded.

"I know she's probably a sweet little girl who loves her daddy."

"Stop talking about her." He was visibly shaken that she knew about his daughter. Z's t-com remained safely in his hand.

"Okay…but…" Z hesitated, watching him. "But did you know that we, my partner and I, were on our way to saving some young girls from some very bad men. Young girls probably around the same age as your Alice."

"Stop saying her name!"

"These men. They abduct young girls and then they sell them as slaves for work or for sex—most likely to people outside this country. And then these girls are never heard from again. How would you feel if one of those girls was your Alice?"

"I told you to stop saying her name!" Big Ugly was becoming very agitated and began pacing the floor in front of the handcuffed Zakaya. He absent-mindedly shoved her t-com into his pocket as he paced.

ↁↁↁ

The moment Big Ugly pressed the red button on Z's t-com, all members of the team received an emergency alert with the ID of the broadcasting t-com and its exact geographic coordinates. Even Tillerman and the team members back in Cascadia were alerted.

When Viking saw the alert, he buzzed Gray and Parker. "Z needs help!"

"We saw it! We're on our way!" Parker yelled as he slung his backpack onto his shoulder. "It's not far from where we have been watching the trafficking house here. Gray estimates it's about a mile and a quarter, straight."

"Do not let anything happen to her, you hear me?!"

"Like you need to tell us?" Parker was nearly breathless as he and Gray were huffing it through the woods and checking directions on their own t-coms with the coordinates Z's t-com had broadcast.

"Keep me informed!" Viking hated not being there. He hated having to wait for word. But he knew if there was any way to save Zakaya Kalu, Gray and Parker would do it. They were the best of the best of CIMA. Meanwhile, he was still in Mexico working on transportation for them out of the US once the mission was over.

Viking clicked off as Gray and Parker emerged from the woods onto a secondary, paved road. They followed the road for half a mile and then left it, heading west.

"How far?" Parker asked Gray.

"About another quarter mile." Gray hesitated and looked at his t-com. He indicated the direction with a hand-chop. "That way!"

Minutes later, Gray held up a warning hand. "Looks like some kind of farm. She's not at the house there, though. She's over there." He pointed in the direction of the barn.

"Quiet. Quiet." Gray warned and signaled to Parker. "Circle around to the other side where there's cover." He pointed to a stand of trees on the far side of the barn.

They made their way carefully around the barn, giving it a wide berth. Once on the other side, among the scrub oaks and high weeds, they hunkered down and Parker dropped his backpack to his side and opened it. He began assembling his rifle. He snapped and locked the barrel and then the optics. Optics in place, he took a look.

The only window on his side was either well-placed or Zakaya was. The problem was the window was dirty. He doubted it had ever been cleaned and its age had left waves in the ever-moving liquid of the glass. Still, with light from the far side window he could make out the silhouettes of two figures inside.

"There's a man in there. He's standing over Z. Looks like she's in a chair but I can only see her head and shoulders. Maybe he has her tied up."

"You have a shot?" Gray asked.

"No. He keeps walking around. When he stops…" Parker shifted his position slightly and moved his finger to the trigger. "Come on…come on…"

⌘

Z watched as Big Ugly paced the floor. He was thinking. That was good for her. She hoped. Gray and Parker were on the way. She only needed to stall this man until they arrived.

She asked, "Why does a successful guy like you feel it necessary to pick on someone like me?"

This question stopped the big man in his tracks. "What the hell are you talking about? Do I look successful to you?"

Z found his response interesting in that, for a moment, he dropped her completely from thought, and focused entirely on the description of himself as successful. It seemed to have caught him by as much surprise as a punch in the gut might have done. This was good.

"Looks don't mean anything, Will. Appears to me you have a farm here that could be productive with a little work. And it wasn't your fault you were laid off from the lumber mill. Lots of people lost their jobs at that time. The economy here isn't very good at the moment. That's not your fault, either."

"Yeah. We're all big successes." He continued pacing back and forth.

Z kept trying. "Look how you have taken care of Alice and her mother with such love and care. That's the mark of a successful man, Will."

She had used his name twice now and he had said nothing, but the mention of Alice and his wife once again stirred his anger.

"They deserve the best. And I told you to stop saying her name, damn you!"

When Z said nothing to that, he stopped pacing and turned to her. "I hate all you Blacks. Every last one of you. You are all worthless!"

"I don't feel worthless, Will."

He laughed. "Well, look at where Miss High-And-Mighty is right now!"

"Not my choice," she said, her voice steady.

"Not my choice one of your kind, drunk as a lord, ran into my car and paralyzed my little girl. You Black people are all alike! Shiftless! Reckless! Worthless!"

"I didn't run into your car."

"Shut up!"

"You know, Will," she said, once again using his given name, "if you harm me you will go to prison. Then what will your wife do? How will she take care of Alice all by herself?"

"Damn you!" He waved the pistol in the air and came really close to her. He leaned over, his face so close his whiskers touched her lips. "I told you not to talk about my daughter, you Black bitch!"

It occurred to Z that his sidekick had never shown up the whole time she had been here. She decided to change direction and asked, "Where's your buddy? He abandon you? You really have nobody to count on, do you?"

"Shut up!"

"He's had plenty of time to come help you out with your dirty deed. Where is he?"

"I told you to shut up!"

Where the hell are Gray and Parker?

Z needed more time. She picked up the taunting of Big Ugly about his little girl. "Poor little Alice. She won't have a father to help take care of her." She wasn't about to let up now. She was gauging the time since he had depressed the emergency t-com button. She could only guess how long it had been. And she could only guess where Parker and Gray were when they got the call. She suspected they were not far from the blue house, and she knew she and Blaze had been less than a couple of miles from there when ambushed. She decided they should be here very soon. If they weren't here already.

"Poor Alice. She will have no one at all."

Big Ugly backed off and slapped her so hard her left ear rang. Determined, she continued, "Poor Alice. It will be hard for her."

At this, he let out an animal growl and lifted her own SIG to her head.

Z closed her eyes.

"Goodbye, you Black witch!" He was smiling when a shot rang out, the window's glass shattered, and the SIG flew into the air. Blood spurted from his hand. He screamed, dropping the pistol to the floor at the same time Gray came bursting through the barn doors. Parker was no more than five seconds behind him, his rifle aimed square on Big Ugly who was still groaning in pain.

"I'll have the keys to the handcuffs." Gray held out a hand and gave Big Ugly a withering look as the big guy clumsily burrowed his one good hand into his opposite side pocket and withdrew the key.

Gray wasted no time freeing Z who immediately scrambled for her SIG, then turned and kicked the big guy in the shin. "That's for calling me names, you sorry trash."

Big Ugly only grimaced, holding onto his bleeding hand.

"I'll have my t-com back, too, asshole."

With her t-com, she punched up JJ with their coordinates and a quick description of the situation. "You need to get some…*special* help out here to take this guy in. Get his sidekick, too. Another kick in the shin and I'll have his address for you."

No kick was necessary. Big Ugly was more than willing to give up his friend and Z relayed the information to JJ who told her he would call on the Selma Blues to come and get them since they were closer.

Not fifteen minutes later, Eli McClain came barging through the barn doors with his Selma Blues buddies. After giving Zakaya one of his most endearing smiles, he took charge of Ugly and whisked him away in less than a minute.

Z and her team headed outside. "We've been held up too long. We were already cutting it close. What if we've missed them…?" she muttered under her breath as they exited the barn. Once outside, she turned to Parker.

"That was one helluva shot, Parks."

He grinned at her. "It was a terrible shot."

"What are you talking about? It was perfect!"

"I was aiming at his head."

She friendly-punched him in the shoulder and laughed. Then raised a hand. "Hold up!"

"What's wrong?" Gray wanted to know.

"I need some things from my rental car here. Just a second."

She opened the trunk, ripped off her jeans, grabbed the cargo pants, and slid into them. She donned the boots and grabbed the already-loaded extra magazines, stuffing them into the extra pockets of her cargoes, then turned back.

"Let's go!"

She started to get into the rental when Gray held her up.

"Z! Straight line will be quicker." He nodded in the direction from which he and Parker had come earlier.

She nodded. She had never known the usually quiet Gray to be wrong when he spoke up on a mission and she was not about to second-guess him now. Time was critical.

They started off at a trot but soon began to pick up the pace with Gray leading the way via the shortest distance to the house.

Halfway there, crossing a short stint of paved road, they saw Blaze trotting toward them.

The moment he saw Parker and Gray he pulled his weapon.

Z stepped in front of them and held up her hand. "Stop!"

"You know these guys?"

"You might say that." She turned to look at them and then turned back to Blaze. "This is Gray, my partner back in Cascadia." She indicated Gray Hawk with a nod. "And this is Parker who just saved my ass from that big ugly moron." She turned back to Parker and Gray and said, "This is Martin Blaze, my sort-of partner here who just got pistol-whipped by the moron's sidekick."

Blaze holstered his weapon and said, "How...?" but then stopped.

Z could see he was curious about how these two had suddenly shown up, but apparently decided not to pursue the question. At least for now. That suited Z. She had too much on her mind for explanations right this minute.

Blaze grimaced and rubbed his head.

"Are you okay?" Z asked him.

"I have a headache."

"Yeah, tell me about it." Her left ear was still ringing.

46

The four of them slowed their pace as they arrived near the blue house and slowly negotiated the woods to the backside where Gray and Parker had been hunkered down when Z's distress call came in. There was still no discernible movement at or around the place. Worse, everything was silent.

Z's heart sank. "We've missed them. Zeena...."

"Maybe." Gray motioned for them to split up and move around the sides of the house, meeting at the front. Parker and Blaze took the left side of the house while he and Z circled the other.

Parker and Blaze were keeping a low profile as they moved carefully through the high weeds that surrounded the house. They moved as silently as they could. Blaze was several yards behind him when Parker heard a halfway-muffled, "Oof!" He looked back to see Blaze lying in the weeds and quickly backtracked to see what had happened.

Blaze was lying perpendicular to, and across the body of, a uniformed policeman.

"Shit!" Blaze swore under his breath and rolled off the body onto his knees and took a look. The officer had been shot in the head at close range. "No wonder he never called in last night. Why wasn't someone sent down here with him?"

Parker let out a breath. "Then you would have had two dead policemen instead of one."

Blaze looked up at him. "Right." He got up and checked himself over but found no blood. He had fallen across the man's legs, away from the carnage of his head. He said to Parker, "Where is his vehicle? And how are we going to tell Zakaya?"

"The car will be found, wherever it is. And Z's going to know everything soon enough. Let's go."

❧❧❧

As Gray and Z moved cautiously around the other side of the house, they heard the ominous sound of…silence. Even the birds had ceased their chirping. As they turned the corner at the front of the house they had expected to meet Parker and Blaze, but were met, instead, with the sound of a low chuckle.

Z stopped cold. There, sitting on the front doorsteps was her Uncle Bo, humming to himself and happily counting a huge fistful of dollars. He looked up to see Parker and Blaze come into view around the left corner of the house and froze. Parker's sniper rifle was pointed dead at him. He looked to escape to his right only to find Z's SIG in his face.

Blaze had started to unholster his own weapon but decided it wasn't needed and slid it back into its leather.

"You low-life piece of scum!" Z screamed at him, waving the SIG. "Where are the girls?"

"What girls?" Bo smiled through his feigned ignorance.

"Where are they?" Z shouted again and lunged for him. Gray held her back.

"Let me go!" she shouted. "I'm going to kill him!"

Her Uncle Bo did the worst thing he could have done at that moment. He laughed at her.

With Gray still holding her around the waist, she raised her arm and shot him in the knee. He screamed and dropped the money. It flew all over the steps and down into the yard like gray-green leaves in a small whirlwind.

"I will shoot the other one if you don't tell me where those girls are! You've got just about two seconds!"

"Okay! Okay!" Bo was moaning and holding his leg.

"Where are they?"

Uncle Bo looked up and whined. "I don't know exactly. They just rent the house from me and I don't ask questions."

"I'll just bet." Z didn't believe a word falling out of his lying mouth. "So tell us what you *do* know, asshole!"

"I need help with my leg here, Z!" Bo whine-begged her.

"You'll get help when we get the information. Now where are those girls?"

"I told you. I don't know."

Z aimed the SIG at his remaining good knee and Bo held up a defending hand.

"Okay! Okay! All I know is two guys rent this place and they bring girls here. They keep guards here when there are girls in the house but I don't know who they are."

"What else? Who are the guys who rent the house? Names!"

"Two police officers. Hadeon Cook is the one who does all the business, and the other one is Donny something. I can't remember his name. He wasn't around much. Cook did all the talking and payments and stuff."

"What else?"

"They rent the house all year. And twice a year they leave. Everybody leaves."

"When do they leave?"

"May. And November. Now." Bo continued to moan and hold his bleeding leg. "I need help, Z!"

She ignored him. "How do they take the girls away?"

"A van comes and they load them up and head out."

"Where do they go?"

"I don't know."

"It would give me the greatest pleasure for my next shot to go right between your legs." Z half-whispered the threat and Bo's eyes grew wide.

"They go somewhere on the coast. Mobile. Yeah, yeah! Mobile! They take a fishing boat—trawler—whatever those things are called."

"What's the name of the fishing boat?"

"Something like *Big Minnow*. No...I think it's the *Giant Minnow*. I heard the guards laughing about the name once."

"Then what? Where does this *Giant Minnow* go?

"They go out in the Gulf and meet up with a yacht. I don't know who owns the yacht. Some guy with lots of money."

"The hand-off is on a yacht?"

"Yes. As far as I know. I've never been."

"Who owns the yacht? He American?"

"I don't know."

"What happens then?"

"I've heard the rich guy turns around and sells the girls to individual buyers. Probably in some other country. I don't know."

Z backed off and looked around at Blaze. "You familiar with Mobile? Fishing boats and docks?"

"Not really, but we'll find them."

"You better hurry then," Bo said, again taunting Z. "They left in the middle of the night last night. They probably already on the water and heading out for that yacht with all that sweet, young merchandise."

Z's head began to spin and Bo's face faded into a blur. She thought back to the mission two years ago when she had freed Zeena. On the coast. That was in November, too. Right about this time of year. Questions crowded her mind. Why wasn't Zeena taken to the yacht? How did she end up at a Florida motel? Did she escape? No…she couldn't have escaped. Was she sold off before the fishing boat set out to meet the yacht? Horrible thought! She might never know. Right now she didn't even want to know. She just wanted to find Zeena.

Z was angry and turned to Blaze. "Why didn't that officer the captain sent down here to keep watch call it in when they took the girls? What was he doing? Sleeping?"

Blaze reached out a hand but she backed away. He said, "He was dead, Z. They must have discovered him here. They shot him."

She put her hand to her forehead and looked around. She started to speak but stopped when she heard a siren sounding in the near distance. Within seconds, JJ in his own squad car and a couple of other police vehicles pulled into the weedy drive and stopped not ten yards from them.

"JJ!" Z looked puzzled. "How"—"

"I called him when I found the officer's body." Blaze told her. "We need to save as much time as we can now."

Z nodded at Blaze, then turned to JJ. "JJ, take my—this *person*—to jail and charge him with aiding and abetting human trafficking and anything else you can think of. He's done more than just rent a house. I'd bet my life on it. Charge him with the murder of that police officer, too, until we find out otherwise from forensics and the M.E."

"You got it, Z." JJ turned to Bo who was loudly protesting his innocence. "Let's go."

"JJ! Wait!" Z called to him as he was about to shove Bo into the squad car. "We need transportation to the coast. Fast transportation!"

"Okay! Hang on!" JJ punched up someone on his t-com. A bit of mumbling, hand gestures, and head shaking and he turned to Z and the rest. "You'll have a chopper out on the main road in a matter of minutes." He pointed over his shoulder, thumbing the direction of the paved county road just beyond Forest Lane.

"How did you manage that?" Z asked.

"The captain. He said he would send anything you need. There's an Army support base over in Birmingham. Captain called in a favor." He grinned at Z. "I told you the captain was a good guy."

"Thanks, JJ." She started to walk away, then stopped and turned back. She walked up to her uncle and looked him steadily in the eye for a long moment, then kicked him in the same knee she had shot just minutes earlier. Hard. "Rot, you sorry bastard!"

JJ pushed the screaming Bo into the squad car and slammed the door. "Good luck, Z!"

She nodded to him as he slid into the driver's seat. The squad cars backed away and drove back to Crimson City. One remained to wait for forensics and the medical examiner to arrive for the downed officer.

Z turned to her team and the four of them walked out to the paved road to meet the chopper.

They had trudged, without noticing, over Bo's money still strewn about on the steps and the weedy drive.

47

The chopper landed in the middle of the paved road. They had heard it coming for nearly a minute. Z's jaw dropped as the wind whipped up by the monster aircraft bent the nearby treetops close to cracking. She landed a few yards from them, looking ominous with the words "Mighty Kong" across her nose and a painting of a huge gorilla on her sides.

Z shook her head. "No one in this country can afford a decent car anymore, but the government always has military equipment bursting at the seams. Glad to get it, though. This thing looks fast."

Blaze looked it over. "It is. It does over two hundred miles per hour and will get us to the coast in less than an hour if my guess is correct."

The four of them climbed aboard and, true to Blaze's guess, they were in Mobile in record time. The chopper was left on stand-by while they made their way to the harbor via the services of the local police—transportation arranged mysteriously by Blaze after speaking privately to the pilot.

Z, ever suspicious, decided that Blaze sure did have a lot of pull with authorities for a private detective. But hot on the trail of traffickers who had Zeena, she wasn't about to question it. Not right now, anyway.

In fewer than ten minutes they were at the harbor. The murky water lapping the docks smelled of fish and glistened with the iridescent rainbow sheen of motor oil and gasoline. They located the Harbormaster's office and inquired about the *Giant Minnow*.

"Lemme check on that," he said. He eyed the team suspiciously but the presence of the red and blues whirling atop the police car just outside the office windows convinced him they were probably okay. He checked his log.

"Yep. The *Giant Minnow*. She left about noon. Eleven forty-two to be exact."

"Her destination?" Z was wasting no time with niceties.

The Harbormaster eyed her curiously. "Well, she's a fishing trawler so my guess is she went out fishing in the Gulf."

"How big?"

"Ummm. She's a big 'un. Carries maybe thirty, forty people."

"How many were aboard?"

"Just the crew and a couple of passengers."

Blaze and Z gave each other a look. Only two passengers? On a boat that could take thirty or forty? Z was worried. Had they missed them? Was her uncle's information deliberately wrong?

"Where are the girls, Blaze?"

Blaze looked just as worried as she was and shook his head. He didn't know.

Z turned back to the Harbormaster. "You're sure there were just two passengers? They didn't have a group of young girls with them?"

"No, Ma'am. Just the two passengers." the Harbormaster assured her.

Z flashed a worried look at Blaze.

"Maybe the girls are on another boat and they meet up with them out in the Gulf," he suggested.

She thought about that for a minute then turned to Parker whose family in Cascadia was quite wealthy and was familiar with watercraft.

"Parks, a fishing trawler can't be too fast, can it? I mean, it can't have gotten very far out into the Gulf yet, can it?"

Parker took a breath in preparation to speak but was interrupted by the harbormaster.

"Oh, she's pretty fast, the *Minnow* is," Harbormaster said. "The owner had 'er special built. Not sure just how fast, but I swear if she had wings she could fly."

Z looked at each of the team. She whispered more to herself than to anyone else, "Must be a Surface Effect..."

Parker nodded agreement and the harbormaster picked up his thought as though there had been no interruption. "I'd wager she can do upwards of ninety-five knots in calm waters. Be a bit slower in chop, though."

Z thought on that for a second then asked, "What kind of passengers?"

"Beg pardon?" Harbormaster knitted his brows at the sudden change of direction.

"You said there were just two passengers. What kind of passengers were on board the *Minnow* when she left harbor today?"

"Oh. Just two guys. I've seen 'em before. They come twice a year like clockwork, those two. They must really like fishing."

"You see them this time?"

"Oh, sure. The *Minnow* docks just two slips down." He pointed to his left.

"What did they look like?"

"Just guys. Say...what's this all about anyway?"

Z ignored the question and repeated. "What did they look like?"

"They just look like regular guys. One is tall and fairly slim. The other is shorter and a bit on the pudgy side."

"Anything else?"

"Well, I hate to say, but the taller one has this look about him."

"What kind of look?"

"Dunno. I mean I don't know what other people would say, but to me, he looks kind of mean. Don't think I've ever seen 'im smile."

Z turned to Blaze. "Cook and Swift."

He nodded, then asked the harbormaster, "Who owns her?"

"The *Minnow*?"

The four of them looked at him impatiently. Parker and Gray were standing behind Z and Blaze, blocking the entrance. They shifted menacingly while Z and Blaze waited for an answer.

The harbormaster tore a worried gaze from the two by the door and looked once again at Blaze and Z. "Well, I don't know why the police are here...."

"Who owns the *Minnow*?" Z raised her voice. "Look. We are in a very big hurry here and don't have time for you to pussy-foot around. Now who owns that boat?"

Harbormaster sighed. "Senator Hodwin." He shoved his hands in his pockets.

"H*odwin*?" Blaze was gobsmacked. "You mean State Senator Hodwin? From Birmingham?"

"Yes, sir. He's the one."

"Was he on board when the boat left harbor?"

"No. Not him. I've never known him to go fishing. He just owns the boat and collects the money, I guess."

Blaze shifted his weight, turned to Z, then turned back to the harbormaster. "You would think a rich guy like

Hodwin would have a pleasure boat rather than a fishing trawler."

"Oh, he does." Harbormaster took one hand out of his pocket and scratched his whiskered chin. He eyed Z and then Blaze who had both perked up at this news. "He keeps that one over to his vacation house across the bay."

"The name of the boat?"

"I think he calls her the *So Rare*. She's a beauty. I've never been aboard, of course, but from the outside, she's a humdinger."

Z, anxious now, asked, "Where's this vacation house of his?"

"Across the bay. Right on the water—big old thing— over in Point Clear." He pointed.

"And that's all you can tell us about the comings and goings of the *Minnow*?"

"Yep. Not a lot to tell about a fishing boat."

Z's eyes narrowed. "You ever know of any young girls or boys on that boat?"

"Sometimes. Their parents drag them along kicking and screaming. You know kids. They don't much like being trapped on a boat when they could be out with their friends."

"Any other times?"

"Not really. Mostly just adults rent for a day of fishing. Usually guys. But sometimes women. Not often, though."

Z asked again. "You've never seen a group of young girls go out on that boat. Is that right?"

"No. Never. Why—"

"Thank you. That's all we need." She turned to leave and then turned back. "For the moment." She wasn't letting this guy off the hook for a second. Even if she never saw him again, if he was in any way tangled up in this trafficking business, the authorities would want to know about it—and about him.

"And by the way," she added, "we need a fast boat to take us across the bay to the Senator's house. Someone who knows exactly where it is. You have anyone in mind?"

The harbormaster nodded and pointed to a red and white speedboat moored three docks down. "My son-in-law. He'll take you over."

48

The Harbormaster's son-in-law was all too happy to make some cash so they were off in a churn, leaving a white foamy trail across the gray water of the harbor. The November air was crisp and much colder on the open water than on land. Z wished she had brought a jacket, but soon forgot the temperature as the speedboat slowed near the shore.

As they approached the Senator's home on the opposite side of the bay, they slowly coasted up to an empty dock at the water's edge. A long, lush lawn swept down from a white-columned mansion that sported a wide, curved row of windows facing the water.

"Where's the boat?" Z was beside herself. "Damn it! Where's the boat?"

"Looks like the Senator could be part of this whole thing in a bigger way than just owning a fishing trawler," Blaze said.

"Well, that's just great." Z was becoming extremely agitated. She repeated, "That's just great. Now we are looking for two boats and a freaking yacht somewhere out there in the middle of the Gulf of Mexico."

Gray moved to Z's side. "It makes sense, Z. They hold the girls upstate in that blue house then truck them down here and load them onto the Senator's private boat. Quick-quick. Hush-hush. Any noise and anybody looking would think it's just a party. But most likely no one would be looking. This estate looks pretty private. And they probably make the transfer of the girls from the truck to the boat as quick as they can. Then the boat leaves just as fast."

Z nodded, waiting to hear the rest of what Gray had to say. Gray never spoke unless he had something serious on his mind. And he was usually right in his analyses of people and situations.

He continued. "So the fishing trawler heads out with just your two perps on board. Nothing suspicious, right? Twice a year the trawler leaves the harbor with two ordinary-looking guys for a day of deep-sea fishing. Like any other customer on any other day. Then the Senator, on his boat with the girls, meets up with the trawler somewhere—probably well out of the bay but not too far out in the Gulf—still, far enough—and transfers the girls to the trawler. Then the Senator's boat heads back, empty, while the trawler continues into the Gulf to meet the yacht where they off-load the girls, collect a big paycheck, and head back the same as they left with just the two passengers. Except the two passengers and the Senator are now a lot richer."

Blaze spoke up. "One big question—aside from where in the Gulf this initial transfer takes place—is how involved the Senator is in all of this. His boat isn't back yet. So…does he float around in the Gulf for a while and come back later with his empty pleasure craft once the girls are offloaded? Does he give orders to have his boat wait for him while he goes with the trawler to meet the yacht and collect his cut of the big payday?"

"Good questions." Z frowned. "But it doesn't really matter, does it? The Senator is up to his neck in this and he's going down no matter where he is. Or how he gets back." She narrowed her eyes. "Right, Blaze?"

He smiled at her. Her suspicion of him was obvious. "That's right Zakaya-Zee."

She ignored the formerly welcome familiarity and became immediately thoughtful. She ran her right thumbnail along her teeth, thinking. She looked at Blaze. "Now what?"

"Now we go after them. All of them."

Z grew agitated. "We can't just go out into the Gulf without some kind of plan. We need to figure out exactly how we are going to do this. And it's already getting late. She checked her t-com. "Sunset is in less than two and a half hours. They moved those girls down here from upstate last night. The trawler left just before noon. According to the harbormaster, it does about ninety-five knots. We can discount a few for rough water. So let's say she does eighty-five knots. That would put her out of federal waters in a little over two hours."

Gray watched Z as she worried the problem, then spoke up. "We should figure longer than two hours since it has to meet up with the Senator's boat to take on the girls. Maybe the transfer goes smoothly and doesn't take much time. But maybe not. No way we can know."

"Okay…" Z turned to Blaze. "We figure forty-five minutes to transfer the girls. So about three hours for them to exit federal waters. And we are assuming the yacht is actually outside federal waters."

"Of course she is. The owner wouldn't be crazy enough—or bold enough—not to be well out there for this kind of thing." Blaze seemed to be puzzling through it as he spoke.

"Still, it's an assumption," Z answered him. "And we have a lot of assumptions going here. We don't even know if the Senator is really involved."

"It's a good assumption, though. No way Cook and Swift are actually going fishing. And since they didn't have the girls with them, they have to pick them up somewhere. The Senator's pleasure boat fits this like a glove. Especially since he's also the owner of the trawler."

Z turned to Gray and Parker. "What do you two think?"

"It's the most logical," Gray told her.

Parker agreed.

"Let's work this out on the other side." Z glanced and nodded sideways toward the Harbormaster's son-in-law.

The others turned toward him and the poor fellow held up his hands. "Look," he said, "I just drive the boat. I have no interest in anybody's plans about anything. And I didn't vote for the Senator."

Z nodded. "Take us back."

Blaze held up a finger to give himself a moment and turned his back to the other three while he made a call.

When he turned back to the rest of the team, Z asked, "What was that all about?"

"The chopper. I requested the pilot to load an inflatable. It should be ready by the time we get there."

49

The speedboat owner paid, and the police car dismissed, the team prepared to board the *Mighty Kong*.

While Blaze was busy getting the thumbs-up from the pilot with regard to the inflatable, Z turned away to punch up Viking on her t-com.

"That's good news, Z," he told her when she had finished explaining where they were, where they were going, and what they were looking for."

"How is that?" she asked.

"Your guess about the yacht being just outside federal waters is probably spot on. This gives me a fairly straight line to find you and get you out of there. We'll have a satellite tie-in until after midnight so you can signal me at any time and I'll be close by waiting to pick you up. Just one thing…"

"What's that?"

"These people. These traffickers. There's a shitload of money in that business and they're dangerous. Don't take any chances."

She laughed. "Viking, this whole thing is nothing but one huge chance after another. We're looking for three boats and we only know the names of two of them. If the fishing trawler is not close by the yacht, we may not even be able to identify her. But I'll tell you one thing."

"Yeah?"

"I'm not stopping until I get these slime…and get Zeena back."

"You just take care. I don't know about this so-called local partner of yours, but Parker and Gray will have your back. You make sure you have theirs, you hear?"

"I hear. Have I ever failed you?"

"There's a first time for everything."

"This is not going to be the time."

"When are you heading out?"

"We're boarding the chopper now. Should be heading into the Gulf in just a few minutes. She's really fast so we should be out there in maybe ninety minutes. But don't start out until I send you the yacht's coordinates. Assuming we can find it. I don't want the pilot or my local partner to know anything about you so I'll send the coordinates via the emergency button on my t-com. Then we will need time to get aboard the yacht and get the girls. Inform the CIB to disregard the emergency aspect of the transmission."

"How will I recognize your chopper?"

"You can't miss it. It's the size of a freaking freight train with a big gorilla painted on the sides. You coming in a tiltrotor?"

"Not this time. I've got a rescue chopper flying out of Mexico. Right on the straight line of the U.S. Federal waters limit. Just signal a second time when you have it under control down there and I will pick you up. And Z?"

"What?"

"Next time, have your mother come to Cascadia when you want to visit, okay?"

She laughed. "We'll signal for you."

"Take care."

"Yep."

ⲉⲱⲉⱺ

Z and her team climbed aboard the *Mighty Kong* behind Blaze who was already conversing with the pilot in animated fashion. The pilot was nodding in the affirmative—much like a subordinate to an officer—as Blaze spoke to him.

As she stepped up into the chopper behind Parker, she never took her eyes off Blaze who turned, at last, toward the team.

"Blaze," she said, her voice lowered, "I don't know who the hell you are. But you are not a private detective."

"No," he admitted. "No more than you are an ordinary police detective. But we can talk about it later, Zakaya-Zee. Right now we have some criminals to catch and some innocent girls to rescue. Can we agree on that?"

Zakaya narrowed her eyes and stared at him. He knew she was probably CIMA. Yet he had never said anything. She never really trusted him. Not fully. But there was a kind of trust there. A tiny something. Something she couldn't name. She slowly nodded agreement.

She said, "We have to have a fixed plan—at least as fixed as we can get it before we lift off here. So what's it going to be?"

Blaze answered. "What we have here is a very special chopper. Besides being hella fast, this thing…this *Mighty Kong*…is amphibious. When we find the *Giant Minnow*, she will most likely be very near the yacht. We set 'er down in the water, push out the inflatable—"

Z held up her hand. "Wait. We need to be really careful with this. Gray, what do you think?"

There was no person on the entire planet she trusted more than her CIMA-2 partner, Gray Hawk. Even Viking came in a close second.

Gray thought for a moment. "First we locate the *Minnow*. If the Senator's boat is nearby, it will just serve as further verification that we are in the right place, but it won't matter in the long run where she is. The *Minnow* will most likely be near the yacht. Once we find her, we identify the yacht by name, get her coordinates, and fly on past her as though she is of no interest to us. The pilot," he nodded to the pilot up front in the chopper, "sets the *Kong* down about a mile away, we push the inflatable into the water, and we paddle back. It will be after sunset by then and we will be less likely to be noticed in the twilight."

"We won't have to paddle," Blaze said. "The inflatable has a small motor. Not fast, but very quiet."

"Even better." Gray nodded to Z. "What do you think, Z?"

"That part sounds doable. How we get aboard the yacht could be a puzzle, but we will manage it. We don't really know what to expect, though, when we do get aboard. That part we will have to just meet as it comes. But…"

"But what?" Blaze asked.

"But if we get control of the vessel and get the girls, what then? There aren't enough of us to fight off the crew and keep the girls safe at the same time."

"I've notified the Coast Guard," Blaze told her. "They have a cutter out in the Gulf. She's about a hundred and fifty miles out and is right now heading to the federal waters limit. So a bit of help is already on the way. When we find the trawler and the yacht, we send their coordinates to the cutter. Then, when we get the girls—and we *will* get the girls—the Coast Guard will take them aboard to safety and bring us all back home. She even has a helipad so the *Kong* gets to ride back with us."

"Sounds like the private detective has a handle on this." Z didn't smile when she said it. She knew her team was not going back to the mainland. Viking would be out there waiting to take them back to the safety of Cascadia, out of the reach of the United States authorities.

"It's as close as we can come. Here's hoping it will be enough." Blaze ignored the "private detective" dig.

"Sounds workable." Gray looked to Parker and Z for agreement. On their nods, he added, "But time is short. We need to get underway." He strapped himself into his seat and tied back his long, black hair with a string of leather.

Z glanced first at Gray. He had been her partner since she first joined CIMA-2 and was the most beautiful man she had ever seen. Strong Native American features, long legs, clear, sienna skin tanned to a golden hue, eyes wise and dark as her own. And brave. No one on this planet could have had a better partner. She turned toward Blaze. Handsome and rugged at the same time, Blaze had green eyes, like Zeena, and sandy brown hair cut short. Square of jaw and taller than Gray, he had long, slender fingers and neat, dark brows that shaded his eyes. Two men. Her life could depend on either one of them.

When she turned, she had caught Blaze looking at Gray before he quickly looked away. What was he thinking, she wondered. What does a man think when he sees another man so nearly perfect in both physique and intellect? No time to find out now. She reached for her boot knives, checking the ease with which they could be accessed, then reached for the harness to strap herself into her seat.

Everyone secured themselves and donned headsets as the pilot revved up the chopper and lifted off, banking sharply as it headed out over the aqua waters of the Gulf.

The *Kong* thundered over the Gulf for over an hour on a straight line out from Mobile.

Reaching the limit of federal waters, they saw no sign of a yacht or the *Minnow*, but they had passed the Coast Guard cutter about forty miles back and to the east. They had flown close enough for the chopper and the ship to identify each other.

With the *Minnow* missing, the pilot asked, "What now?" His question came through their headsets loud and clear.

"Gotta be either east or west," Z said. "Flip a coin."

"East." Blaze thumbed the direction to his left. "Less distance for the Coast Guard to travel."

"That's wishful thinking, Blaze. When has anything ever been that easy?"

"Gotta go one way or the other. Might as well be east."

On Z's nodded agreement, Blaze spoke to the pilot and the chopper banked hard to port, heading east as the pilot relayed their intentions to the Coast Guard cutter pushing hard for the federal waters limit below.

Within seven minutes on their easterly course, they spotted a fishing trawler in the water below. No churn. The water around the vessel was calm. Close by was a yacht, floating like a proud white swan on the golden sparkle of the reflected sunset. It was huge.

Parker grabbed the optics from his backpack and took a look. "It's the *Minnow*! And the yacht…is…"

"The *Ocean Pearl*!" Blaze shouted as he peered through tactical binocs when the chopper eased slightly sideways. "She's motor-driven. One of those luxury things. Mega yacht. Must be over a hundred meters long. Looks to have at least four decks. Maybe more. And she sports a helipad."

"Notify the Coast Guard of their coordinates and identities!" Z shouted back, giving a thumbs up. The presence of the yacht's helipad was good news to Z. Viking would be able to make use of it. Maybe.

While Blaze gave the order to the pilot, she flipped up the top of her t-com and pressed the emergency button to inform Viking of the yacht's coordinates, and quickly closed it once again. This action was not lost on either Gray or Parker who nodded their understanding.

The *Mighty Kong* roared on past the two vessels below for another mile and three quarters, then settled itself softly into the water, cutting the rotors back to idle to wait out the time until the team called for it to rejoin them on the Coast Guard cutter. Blaze slid open the rear hatch and popped the inflatable into life. The four of them maneuvered it until it splashed into the water, then each jumped in and began preparing for what lay ahead of them. Blaze fiddled around with the tiny motor until he got it going and they slowly turned west, heading back toward the yacht and into the last dregs of the sunset.

50

It took them a good fifteen minutes to cover the distance from the chopper to the yacht, the sky becoming darker and darker with every second. A safe distance from the sleek, white vessel, they cut the motor to avoid discovery. Even though it was small and quiet, sound travels extremely well over water. They couldn't be too careful.

Z nudged Blaze. "We're in luck," she whispered. "The lights are off in the stern and they've left the swim platform down. Pretty good sign they are here for a good time and not expecting trouble."

Their forward inertia carried the inflatable near the stern of the yacht so slowly that Z became nervous of discovery. Gray put out a hand to calm her as Parker and Blaze took up the paddles to silently move the inflatable forward the final few meters.

Just inches from the swim ladder, Blaze reached out to grab hold of it to secure the inflatable. Gray was first up the ladder and as he reached back for Z they heard another chopper in the distance to the west. Parker followed Z onto the platform with Blaze coming aboard last. Z turned in the direction of the distant chopper. They heard it pass on by. Z looked at Gray. "Viking," she whispered. He nodded.

In the silence of the calm Gulf, a loud thump startled them. They turned to find a crewman coming toward them and he did not look friendly.

Gray moved quickly away from Z, reached with his left hand to the K-Bar nestled in its sheath on his back, and silently withdrew the knife. The crewman opened his mouth to shout a warning but no sound ever came. From over ten feet away, Gray dispatched him swiftly and silently, then tucked the body to the side of the platform and motioned the others forward.

The four of them made their way through the yacht. It was odd there was no one about. Parker and Gray guarded the area that led into what appeared to be the cabin deck while Z and Blaze began silently opening doors, one after the other until they reached what appeared to be the main cabin near midship.

When Z opened this last door, she startled a woman who was attending to one of several girls in the suite. She appeared to be dressing her in some kind of filmy pink fabric and fluffing her hair. She froze and her eyes grew wide. Z's eyes also grew wide. She had found the girls.

Z looked around the cabin. Purple and pink tapestries lay about and the huge bed was draped in white satin bordered in gold brocade. It was as lavish as anything Z had ever seen. There were several girls ranging in age from about twelve to seventeen sitting about the room. All of them looked petrified and were completely silent as Z and Blaze looked them over, Z searching for the one familiar face. But Zeena was not among them.

Z's heart fell and her stomach churned. She had known there was a possibility Zeena would not be here, but she had hoped to the point of convincing herself that she would be. Now those hopes were dashed. Still, there were girls here just as frightened as Zeena would have been—and maybe still was. Somewhere.

"Do you speak English?" Z asked the woman.

The woman nodded.

"Where is everyone?" Z demanded.

The woman pointed up, above her head.

Z turned to the girl who was being enveloped in pink. "What is your name?"

"Kit Deming." Tears began to flow. Z reached out and took her hand. Relief flooded her. She had found Connie Latham's friend. She had found the girl who had been taken from the dress shop by Cook and Swift.

"Kit, is there a small, Black girl somewhere on board here named Zeena?" Z was hopeful to the last, but Kit only shook her head and continued to cry.

Z took a deep breath. She couldn't save Zeena. At least not right now. And not here. But she could save these girls. And that's exactly what she intended to do.

"It's okay, Kit. Nothing is going to happen to you now that I'm here. I promised your friend, Connie, that I would find you and bring you home. And that is a promise I'm also making to you now."

"You know Connie?" Kit appeared both amazed and overjoyed at the same time.

Z placed her right hand on Kit's shoulder. "Yes. I met her. She misses you terribly. I promised her I would find you and bring you home. Just be very quiet while I do my work here, okay?"

The girl nodded, wide-eyed.

Z looked around the room at the other girls. Just beyond them stood an elegant, glass cylinder. An elevator. It was wrapped by a staircase that wound around it leading to the upper decks. Z eyed it with suspicious curiosity.

"Where does this elevator go?" she demanded of the panic-stricken woman.

The woman again pointed up.

"What are you supposed to do here?"

The woman took Kit by the hand and led her to the elevator. Kit squirmed, trying to break free. She shouted, "No! No!"

"Kit!" Z tried to calm her. "It's okay. There are a lot of people on their way to rescue you right this minute. But I need you to go ahead and get in the elevator so that everything appears normal. Can you summon up enough courage to do that for me?"

The girl nodded but swallowed hard. Her breathing was heavy. Fear exuded from every pore.

Z turned to the woman. "How many girls have been sent up there before this one?"

"No one." The woman's eyes darted from Z to the elevator and back again.

Z took the woman by the hand to calm her, then nodded toward Kit Deming. "Send her up."

The woman put the girl into the elevator and closed the curved glass door. She pushed one of the metal buttons, but the elevator didn't rise.

"What's wrong?" Z demanded of the woman.

The woman pointed to a small, glass-covered button on the side of the elevator located between two other metal buttons. "I wait for green," she said.

While they waited, Z kept eye contact with Kit. The girl was absolutely beautiful. And terrified. Within less than a minute, the green light came on.

"Now what?"

"I send up," the woman said.

"Which deck?" Z was growing more anxious by the second.

The woman held up two fingers.

"Do it!"

Z watched as the terrified Kit inside the glass tube of the elevator rose through the ceiling on her way to deck two of this beautiful, wretched vessel. Her mind was racing. She turned and nearly ran over Blaze who had been standing behind her, giving her free rein on handling this situation with the girls. Girls. A woman. It was better in this situation. Much better. She was glad he had stood back while she took point on this.

"Blaze, we have to get the rest of these girls out of here *now* and into the inflatable." She grabbed the woman by the arm and looked her in the eye. "Do you want to get away from here?"

The woman stared wide-eyed at Z and quickly nodded in the affirmative.

"Take this woman with them," she said to Blaze. "Then cut it loose and get them away from this…thing. Then notify the Coast Guard to pick them up. I'm going up to deck two and catch me some criminals."

"No! You will wait for the rest of us. You have no idea what's going on up there or how many men you will encounter. I'm not losing you."

She gave him the Zakaya stare for a split second before nodding her understanding that he was right.

Parker and Gray, who had been guarding the entrance to this particular deck, motioned the girls forward and led them quietly down the passageways and out onto the swim platform where the secured inflatable remained tied to the swim ladder. Z and Blaze guarded the end of this small procession and saw the woman and the last of the girls into the inflatable before it was cut loose and pushed hard away from the yacht.

There was still no one about. Apparently, the lone guard eliminated by Gray was the only one on duty. It was dark here at the stern away from the setting sun in the west, but they could see lights shining brightly onto the surface of the water from one of the decks above them.

"Must be deck two. Having a party." Blaze said between clenched teeth.

Z gave him a look. "Or an auction."

51

They watched as the inflatable of silent, frightened girls floated gently away some distance from the yacht before Z turned to Gray and Parker with an idea that had been lurking just beyond her reach but now erupted full-blown.

"Gray!" Her voice was low in spite of the urgency. "Those bastards up there," she whispered and nodded toward the upper decks, "will be expecting the next girl to be sent up on that elevator. If no one is sent up, they will send someone down here to find out what's wrong. So let's not disappoint them."

"Whoa! You? Trapped in that little glass coffin?" Gray was not happy with this idea, but Z was zeroed in on her plan.

"Gray…Think about it. I won't go up until they give the green light on that thing. They will think everything is perfectly normal for their disgusting little party and they'll believe their next victim is on her way up. But you and Parker will already be up there, and when I arrive in the elevator they are going to get the surprise of their lives. Blaze can send me up and then take the circular stairs. The stairs wrap around the glass elevator cylinder so it's plainly visible all the way up. He can keep an eye on me the whole time." She turned to Blaze and asked, "What do you think?"

"I think this is one damned risky idea, Zakaya-Zee." He hesitated, thinking. "But it might just work. As long as everything is proceeding exactly as they expect, we will have the element of surprise. That will give us an advantage. But…"

"But what?"

"It's very dangerous. If anything happens to you…"

"I'll be fine."

Parker groaned. "Right. You'll be fine. Damn it, Z. This is way too chancy. What if all those scumwads are sitting up there with pistols and knives?"

"That's why you will be there, Parks." Z smiled at him. "We've got this. Let's do it before they get suspicious and wonder why the woman hasn't signaled the next girl is ready."

Timing was the crucial part of this plan, Z knew. The Coast Guard cutter was barreling through the water on its way to them right this moment and when they arrived they would waste no time boarding this yacht. She needed to be sure Viking had her team on the rescue chopper and on their way back to Cascadia before the Americans had a chance to arrest them along with the rest of the *Ocean Pearl's* passengers and crew.

ৎৎৎ

In the salon on deck two, Hadeon Cook and Donny Ray Swift sat at the back of the room near the salon doors along with the State Senator from Alabama. They were sellers, not buyers. They were there to watch and wait until the end to receive their cut of the sales. More important and much wealthier people—the buyers of human beings—sat or lounged on more luxurious furnishings toward the front of the salon with a good view of the elevator.

The atmosphere was festive with champagne being passed on golden trays to men arrayed in various styles of ethnic garb—most of which was rather a mystery to the two Alabama detectives.

It irked Cook that he was looked down upon by these foreign moguls. He found them dirty and disgusting with their facial hair and questionable manners when compared to himself. Fastidious in his person and clean-shaven, Cook considered himself well above this rich rabble. But the money that flowed through them was so great he could put up with anything for one evening's unpalatable contact twice a year.

He leaned back into the velvety seating alongside Donny Ray who hadn't wanted to come at all, was embarrassed to be here, and would rather have been nearly anywhere else on the planet.

"Why do I have to be there?" he had asked.

"Because I don't trust you," had been Hadeon's answer. And so Donny Ray Swift, frankly afraid of his psychopathic partner, and whose intellect had never lived up to his name, had come along once again. Just as he had several times before. Though a man of some conscience, his guilt was as certain as Cook's. And he knew it.

Now, side-by-side, sipping champagne from elegant crystal flutes, they waited for the event of the evening to begin.

The rather rotund owner of the yacht stepped up to the front of the room and to the side of the elevator with a huge smile on his face. He announced the opening of the festivities, then turned and watched as the elevator rose through the floor and into the room of leering and smiling men.

Hadeon leaned forward on his seat. This slowly rising vision in pink was the girl he had taken from his sister's dress shop so many months ago. He was certain of it. She was gorgeous. Her long, dark hair barely covered her shoulders and her breasts were plainly visible through the filmy pink of her garment. A pang of regret flooded through him. Why hadn't he kept her for himself? But he knew why. Keeping her near her home and in the same town as himself was risky. Then, too, the money was just too great. There would be lots of other girls. Lots. None of them had ever wanted him, anyway, so what did he care? Bits of flesh. That's all they were.

Fingers were raised silently as a man in an ordinary business suit stood behind a podium to the side of the room and, much as he might have done at a high-class auction house, called for bids. When the bidding reached four hundred and fifty thousand dollars, Kit Deming was sold and taken from the glass enclosure of the elevator by a fat man pushing sixty.

The purchase was recorded, and the owner of the yacht announced the next girl would soon rise in the elevator.

The men were in party mode, giddy with expectation.

ഇരുന

Kit Deming shivered inside the glass enclosure. But not from the cold. She looked back at Z in the cabin as the elevator began to rise. That kind, Black woman had promised nothing was going to happen to her. People were coming to save her. But who? And when? She needed them now!

She kept eye contact with Z until the elevator rose through the cabin ceiling and kept slowly rising through another cabin and, finally, into a large room full of men lounging on huge, over-stuffed sofas.

When the elevator finally stopped rising, the men began applauding and laughing. They pointed at her and smiled at each other. She felt as though she would throw up. She tried covering herself with her arms and turned her face away from them. Her entire being burned with embarrassment and fear.

Some man at a podium over to the left of the room began speaking and the men on the sofas began raising their fingers in turn. At last a finger was raised that seemed to satisfy the man at the podium and he made some kind of announcement. The man who had last raised his finger clapped his hands and leaped up from the sofa, his companions all rising and shaking his hand. Finally, he approached the elevator, opened the glass door, and took her by the arm. She resisted, but he pulled harder, attempting to make soothing sounds to her. She could not break his grip as he pulled her through the room and out the salon doors past the seated Cook, Swift, and the Senator from Alabama.

Donny Ray Swift was the only one of the three who looked away.

ℭℜℭ

While Z and Blaze headed back to the cabin containing the elevator, Parker and Gray made their way up to the second deck. The darkness assisted them in locating the one area that seemed to be alive with both illumination and party-like sounds.

Emerging stealthily from the third deck onto the second, they encountered no one. Gray was suspicious of this and whispered to Parker, "No one guarding. This is odd. Can they really be that arrogant?"

"You would be surprised how arrogant the super-rich can be. Watch my back." Gray acknowledged with a nod and Parker moved around the corner from the stairs. He took a look and darted back again.

"There's a guard. Looks to be a large salon just inside double doors about eight feet away. Well lit. Sounds like a party going on in there. The doors have circular windows, like portholes, and the guard seems fascinated by whatever is going on inside. He's not looking this way. No other doors on the hallway. Just a sofa on each side with small side tables and lamps on each end."

"I'll take care of him," Gray whispered as he retrieved the K-bar from its sheath and stepped silently around the corner.

The guard never saw him. Or heard him. He was dead before his knees buckled. Gray eased his body onto one of the sofas and stepped up to the left-hand circular window to take a look. There were doors on either side about midway down the salon that opened onto the upper port and starboard decks. Inside, there were a dozen or more men lounging comfortably among cushioned sofas.

Gray pushed lightly on the door. It didn't budge. He held his breath and gripped the door's gold-plated handle and pulled almost imperceptibly. It gave! The doors opened out from the salon. Releasing the door handle, he turned to the sofa that was unoccupied and eyed its dimensions. Satisfied with his calculations, he turned and motioned for Parker to join him.

The two of them quietly lifted the sofa and turned it parallel to the salon doors. It didn't fit. Slightly too long. Perfect. They pushed the overstuffed piece until it was firmly jammed between the two walls, blocking the salon doors Kit Deming had been escorted through only moments before they had arrived on this deck.

"There are doors on either side of the room in there," Gray said. "They open onto the port and starboard decks. You take the port side and I'll take starboard. Then we wait until Z comes up in the elevator at the far end of the room. No one is getting past us."

Turning their separate ways, the two of them exited the hallway and headed for the decks on either side of the salon.

52

As soon as Gray and Parker left them on the swim platform and headed up to deck two, Z and Blaze wasted no time returning to the cabin area to find the elevator had already been sent back down for the next girl. This meant Kit Deming had been sold. Z shivered but quickly snapped out of it. There was no time to lose now. This was it.

She eyed the filmy material draped about the room that was supposed to suffice for the girls' clothing. She frowned and looked away. No way she was getting into any of that.

"Blaze," she said, turning to him, "we need to press the ready-button, or whatever it is the woman pushed before. Do you remember which one that was?"

"Nope. I was behind you, remember?"

"Damn!" She ran her finger along the several buttons on the panel to the side of the elevator. "One seems to be for 'ready' and the other seems to be for sending the elevator up. But which is which?"

Blaze looked the panel over alongside her. "Three buttons. Well, actually, two buttons and a light in the middle covered with green glass. You have a fifty-fifty chance. Take your pick."

Z held her hand above the panel. She closed her eyes trying to remember which the woman had pushed. "I think maybe this one, farthest from the elevator door might be the ready-button. The one nearest is probably the send-up button."

"Good a guess as any. Go for it."

She held her breath and pushed the button farthest from the elevator door. Nothing happened. She exhaled.

They waited.

And waited. Seconds dragged into minutes.

What the hell were they doing up there? Whipping up a drooling frenzy over the next victim?

At last, the green light came on.

"The perps must be primed and ready for their next victim," Blaze said, parroting Z's thoughts. "Just make sure it isn't you, Zakaya-Zee."

"Okay, here we go," she said. "You push the send button and then follow me up the stairs. Take care that your head doesn't pop up into view when the elevator breaks the floor of deck two."

Their eyes met and Blaze nodded. Z checked the magazine in her SIG, tapped her cargo pockets checking for the loaded extras, took a look at the boot knives sheathed in her boots, and stepped inside the glass cylinder. She closed the door. One last look between them and Blaze pushed the send-up button.

The elevator slowly began to rise. When Blaze turned to take the stairs, Z popped her t-com and pressed the emergency button. Things would happen fast now, and Viking needed time to get to the yacht to pick up Gray and Parker before the Coast Guard arrived.

❧

The moment Viking received Z's alert, he commanded the chopper pilot to turn back to the coordinates of the yacht. They had passed it about fifteen minutes earlier. It was almost time to pick up his team and get them safely back to Cascadia.

A thunderstorm had come up and the helicopter banked and headed back through sheets of rain, passing the Coast Guard cutter chopping through the water at a foam-churning pace.

ⱷᔢⱷᔢ

The elevator rose at a slow, nerve-wracking pace. Z kept eye contact with Blaze, who was taking slow, single stair steps to stay even with her and keeping eye contact as she rose.

At last, the elevator broke the plane of the salon floor on deck two, and Z's dark head with its twisted 'fro slowly came into view. This, she knew, was the most vulnerable she would be—enclosed in a glass cylinder with Blaze behind and somewhat below her and out of sight, unable to help for what could be urgent seconds. She held her breath and swept the room with her eyes as the elevator slowly inched upwards into the room.

All men here. Lounging carelessly. Smiling. Leering. Happy. Some guy in a business suit at a podium to her left. A fairly rotund guy in ethnic garb—perhaps Arabian, perhaps not. She couldn't readily tell. He stood with his back to her, also to her left and several feet closer than the business suit. The room appeared warm and cozy, defying the coldness of the rain now whipping the port side of the yacht.

She quickly assessed the layout of the room. There were several ways into and out of this salon. One large rear double-door and a smaller door on either side. A shock of blond hair was barely visible through the glass of the port-side salon door. Parker.

Gray's majestic profile was visible through the salon door to her right. It seemed that only she had noticed either of them. All eyes inside the salon at this moment were on her, save for the large man with his back to her. The men were lounging comfortably. Smiling. Sipping champagne.

As the elevator continued to rise, revealing her in full-form and clad in camouflage, the men's smiles faded and furrowed brows formed puzzled looks.

Someone sitting at the back of the room near the double doors leaped up and pointed at her. He shouted, "I know her! We've been boarded!" It was Hadeon Cook.

Gotcha!

There would be no getting out of this for the so-called fast food duo now. Even if his DNA wasn't found on those pink panties, this guy was toast. And his buddy, Donny Ray, was right there beside him.

At Hadeon's shout, the rotund guy turned around to see what was causing the commotion at the same moment Z stepped out of the elevator. She stood straight, but lifted her right knee and withdrew the boot knife. On seeing the stubby knife, the big guy laughed at her and pulled from his own waist a curved blade several times longer than the K-bar. Her knee still up, she rapidly kicked him hard, once in the chin and a second blow to the crotch, doubling him over and sending his scimitar spinning across the polished marble of the salon floor.

The men began leaping from their sofas and heading for the double doors behind them only to find that way firmly blocked. Turning, they headed for the deck doors on either side of the salon, the state senator from Alabama knocking people out of his way as he advanced. Their attempts, however, proved fruitless and they were halted in their tracks as Gray and Parker stepped inside, weapons at the fore, their backs to the doors, blocking egress.

The auctioneer behind the podium began quickly gathering up papers and eyeing the only way left out of the salon: the staircase that wrapped around the elevator.

With his papers in hand, he bolted for the stairs, dashed behind Z, and found himself face-to-face with a nine-millimeter Glock in the hand of a scowling Martin Blaze. At this point, he dropped the papers and backed up into the room with the rest of the trapped men.

"Gentlemen! Gentlemen!" Z shouted, her own SIG now in her right hand, supported by her left hand and forearm sweeping the room like a security camera. "Please take your seats. This party is over."

The rotund guy, whom she took to be the owner of the yacht, stood up now, screamed something in a language she neither spoke nor understood and, in a rage, threw himself toward her. Parker leveled his SIG and took out his right knee. The man fell and literally rolled backward, screaming.

Another shot rang out. It had been aimed at Z. The bullet missed her face by a fraction of an inch, and ripped a hole in the curved wall of the elevator behind her sending several large cracks shooting through the glass in various directions like bolts of silver lightning. Z dodged reflexively when she saw Hadeon Cook readying to fire again. But he never got the chance. Gray took him down from across the room with a bullet to the shoulder that knocked him backward and onto the cowering Donny Ray still seated next to him, his hands covering his face.

There were now at least three hostile weapons in this room. Z shouted out, "Swift! Bring Cook's pistol up here! And your own! Parker, take charge of this guy's knife over here, will you?" She nodded at Mr. Rotund still moaning and holding his shattered and bleeding knee.

While Parker gathered the scimitar that had slid nearly to the podium on the slick marble of the floor, Donny Ray

Swift gave an apologetic look toward Cook and gathered up his pistol, now several feet from where he sat. He walked to the front of the salon and handed it over to Z.

"I'll have yours, as well, Swift." Z held out her hand for the weapon and stared him down.

Donny Ray met her gaze for one pregnant moment, then reached to his side and withdrew his weapon, clicked off the safety, placed the barrel to his temple, and pulled the trigger.

Z let out an involuntary yelp at the shot and watched in horror as he dropped to the floor beside her, blood slowly spreading across the white of the marble. She quickly shook off the shock and handed Hadeon's pistol behind her to Blaze.

The roar of helicopter rotors cut through the steady ping of rain and permeated the salon as it made one pass around the yacht before settling down on the foredeck helipad.

Viking had arrived.

But where was the Coast Guard? Did they pick up the girls?

Z's mind raced now. It was imperative that Parker and Gray leave this vessel with Viking before the Americans had a chance to confront them. Both, like herself, were still high on their "wanted" list for their part in the mission two years earlier that had denied them the possibility of a horrific weapon of war.

She spoke with Blaze momentarily. "I'm going out to check on the Coast Guard. Back in a flash."

Blaze nodded as she passed behind Gray at the starboard side salon door and out onto the deck. The rain was whipping in from the port side, so she was somewhat shielded from the pummeling. Through the remaining dregs of twilight, she could just make out the cutter about a half-mile out. It seemed to be still in the water. Good. If it was not moving, it would be picking up the girls.

She darted back inside the salon to speak with Blaze.

"The cutter should be here in just a few minutes. Looks like they are picking up the girls right now. Keep these people under control, will you? I have one more thing to do."

Before Blaze could object, she took the stairs behind him and raced down the decks and through the cabins until she reached the cabin where she had found the girls.

No one was there.

Where is Kit?

She left the cabin and began flinging open the other cabin doors one after the other. Four cabins down, she opened the door to a very surprised man who had a crying and half-naked Kit Deming in his grasp.

Z was in no mood to negotiate. She shouted, "Let her go!"

The man, at first shocked, froze. Then, on sizing up her small stature and, as Z guessed he had done all his life, dismissed her as just another woman, he smiled at her and pulled Kit closer.

She never hesitated for an instant. She took aim and shot him in the left arm. He reeled but reached with his right hand to his side. Before he could lay his hand on his own weapon, Z's next shot rang out. He was dead before he hit the floor.

She watched him fall.

Kit ran to her, crying. "I thought you weren't coming!"

"I told you I would. I always keep my word." Z hugged the girl to her and then backed away and ripped her own t-shirt over her head and helped the girl into it.

"Let's go! Help is on the way now. You're safe. You'll be home soon." Z took her hand and they headed up to the salon via the winding staircase in the first cabin, the girl in Z's t-shirt and filmy fabric coving her legs, and Z in camouflage cargoes and a black sports bra.

Emerging from the staircase, she handed Kit off to Blaze as shouts came over a bullhorn announcing an intention to board. The Coast Guard had arrived.

She had to get Parker and Gray to safety. Now.

Panicked on hearing the Coast Guard, the men in the room stampeded to the unguarded double-doors at the rear in an effort to break through whatever was blocking them. When the doors finally gave, they found themselves tripping over each other and the huge overstuffed sofa, suddenly free, yet with nowhere to go in the middle of the Gulf of Mexico.

Z signaled with hand chops to Parker and Gray to go.

They backed out their respective side doors and headed for the helipad. Leaving Kit with Blaze, who looked somewhat puzzled at the unexpected departure of the Cascadian team, Z headed out after them. Blaze, with Kit in tow, followed them.

The din of the chopper blades had never stopped and Viking, his bulk nearly filling the hatch, was hurrying his team aboard. Parker jumped aboard first, followed by Gray who reached back for Z.

She backed away.

"Z!" Viking shouted. "Come on! We have to go!"

She shook her head.

"Damn it, Z! Get your ass on board! That's an order!"

She shook her head again and shouted over the deafening whop-whop of the chopper, "I can't! I'll come when I find Zeena!"

"Z! Don't be a fool! She could be anywhere!"

The chopper pilot yelled at Viking. "We have to go. Now!"

Gray, who had been her partner since she had joined CIMA, nodded. He understood. Gray had always had her back. She knew he would make her case back in Cascadia and, if necessary, he would come back for her.

He pulled Viking away from the hatch and, with a final nod to Z, he slid it shut. The chopper lifted off, banking hard to starboard.

The Coast Guard, unaware this chopper was not part and parcel of the criminal coterie of the yacht, fired at it. Z held her breath as the pilot dodged and wove causing them to miss, then headed straight west at full speed.

Z stood beside Blaze and Kit Deming. The three of them watched the chopper growing smaller as it headed back to Mexico carrying CIMA's best—minus one.

53

The Coast Guard paused long enough to pick up the woman and the girls, then wasted no time covering the distance between the free-floating inflatable and the *Ocean Pearl*. Blaze had kept contact, informing them of the status on board and what they would be encountering so they did not hesitate. They blasted their intentions over the bullhorn only moments before they boarded the *Pearl*.

Hadeon Cook, dismissing with zero remorse the sight of his partner sprawled stone-dead on the salon floor, joined the stampede for the salon's double doors.

Once out of the salon, the men were soon smacked soundly down by reality. There was no place to go. The armed Guardsmen easily took them one-by-one into custody.

Along with the other passengers, Cook and the Senator, were rounded up, arrested, and taken aboard the cutter. The Senator, unaccustomed to being treated with anything other than deference, attempted to pull the "do-you-know-who-I-am" threat—a threat that fell on deaf ears as he was locked up securely, and without hesitation, along with the rest of the criminals in the cutter's brig.

When everyone had been herded on board the cutter, Blaze gave Z a nod, then called the *Mighty Kong* to catch up with them for the ride back to Mobile.

Kit Deming still safely between them, Z and Blaze were the last to board.

⁂

Once Kit was handed off to a guardsman to be pampered along with the rest of the girls, Z and Blaze remained on deck watching the *Ocean Pearl* and the *Minnow* behind them.

Z sensed something was amiss. Of all the people rounded up and arrested, she had not seen the rotund man she had taken to be the yacht's owner, whom she had kicked, and Parker had shot, in the knee. She told Blaze of her concern as they stood on the deck looking back at the two vessels.

"Don't worry. He won't get away."

"You seem pretty sure of that."

"I am. Look there!" Blaze pointed to the yacht that was now about a quarter mile away from the cutter.

From the side of the huge vessel, a bay door opened and a speedboat emerged. Mr. Rotund was at the helm whipping up a froth behind him as the small craft roared out into the Gulf on its own.

"Where the heck does he think he's going?"

"I doubt he even knows at this point. We'll pick him up. Look." Blaze nodded toward the small white craft just visible in the distance. "He's already just drifting. He knows he has nowhere to go. It's over."

"What if the *Minnow* decides to make a run for it? If she's really an SES, she can outrun this cutter."

Blaze laughed. "True. But she can't outrun a shelling by the cannons."

"Good point." Z watched the boats for a couple of minutes longer, then asked, "What about the Senator's boat, the *So Rare*? We never saw her."

"She'll have to go home sometime. May already be there. She'll be picked up soon if she isn't already."

"So what will happen now?"

"The trawler and the yacht will both be piloted in under guard where they will be held and gone over for every speck of evidence on them. Then, maybe they will be auctioned off in the future when all of this is history. Same for the Senator's boat."

Z shook her head. "Such a gorgeous yacht for such an ugly purpose," she said quietly.

"She won't be auctioning off another young girl. That's for certain." Blaze grew quiet as he watched the two vessels behind them.

There was something in Blaze's voice. Z sensed more than satisfaction in a job well done on this mission. Somehow, she sensed that, for him, this was personal. As personal as it had been for her even though she had not found Zeena. She found herself wondering about the sister he had said was gone, but her thoughts were interrupted as he suddenly turned away from the scene.

He said, quietly, "I'll go up to the bridge and tell the captain to pick up the guy in the speedboat just in case he didn't see him."

While Blaze made his way up to the bridge, Z called JJ who informed her the DNA results came back. Blood was found on the back of the chair in the secret room of the dress shop and it belonged to Hadeon Cook. His DNA was also found on the pink panties. And DNA from one other—her Uncle Bo.

At this point, that news came as no surprise to Z. Still...*What did he do to that girl? Did he kill her?*

She closed her eyes and shook her head. She said, "It's over, JJ. We've got them. Both Cook and Senator Hodwin. They are under arrest along with the rest of the rabble dealing in young girls. They are in the Coast Guard brig here on the cutter. We're on our way back now. Just make sure you keep Bo Kalu locked up tight."

"Will do, Z. You said Cook and Senator Hodwin. What about Swift?"

"He shot himself on the yacht. The Coast Guard has his body. I guess the shame of the whole thing was too much for him. I always thought he was under the thumb of Cook a bit involuntarily. Hard to feel sorry for him, though. He was a grown man and made his choices."

"Yep. I think you're right about that."

"And JJ?"

"Yes?"

"Tell the captain we have Kit Deming so he can inform her parents."

She next punched up a number she had saved on her t-com. Connie Latham's.

"I've found Kit, Connie!" she told the elated girl. "We're bringing her home."

❧❧❧

As the Coast Guard cutter pulled into Mobile, it was met by three official-looking people standing beside a police car. Z instantly recognized the two FBI agents she had foiled in Atlanta two years ago and had recently run off the road back in Crimson City, but she didn't recognize the third person: a tall woman with bobbed, blonde hair.

Blaze took one look as they disembarked onto the docks and groaned. Z asked him what was the matter but he didn't answer.

The woman stepped up to greet them.

"Blaze! You are in a helluva lot of trouble, Partner." She looked from Blaze to Z and back again.

Z turned to Blaze, somewhat puzzled. The word "partner" had given her a start, yet she had always known there was more to Blaze than he had revealed.

Blaze winced at the greeting. "You came all the way down here to tell me that?"

"No. Actually, I came for this." She turned to Z. "Miss Zakaya Kalu, you are under arrest for sabotage, espionage, and whatever else the government can find to charge you with."

Z gave Blaze a look. "Partner? So, Mr. Private Detective, this is what it was all along, huh?"

"Sorry, Z." No pet name this time. Just Z.

"I'll take the weapons." The blonde woman held out her hand. "And the t-com, as well."

"I'll take the t-com, Dotty," Blaze told her.

Z handed the woman the weapons, one by one, while still looking Blaze dead in the eyes. As she unfastened her t-com and handed it over, she said, "Call my mother, Blaze. Tell her I'm okay. Then call JJ and ask him to go out to that big, ugly guy's farm and get my car and return it to the rental office in Montgomery. But first, have him get the key out of the pocket of my jeans—they're in the trunk—and return it to Sam's Package Pickup there in Crimson City. Also, if you don't mind, thank Captain Taylor for all his help and tell him it would be in his interest to arrest the sheriff. His case might be harder to prove than his nephew's, but it might scare the bastard straight even if they can't get a conviction. And one last thing…"

"What's that?"

"Check on Charming Billy. Make sure they're treating him right, will you?"

Blaze nodded while the woman commanded Z to hold out her hands to be cuffed.

Blaze said, "Look, Hightower, is this really necessary?"

She didn't answer so he said again, "Dotty?"

"Sorry, Blaze. I'm under orders from headquarters."

"Yeah, right. And you always obey orders from headquarters. Right, Agent Hightower?"

She ignored him and said to Z, "This way." She held the police car door open and directed Z to get in. Blaze got in beside her and the door was slammed shut behind them.

Z looked out the window on her side of the squad car. Silent. Her cuffed hands in her lap.

Blaze was silent as well. Neither could look at the other.

The woman, Dotty Hightower, got in the front beside the police officer while the two FBI men plopped themselves into a second police car parked nearby. The small entourage slowly rolled out of the area and onto the highway that led to the Mobile airport where they boarded a small plane to Atlanta.

Z could only think of one thing on the flight: Zeena.

Where was she? What had happened to her? Was she okay? And how was she going to find her if she was in an American prison?

Z had learned long ago that the imagination is a very powerful thing. It can de-rail you if you let it. She cautioned herself not to imagine the worst, but it was hard advice to take. The girl was just fifteen. A very young fifteen, ripe for some scumwad—as Parker called them— to take advantage of. And she had been in her care. How could she have let this happen? She should have just packed up and flown back to Cascadia with her. She should have just let the Americans handle their own cases. But the thoughts fizzed away as she knew those girls being trafficked on that yacht would never have been saved if it had not been for her. And Blaze—as much as she hated to admit it.

Blaze. She could hardly stand to think of him at this moment.

She raised her cuffed hands and wiped away a very unusual tear for Zakaya Kalu.

54

In the Atlanta airport, Agent Hightower herded them into the waiting area for their flight to Virginia. Like all airports, the place smelled stale and slightly rank with the odors of human sweat and mildew. Z ignored it all and sat stoically between her two captors in one of a row of plastic chairs bolted firmly to the floor. She had refused to speak to Blaze, or even look at him, throughout the entire flight. But she had studied the rigid mannequin of Dotty Hightower.

Tall woman. Stiff. Unyielding. Probably clawed her way up the ladder until earning the title "Special Agent." She seemed to actually like Blaze. They had chatted informally during the flight about nothing of import or consequence. But it was obvious to Z that she was not someone Blaze would ever choose to be intimate with. And it seemed that, right now, this Dotty Hightower definitely had the upper hand. Blaze was in trouble, she had said. Z wondered what he had done. Or not done.

She found herself wishing she had asked him more about himself when they were in conversation back in Brassy's Bar and Grille in Crimson City. Too late, now, of course. But there were hints of things that could have explained more about the person of this man whom she had never fully trusted yet found herself oddly attracted to.

They sat in silence for a while until Blaze became restless after checking the time. He got up and told Hightower he was going to stretch his legs and sauntered off down the concourse. Z noticed him calling someone on his t-com. She wondered who it was. If he was in trouble, it was probably not his boss. And she doubted very much that he had a wife or significant other person in his life. This conversation seemed serious. Business-like.

She watched him for a minute or two then looked away as he turned and walked back to where they were sitting. He seemed…happy, which Z found very strange under the current circumstances. Well, he wasn't the one in cuffs and under arrest so why shouldn't he be?

He smiled at her as he took his seat once again, but she looked away.

He leaned forward and inquired of Hightower, "How long to the flight?"

"About half an hour." Long legs crossed, and obviously bored, she was flipping through a magazine.

Blaze leaned back and waited for a minute before speaking up again. "Maybe Miss Kalu would like to use the ladies' room." He turned to Z, "Miss Kalu?"

There was something in his eyes. Something…

She nodded and finally spoke to him for the first time since she had been arrested in Mobile. "Yes. Thank you."

"Let me check your bag first," he told her. The look was still there.

Z handed him her bag and watched as he went through the contents. They had already done this in Mobile so this unnecessary second check piqued her interest. He slipped something inside when he was turned sideways from Hightower who was rising from her own plastic chair to act as escort.

"Looks okay." He handed the bag over to Hightower. "You want to take a look, too?"

"No." She gave him an exasperated look. "I'm sure you know how to inspect a woman's bag, Blaze. And I already checked it before."

He turned back to Z. "You will have to go with Agent Hightower. She will take you down there to the restroom." He pointed down the concourse. "I'll just wait here for you."

The look. It was undeniable. Unmissable. What was up?

"Let's go." Hightower was all business and stayed just behind her as they made their way down the concourse and into the ladies' restroom.

Once inside, Hightower looked her over. "Can you manage in those cuffs?"

"Yes. I think so. Thanks."

Z entered one of the stalls, slid the lock to hold the door closed, and looked back out through the crack where the door met the locking post. Dotty Hightower was admiring herself in the mirror on the opposite side of the room at the row of washbasins. Z quickly went through her bag. There, on the bottom, was the small key to the cuffs. She could not suppress a smile as she took it out and put it between her teeth in order to work the lock on the cuffs. Maneuvering the key into the lock was difficult and just as she thought she had it secured, it slipped and fell to the floor with a clink.

She froze. The key was just under the door and clearly visible both inside the stall and outside where Hightower was waiting for her. Worst of all, the damned thing was silver and glinted brightly in the lights over the washbasins.

Z quickly put her shoe over the offending key and peeked through the crack in the door just as Hightower turned her way. "Are you okay in there?" Hightower called to her.

"Yes. Just a little slow. I'm fine."

She watched as the woman turned back to the mirror then bent down and retrieved the key for a second go at it. This time she held the key tightly between her teeth and carefully maneuvered it around a tiny fraction at a time until the cuffs released. Free now from the hindrance of physical restraint, she turned back to the crack between stall door and post to check on the exact whereabouts of Hightower.

The woman was still looking at herself, pressing a little finger to the edge of her mouth to vanquish an errant speck of lipstick.

It was now or never.

She waited a second or two longer until another woman passed between them on her way to an empty stall, then quickly opened the door. As the other woman was blocking Hightower's view, Z covered the several feet between them. Hightower saw her coming at the last second, but it was too late.

Z cuffed the unconscious Hightower to the pipes beneath one of the washbasins and quickly exited the restroom, tossing the key to the cuffs in the trashcan by the door. As she stepped outside the restroom, she heard her name being called over the intercom system.

Miss Zakaya Kalu was to please go to gate seventeen immediately.

Cautiously, she headed for the gate. When she saw that it was the Cascadian airline's gate, she began walking a bit more briskly. She looked around but saw no one remotely suspicious so she approached the gate attendant who informed her the flight was being held for her.

"Please go on board, Miss Kalu."

Z nodded at the attendant and made her way past the gate. She had almost decided nothing could surprise her anymore until she entered the boarding tunnel to find Blaze casually leaning up against the wall.

He stood up straighter when he saw her. "Hightower?"

"You mean Bandbox Barbie?"

Blaze laughed. "Yeah. She okay?"

"She'll live."

"Good."

Still laughing, he handed the SIG and boot knives back to her.

"Keep them. Return them to Eli McClain, will you?"

"No need to return them to anyone. You're cleared to take them. Seems you are an important person, Zakaya-Zee."

"My t-com?" She raised an eyebrow and tilted her head.

He fished the t-com out of his pocket and handed it over to her.

"Thanks."

"Oh. One more thing," he said.

"What's that?"

"There's a cute little fifteen-year-old already on board and very excited to see you."

Z's eyes grew wide. Speechless for once in her life, her emotions scattered in every direction imaginable. Then, finding her voice at last. "Zeena! You found Zeena?"

"Not found, exactly," he admitted.

Z could not believe what she was hearing. Her face flushed with anger. "You had her the whole time? *You?*"

He nodded. "Taking Zeena was the only way I could think of to keep her safe, keep you in the country long enough to save those trafficked girls, and protect myself at the same time. She's been in a private boarding school for girls here in Atlanta and has been treated like a princess, I promise you. I'm sorry I couldn't tell you—."

"Damn you, Martin Blaze! You let me worry all this time!" She gave him the Zakaya stare. Then, without warning, she slapped him as hard as she could.

As she was drawing back her hand, he reached out and grabbed her by the wrist. Pulling her close, he kissed her.

She pushed him away, gave him a look, and slapped him again.

He rubbed his face and smiled at her, then handed over her passport and other identification. "You take care of yourself, Zakaya-Zee."

Her emotions were a jumble. She said nothing as she turned to make her way aboard the aircraft.

As she turned, he reached out his hand and she brushed his palm lightly with her own and gave him a last look.

"See you around, Martin Blaze."

55

After many hugs and settling into the four-seater with Zeena who had been overjoyed to once again be with Miss Z, the airline doors were closed and locked with a reassuring hiss and the boarding tunnel was retracted.

Zeena rattled on and on about how some bad guys had tried to kidnap her in the airport, but some good guys stopped them and made them let her go. Then the good guys took her to this wonderful school where she had the best time…she kept happily talking non-stop but her voice gradually trailed away until Z no longer heard it. Her attention was distracted by the last person to board the flight. He came slowly down the center aisle and took his seat two four-seaters ahead of them and across the aisle.

Blaze.

Z watched him. He didn't look back at the two of them as he stowed his small bag.

He looked tired.

Her mind, retracing everything that had happened over the past weeks, settled on one thing. Something he had said to her.

The legacy you leave doesn't have to be a tangible thing. It can be a feeling. It can be a life or a love, or freedom the recipient would never have but for you. Everyone leaves a legacy. Everyone.

She was watching him when her t-com buzzed and a text message began scrolling across its small screen. It was from Alex: *You wanted to know about a guy named Eli McClain and also who the operative was in that region. Nothing much to tell about McClain—just a gang boy turned good-guy—but Budgie, the wunderkind, finally found the identity of the operative*:

There was a long blank space and then the letters began marching across the screen:

....M...A...R...T...I...N...B...L...A...Z...E....

She looked up to see Blaze's head leaning against the window. Asleep.

She smiled.

After a moment she punched up Alex on her t-com and sent a six-word message: *I have Zeena. We're coming home.*

AFTERWORD

To my Readers:

I offer my sincerest gratitude to each of you who gave so generously of one of the most valuable gifts possible: your time. I hope you found this work worthy. You make it all worthwhile.

To Black Opal Books and my editor, Susan Humphreys:

Once again, you made the magic happen. Thanks for everything.

To Lawrence, my indefatigable Beta Reader:

Your knowledge of how things work is like a treasure trove of goodies that make the writing real. And your uncomplaining reading and re-reading of this manuscript was an even greater treasure. Thank you for all of it. You're still the best!

A word about "Cultural Appropriation":

Mrs. Kalu's cooking in this story is not something with which I am unfamiliar. Syrup biscuits, boiled peanuts (mentioned in my first novel, Legacy 627), black-eyed peas, collard greens, and cornbread fresh and hot out of the oven are all fare I found on my own dinner table as I was growing up. My mouth waters just thinking about how good it all was. These things were, and still are, part of my own culture as well as that of the Black men and women who also grew up in the South. Those Black men and women are my brothers and sisters in spirit, if not by blood.

A word about a young man named Elijah McClain:

The lives of many Black people have been cut short in encounters with the police in this country. Some justified. Many not. But there was one life cut short that brought me to great sobs of anguish. When I read of it I cried as though I had lost my own child. That life belonged to a young man named Elijah McClain. If you are unfamiliar with his story, I encourage you to look it up. You can easily find it on the internet. By all accounts, he was a gentle soul who had harmed no one. He was a young man who played his violin for the kittens in a shelter on his lunch hour so they would not be lonely.

The character in this book, Eli McClain, is not Elijah. Nor is anything about him based upon Elijah—except his name.

The name of the young man who needlessly lost his life—the young man who played his violin to keep shelter kittens from being lonely—should never be forgotten.

About the Author

RLM Cooper has been published in literary reviews and print anthologies both domestically and internationally and is a member of the International Thriller Writers (ITW). A Southern gal who grew up along Florida's west coast, she spent over seventeen years writing life-saving application software for a computer graphics company in northern Alabama. She currently lives on the west coast of the United States.

She's an avid fan of Alabama softball and football, plays chess, loves opera, does a bit of quilting, and likes to try out new vegan recipes.

Her venture into the thriller genre was inspired in no small part by several of her favorite authors: Michael Connelly, David Baldacci, and Lee Child.

Z's Legacy is her second novel and the sequel to her debut novel, *Legacy 627*.